BLINKE IT AWAY

Victoria Landis

BLINKE IT AWAY

October 2011

Coming Fall, 2013
Alias Mitzi & Mack

Follow Victoria Landis on Amazon at:
http://tinyurl.com/VictoriaLandis-AuthorPage

Facebook:
http://tinyurl.com/VictoriaLandis-Facebook

Website:
http://victorialandis.com
http://tinyurl.com/VLandisArt

Blog:
http://www.authorvictorialandis.wordpress.com

Praise for *Blinke it Away*

"Victoria Landis delivers a skillfully crafted page-turner with Blinke It Away. Vivid exotic settings and compelling characters come together in an engaging mystery that demands to be read in one sitting. Not to be missed." - Joe Moore, International Bestselling Co-Author of *The Phoenix Apostles*

"I couldn't wait to get home to read more of Blinke It Away. Forget the chores; you'll want to sit down until you finish the story. Five Stars!" - Nancy J. Cohen, author of the Bad Hair Day Mysteries

ACKNOWLEDGMENTS

Thank you to my incredible critique group for the last seven years of (ever so gently) pushing me to better and better writing—in both technique and content. Ann Meier, Gregg Brickman, Randy Rawls, Richard Hodes, and Stephanie Levine, I owe you so much.

Thank you to Mystery Writers of America, an organization of writers I have belonged to since 2003. The dedicated volunteers of our Florida Chapter organize the Sleuthfest writers' conference every year. Attending Sleuthfest enabled me to meet experienced authors and learn from them firsthand in workshops and seminars. In 2003, at my first Sleuthfest, I came with a completed manuscript thinking I knew what I was doing. I found out that, not only did I not know what I didn't know, but my writing was awful. In the second year, I participated in sessions where it felt as though they'd peeled my skin off, then handed it back to me and said, "fix it." They not only told me my baby was ugly, they dismembered my baby. After recovering from the humiliation, I strived to learn the craft. I owe plenty to these amazing authors who have shared so much of their valuable time with aspiring writers, including the PJ Parrish team, Elaine Viets, Christine Kling, and especially the late Barbara Parker. If I'm ever in the position to do so, I will pay it forward.

I am also grateful to the FBI agent on duty who answered my inquiries, the wonderful Honolulu Police Department, and the *local* people of Hawaii—the kindest, most generous and loving people I've ever had the pleasure of sharing a state with. I lived on Oahu for twelve years, my two oldest sons were born there, and every day I want to return. Someday, I will.

AND

My son David—for sharing his experiences of hiking up Mt. Kaala.

My son Christopher—for letting me know when my natural nerdiness needs to be restrained.

My son Andrew—for his whip-smart brain that keeps me on my toes.

And my mommy, Catherine L. Landis. I love you.

Email me at:

Victoria@landisdesignresource.com

www.victorialandis.com

For Ann, Cheryll, Jan, Margie, and Miss Pammy

The best friends any woman ever had. Thank you for being my cheerleaders. Without you, I doubt I would have developed the confidence to persevere.

Map of Oahu locations from Blinke It Away. There are locations that are fictional, but resemble real places. For those, this is where I imagined they'd be.

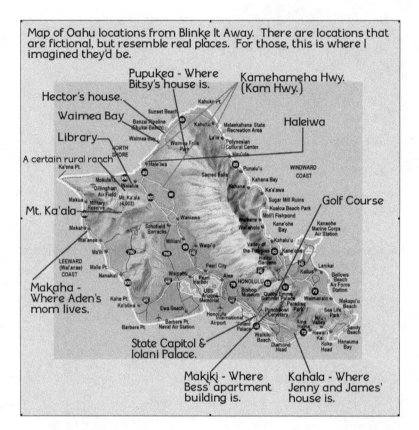

Pupukea - Where Bitsy's house is.

Kamehameha Hwy. (Kam Hwy.)

Hector's house.

Waimea Bay

Haleiwa

Library

A certain rural ranch

Mt. Ka'ala

Golf Course

Makaha - Where Aden's mom lives.

State Capitol & Iolani Palace.

Makiki - Where Bess' apartment building is.

Kahala - Where Jenny and James' house is.

CHAPTER ONE

My flip-flop flew off my foot and sailed backward toward dense bougainvillea.

"Shoot." I flicked the other sandal aside and hoped I'd find the airborne one.

"That was funny, Auntie Bess," Quinn, my nephew, said. "Now make us spin faster."

"Yeah, way faster," Mikey, his buddy, said.

Huge white billowing clouds hung over the Koolaus and the brilliant Hawaiian sun played on the valleys and peaks that formed those magnificent mountains. I leaned on my left knee as my right foot kicked at the red volcanic dirt and pushed the whirling platform into our playground version of hyper-speed.

"Hang on," I shouted.

They shrieked their delight, smiles filling their faces, their small hands gripping the rusty metal bars. I glanced toward the side bench, on a lower level, at my best friend Jenny, Mikey's mom. She laughed and waved at us.

After a few minutes, I slowed the splintery disk, then stopped it. "I need a break, guys. Give me five, okay?"

They wobbled like boozy spring breakers toward the jungle gym.

I retrieved the errant flip-flop and its mate, pleased that I managed it with a minimum of scratches from the bougainvillea thorns, then plopped beside Jenny on the bench. We often brought her kids to that neglected old park with its descending terraced play areas nestled into the side of the mountain. The funding for replacement of its aging playground equipment hadn't made it past the latest Honolulu budget cuts, but the boys enjoyed the place. The newer, safer equipment at other parks wasn't as much fun, they claimed.

Jenny's youngest, Samantha, sat in the sandbox in front of us, buried halfway up her chubby thighs. Her diaper crammed full of sand, she squealed as she threw a fistful onto the grass.

"No, no, Sammy," Jenny said. "No throwing the sand."

"I want their energy level." I pointed to the boys.

"I just want yours," Jenny said. "You should be the one with four kids, not me. I'm exhausted."

She brushed a lock of gleaming auburn hair from her face. A model's face that, even with the dark circles under the eyes, still turned heads. Looks like hers opened many doors if you wanted them to, something I'd never know about firsthand.

I followed her gaze further downhill, to the lowest terrace, where Paul and Richard, her older sons, seemed to be ordering the younger boys off one side of the climbing structure. Jenny wore a weary half-smile, and anyone could see the pride she had in her progeny.

"Richard really thinks he's hot shit now that's he's a third-grader, doesn't he?" I asked.

She sighed. "He's got a lot of his father in him. I'm doing my best to counteract that influence." She uncrossed her legs. "You promised to remind me not to do this." She extended her right leg and pointed at her calf. "My varicose veins are monstrous."

"Sorry. I forgot. Again." I stretched, then held my leg next to hers. "I don't see why you think yours are so bad. Look . . ." I traced the vein in my leg with my finger. "Everybody has veins that are visible. You think yours aren't supposed to be?"

"Bess, it's a wonder you can see at all, with those rose-colored glasses you insist on wearing." She pulled her leg in and stared at me. "But I love you for it. You're the best, no, make that the *only* real friend I've ever had."

"And you exaggerate."

Her fingers played with a macaroni necklace around her neck. She tilted her head upward and closed her eyes.

I took that as a signal indicating a desire for quiet, so I watched Sammy's attempt to fill a bucket with sand. The seven of us were alone in the park. Because it was unkempt, few people bothered to go there, and that suited us fine. The slow-paced afternoon felt peaceful and easy, and the only sounds were birds, wind rustling the surrounding palm fronds and brush, and the happy voices of the children playing. A faint scent of gardenias floated in with the gentle trade winds.

"James' lawyer called my lawyer today." Jenny turned to me. "Said James decided he wants half-custody."

"What's that mean?"

"He gets them for a week, then I get them for a week."

"That's ridiculous. He doesn't show up for the few times he's supposed to take them now."

"I know. My lawyer thinks it's because he'll have to pay less child support."

"That doesn't make sense either. He'll fork over more for a nanny in those weeks than he'd wind up paying you."

"He wants to hurt me. Take away the only thing that matters to me anymore." She wiped at a tear. "I'm not sure how much more of this I can handle." Her voice lowered and took a hesitant edge. "Bess, it's more than the divorce. Maybe worse."

"Like what?"

She clenched her jaw and stared into the sky again. Her eyes watered. With a touch of an empty left ring finger, she wiped away a tear.

Mikey and Quinn ran to us.

"Now they won't let us climb on *any* of the bars," Mikey whined.

"Richard," Jenny yelled.

"Forget it," I said. "I'm rested. Let's finish our ride, boys." I hauled myself off the bench, then twisted to face Jenny. "Whatever it is, you *know* I'll help you. Let's talk later. Get the kids settled at home, and we'll open a bottle of wine. Sound good?"

She nodded, but her eyes seemed blank.

I jogged behind Mikey and Quinn, back to the whirligig. What could be worse than the divorce tangle Jenny was in? Maybe the stress skewed her thinking a bit. Money, I thought. It had to be money at the root of Jenny's problem. Which would make it an extension of the divorce issue, not a separate one.

Tall coconut palms edged the park. The whirligig sat on the highest level of the park, just a few feet below the parking lot. From it I saw through the palms to the distant back of Diamond Head Crater and the sparkling aquamarine Pacific beyond that.

I kicked my flip-flops off. Holding fast to the bars, I ran at first, then jumped on, pushing with my foot when needed to thrust us into the speed zone. Spinning around, I caught glimpses of ocean, trees, mountains, and Jenny on the bench. Flashing by over and over. The boys shouted constant encouragement to keep me working, and the wind whooshed in my ears.

I stopped looking at anything but the blue paint peeling off the wood platform. A couple more minutes passed, and the circling began to affect my stomach. I let the whirligig slow to a stop.

"That's it. Auntie Bess has had enough for now." I tried to stand, the world still spinning around me, and almost fell.

Mikey and Quinn both toppled over, giggling, into the grass.

I heard a man's voice. Couldn't make out words, only deep-toned syllables. I looked for Jenny, but she was no longer on the bench next to the sandbox. Sammy sat playing, but alone.

My eyes darted up the hill to a flash of movement in the parking lot. I didn't see anyone. "Jenny?" I walked to the sandbox, then stopped.

A flock of Iwa birds, squalling and flapping, rose from the tall grass on the east side of the lot and took to the sky. From the swaying of the grass, it looked like maybe a mongoose had startled them. I turned my attention to the lowest terrace.

"Hey, Paul," I yelled. "Where'd your mom go?"

He looked up from the top of the jungle gym. "I don't know."

"Come here for a second, okay?"

Nodding, he descended the metal bars and climbed the hill. I waited until he reached me.

"I'll be right back. Stay here and watch the baby."

"Where's Mommy?" Paul asked.

"Probably in the bathroom, honey. I'll check."

I didn't want to alarm him, but it wasn't like Jenny to leave Sammy alone without at least telling her oldest or me. Paul took pride in the times she let him be in charge for a few minutes. She must have called to him and thought he'd heard her. But then, why'd she leave Sammy before he got there? And I hadn't heard her. As I hiked upward toward the parking lot, on the highest terrace, Jenny's

4

Sequoia came into view. The doors and back hatch were wide open. The children's toys and blankets were strewn about on the crumbling asphalt. I glanced at my van, parked about ten feet away. It looked intact.

My heart skipped a beat. "Jenny?" Why'd she throw everything out of the car? I ran around her car, peering inside at more disarray, then hurried toward the concrete block restrooms at the west end.

It took a moment to adjust to the deep shade of the restroom. The pungent odor of concentrated urine hit my nose. "Jenny? Are you okay? What happened?" I expected to find her in a stall.

The first stall was empty. The second was locked. "Jenny?" I jiggled the door handle. "Are you alright?" Silence followed, so I got on hands and knees and stuck my head under the door. There was no one there.

The third stall's lock was missing and it, too, was empty. Except for the echoing of a constant drip from one of the faucets, silence surrounded me. Where had she gone? For a walk? But she would have told me. And why did she pull all the stuff from the car? Everything felt wrong.

Emerging into daylight, I went to the lot edge to scan the children's play area. Maybe she'd made her way back there.

A crunching sound came from the woods to the north. I raced across the lot in that direction.

"Holy Moses. You had me worried. What are you doing in there?" I came to the edge of the parking lot and peered down the slope through the brush, but didn't see her. I heard a man's voice, talking low, almost in a whisper. I took a few steps in.

He was in a crouch, holding a cell phone to his left ear. A black ski mask covered his head.

"I'm telling you she didn't have it with her," he said.

His voice had a touch of panic.

"I'm getting out of here now." He closed the phone.

I took a step backward.

His head snapped in my direction. He stood and shoved the phone into his back pocket. There was a gun in his right hand and Jenny's lavender Coach purse slung by the strap over his forearm.

His body swiveled as he raised the gun toward me.

I screamed, then dropped to the ground, cringing and praying. I heard twigs breaking, then the swishing of thick brush being pushed aside. He'd run instead of shooting me. My heart pounded as I rose in time to see him crash through the bushes to the parking lot. When he reached the asphalt, he ran to the far east end and disappeared into the tall grass. The same spot where I'd seen the birds scatter.

"Jenny?" Scared to my core, I ventured farther into the broken brush until I saw her.

She lay on her back on the ground, arms and legs splayed outward. Blood spatters marred the grass and the leaves and yellow flowers of a hibiscus behind her. Blood trailed from a jagged hole in her forehead.

I heard a loud guttural sound and realized it came from me. Shivering, I sank to my knees, picked up her wrist, and felt for a pulse I knew wasn't there.

It couldn't be real. I stared at the remains of my beautiful friend. A wad of gum stuck to the bottom of her sandal, a baby food stain—probably carrots—on her white shorts, her fingernails rough and in need of a manicure. Tears dripped down my face. "Oh, God. Oh, God. Oh, God."

The macaroni necklace that Mikey made lay broken beside my knee. I lifted both ends of the string and stared at the painted elbow noodles encrusted with gobs of glue and gold glitter. I'd watched a proud Mikey give it to her the night before during dinner at Jenny's house.

The shouts of children jolted me from my shocked daze to my immediate surroundings. I hurried back to the parking lot.

The boys headed toward me. I wiped my tears, then hustled toward them, arms wide, to stop them from going any further. I needed to be strong for those kids.

"Why did you scream?" Paul asked.

"Mommy," Richard yelled. "Where's Mommy?" He tried to get past me.

"No," I said. "Stay here, honey." I grabbed his green, shark-print shorts. "She's hurt. Come on, we've got to call for help." Trying to calm my trembling, I marshaled them back to the bench where a very much alive Jenny sat moments before.

"Sit," I commanded. "All of you." I checked Sammy, still blissful in her sand kingdom, and dug my cell phone out of my fanny pack. My hands shook, the boys started to cry, and I had never felt so frightened and empty.

CHAPTER TWO

Two squad cars from the Honolulu Police Department arrived within minutes. The four officers approached Jenny's car. Then one of them, a thin Japanese man with gray hair, headed our way.

"I'm Sergeant Onaka, HPD. You the one who called this in?"

I nodded, then made a gesture with my free hand toward Mikey in my lap, and the rest of the kids, imploring him with my eyes to understand. He responded with his own, ever so slight, nod.

"The detectives are on their way, ma'am. May I ask you a few questions?"

Behind him, I could see an officer venturing toward the brush, and one hammering in tall stakes around the Sequoia. Another unrolled yellow crime scene tape.

"Is the ambulance coming soon?" Richard asked from his seat beside me on the bench.

Paul huddled next to him. "Is my mom going to be okay?"

Officer Onaka's eyebrows rose.

"The boys were here on the playground side when it happened. I didn't let them go there," I said.

He nodded again. "It's on its way." He looked at Paul. "We'll do everything we can for her, son."

A van from one of the local television stations raced into the lot. An officer ran to intercept it. A moment later, the van backed up to the entrance driveway and parked in the grass.

"Stay here," I said to the children. I stood and put Mikey in my spot between Quinn and Richard. "Watch your sister."

I stepped about twenty feet away with Officer Onaka. While I relayed the basic facts of what I saw, an ambulance, two black sedans, and more television trucks arrived. "Are those are the detectives in the Fords?"

"Yes," Onaka said.

I took a deep breath and returned to the children.

The detectives walked to where Jenny's body lay, disappearing for a few minutes. Then a petite, pretty woman in black slacks and a white blouse made her way to us.

She seemed quick to assess the situation. "I'm Detective Smalley. I'll stay here with the keikis while you speak to Detective Chang." She pointed to a man standing beside the Sequoia, holding a clipboard.

Onaka escorted me up the hill, keeping a gentle, but firm, hand on my arm.

I hadn't realized how unstable my movements were and appreciated his help. By the far edge of the lot near Jenny's body, they were placing five-foot-high, dark-green plastic screening. Thank God, I thought, there'd be no chance the kids would see her like that. The media wouldn't get any shots of her to broadcast, either.

"Detective Clifford Chang." He was a couple inches shorter than me, and the serious set of his eyes told me he was all business. He offered his hand.

"I'm Bess Blinke." I shook hands with him. "Jenny was my best friend."

His eyes darted to the screened area. "I'm sorry." He pointed to a grouping of well-worn lava rocks nearby. "Why don't we sit?"

"Good idea."

"How are you holding up? Is there anything you need right now?"

I walked to, then sat, on a rock, closed my eyes, and massaged my neck. "I don't know. I think I'm okay. I'm numb."

Detective Chang sat on the rock beside mine. "Tell me about today. Start when you got to the park this afternoon."

He jotted notes while I told him everything I could remember. The facts came out in halting sentences. "I'm feeling very spacey. It's hard to concentrate. Sorry."

"I understand. You didn't hear the gun?"

"No."

"She didn't yell or scream?"

"No. Or if she did, I didn't hear her. Mikey and Quinn, the two smallest boys, were making a lot of noise while we spun around."

He sighed, set down the pen, and rubbed his forehead. "And those kids? All five are hers?"

"Four of them are. The hapa-haole is my nephew, Quinn. Jenny's kids are Paul—he's nine, Richard—who's eight, Mikey is five, and Sammy—Samantha—is eighteen months."

"Where's their father?"

"It's Saturday afternoon. He's likely to be entertaining a woman on his boat—out there somewhere." I pointed to the Pacific. "Spends most every weekend on the boat. He has almost nothing to do with his children. There's . . . there *was* some vile divorce-related fighting going on."

"You have his cell phone number?"

"No. Just his home and office. In my car." I gestured to my minivan. "I'll go get them." My hands shook while unlocking the van, and I took some deep breaths.

I returned with my purse, looked up the numbers, and gave them to him. "Jenny has a sister living on the North Shore."

Bitsy, Jenny's insufferable older sister, was her last living relative beside the kids. I didn't know what I should or could do about them. Jenny and her lawyer fought for months to win temporary primary custody of the kids, until the court decided about permanent custody. I thought the last thing she would want was for Bitsy and me to hand them over to their father, James Dobbins. If we even had that choice.

"What about Mrs. Dobbins' parents?"

"Both dead."

"Mr. Dobbins' parents?"

"Alive. They live in San Francisco."

"Do you have their number?"

"No."

Do you have the sister's number?"

"Sure." I read it to him. "Her name is Susan Cooper-Zeller. She goes by *Bitsy*."

"Do you want to call her?" he asked.

"I don't think I could tell her what happened without falling apart."

"Wait here. I'll be right back." He stood, took his cell phone from the holder on his belt, and stepped out of earshot.

"I called both of Mr. Dobbins' numbers and got voice mails. The sister is near Haleiwa and said she would be here within the hour," he said when he returned.

"How did Bitsy take the news?"

"She sounded upset, but controlled." He retook his seat. "Tell me more about Mrs. Dobbins' husband."

I felt like saying, *James is an asshole. Period.* But I didn't. James Rutherford Dobbins was a trust fund baby. There were a lot of those in Hawaii. He could be the most charming sophisticate or the biggest jerk. You never knew what you were going to get with him. Unfortunately for Jenny, as time went on, she only got the jerk.

I wiped away another tear. "I've known him as long as Jenny has. Did. He's from a rich family. He's extremely handsome. He's spoiled rotten."

"And the divorce? How long has that been in process?"

"Over two years. Since Paul was born, James did nothing but cheat on her. She caught him a few times and threatened to leave, but he always talked her out of it. Then, while she was pregnant with Sammy . . ." I turned to check on the kids. The lady detective looked to be occupying them with a game on her cell phone. "James met someone *special* and moved out."

"Any disagreements between them that stand out in your mind?"

"Most were about money. James' lawyer is a bloodthirsty shark."

"You mean the amount she should be awarded in the divorce?"

"No. The more immediate problem was she didn't have enough to survive right now. The judge awarded her so little temporary support. Her lawyer couldn't get it upped. She and those kids are almost starving."

He gave me a deadpan stare.

"I'm serious. Go check her gas tank. It's less than a quarter-tank, I'll guarantee it. Never put more than ten dollars in at a time. *I've* given her four-thousand."

I filled him in on the status of the divorce, and gave him Jenny's attorney's name.

He told me he'd need to interview me again the next morning after assessing the collected evidence, then let me return to the

10

playground to wait for Child Protective Services and Bitsy with the kids.

"Are they helping mommy?" Paul asked. "Can I see her?"

"Yes, they're with her right now." The words choked in my throat as I saw the Medical Examiner's van pull in. "But, no, you can't see her."

Detective Smalley frowned. "I need to get back there."

"Thanks for staying with them." Maybe she thought I should have told the kids their mom was dead, but I just couldn't. I watched her walk away, then sat on the grass beside the sandbox, picked up a tiny pink plastic shovel, and scooped sand into a pile. I couldn't control my tears.

One by one, the boys joined me around the sandbox. They copied my mindless playing with the sand.

"Why are you still crying?" Quinn asked me.

The other boys looked up.

"It makes me very sad when somebody I love gets hurt." I managed a weak smile.

Forty minutes later, I'd just finished changing Sammy's diaper when I saw Bitsy's silver Mercedes sedan pull into the lot.

Bitsy stepped with great care over the buckled pavement to the taped-off area. She spoke to an officer who pointed at the enclosed area. Bitsy's hand flew to her mouth. The officer gestured toward us. Mikey spotted her first.

"Auntie Bitsy's here." He walked up the hill to her, followed by Paul and Richard. Quinn gathered the sandbox toys while I held Sammy, then we joined them.

Bitsy came toward us, and I saw why she'd seemed so cautious walking across the parking lot. Her spindle legs were made all the more unsteady by ridiculous four-inch pink heels. One wrong step in those things, and she could snap an ankle. Jenny had always made fun of her sister's impractical habits.

Bitsy's eyes were moist, but she smiled at the boys and gave them hugs. She pulled me aside. "How could this happen? What did you see?"

"Great question," I whispered. "I'm not supposed to tell what I saw, but I didn't see it happen. The boys think she's alive, but badly injured."

"What?" She sounded almost angry.

"Do *you* want to tell them their mother is dead?" I gestured toward them.

She conceded that point with a shake of her head. "What are we going to do? I don't know how to take care of four children. And I have a career to think of."

I couldn't believe my ears. Bitsy's sister, her only sibling, lay mutilated on the ground some two hundred feet behind her. I wanted to believe she was in shock.

On rare occasions she'd returned Jenny's phone calls. She was probably afraid Jenny might ask her to help out and babysit the kids once in a while. She had no experience with children and didn't want any. She seemed to have divorced her family. Five years before, when their mom died, Bitsy flew to Sacramento for the day of the funeral. She took an immediate flight out after the wake, leaving Jenny to handle everything alone.

"James isn't going to want them. You know that," I said. "Hire a nanny. You can afford it. James will do that if he gets the children."

"I can't. I don't know the first thing about raising kids. Have you told James?"

"No. I'm letting the police handle that call. Please, Bitsy, just take them to your place for a few days at least? Act like you want them until I can think this through? Otherwise, if the police can't find James, the kids will have to go to some kind of foster home tonight. You don't prefer that option, do you?"

"Well, it's not like I don't *want* them. And of course I don't want them with strangers." She cast a glance at the boys. "It's just I'm clueless about this sort of thing."

I saw a woman with a hanging badge approaching us. "Uh-oh, hope you've got lots of ID on you. Looks like that woman is from Child Protective Services. Detective Chang said there would be paperwork."

I occupied the children for another thirty minutes, fighting more tears while the case worker interviewed Bitsy and had her fill out what seemed to be fifty pages of forms.

The moment I handed over Sammy to Bitsy, the adorable baby threw up the contents of her last meal on Bitsy's pale-pink Chanel suit. Regurgitated peas, carrots, cheese, and lots of sand.

Bitsy shrieked.

I grabbed the baby while flashing Bitsy a look that said, *you should have known better than to wear a suit.*

"I was showing a house." She opened her trunk, pulled a few paper towels from a roll in there, and wiped at the baby barf with a look of revulsion on her face.

She liked to play at being a real estate agent. I think it was an excuse to wear the expensive clothes she bought. Even so, *nobody*, except in court, ever wore a suit in Hawaii. It was such a rare occurrence that it was cause for staring.

We loaded the Dobbins children into her car, and I watched her drive away. She looked more than a little unsure, and the boys bewildered.

By seven I was in my van, with Quinn secured in the back seat, paying for Quinn's dinner, a Mini Pac Chicken Katsu at a Zippy's drive-up window. I had no appetite. My sister Debbie, Quinn's mom, was due in any moment from San Francisco. I decided to drive to her house and wait.

Debbie and her husband, Aden Kaikau, lived in a simple three bedroom house situated on the north side of the Manoa Valley. It sat nestled high on the mountainside and afforded a jaw-dropping view of Honolulu.

My van chugged up the steep driveway. Quinn and I settled at the top of the steps, sitting on the front lanai. He leaned against me.

"Auntie Bess?"

"Yes, sweetie."

"Is Mikey's mom dead?"

He hadn't said much all afternoon, leading me to believe he hadn't suspected the truth. I'd been too afraid to ask him in front of the other boys. "Yes, honey, she is." I said it as gently as I could. I picked him up and placed him on my lap, cuddling him close to me.

"So she's in heaven now." Quinn looked up at me with his soulful green eyes, his long dark lashes wet. "I really, really liked her."

"Me, too." For a six year old, he seemed to put a lot of thought into his words before he said them, a trait I wish I possessed. I'd have more interior design clients and more money.

Ten minutes passed until Debbie's red Highlander appeared in the driveway.

"Why are you sitting out here? And why the glum face, sugarpie?" Debbie asked Quinn. She walked up the steps to the lanai. "How's my most wonderful buddy? Did you miss me?" She spread her arms wide for a hug.

Quinn climbed off my lap and fell into his mother's arms. "Mikey's mom got killed."

Debbie's eyes widened.

"I left a message on your cell phone," I said.

"I forgot to switch it on after we landed." She turned her little boy around, then brushed his brown hair back from his cocoa-colored face. "Quinn honey, I'm sorry. I'm here now." She hugged him tight. She mouthed the words, *did he see it?*

I shook my head.

"Okay. Let's go inside and get you ready for bed, then you'll need some more hugs. I want to talk to Auntie Bess."

We moved indoors. Quinn left to wash up and brush his teeth. We sat at her kitchen table. Once Quinn was out of earshot, I relayed what happened.

"Dear God in Heaven," Debbie said. "I'm so sorry." Tears formed.

Seeing her cry started me going. I'd been doing a pretty good job of holding back, but droplets now splashed onto my bare thighs.

Debbie leaned in and we hugged each other for support.

"What about Jenny's kids?" Debbie asked.

"They called Bitsy. She came and picked them up."

"Oh, no."

"What choice was there? Call James? Well, actually, they couldn't reach him. CPS came. They still might insist on James taking them, when they find him."

"You're right. You had a choice between shitty and shittier. Would you like to stay here tonight?" She grabbed a tissue and handed me the box.

"Thank you, but I want to go home."

"How about a drink?"

"Yes. Make it a vodka and something. Anything."

A minute later, she handed me a vodka and orange juice in a chunky glass, then set hers down.

Fearing I would lose complete control if I said too much more, I tipped my glass in her direction, and drank.

She seemed to understand, and we finished our drinks in silence. We settled Quinn into his parents' bed, always a refuge of safety for him. He fell asleep in minutes with Debbie and me sitting on either side of him.

As we returned to the kitchen, I apologized all over myself for somehow allowing Quinn to be exposed to such a horrible occurrence. "Steve will want to see him."

She grimaced.

"It'll be fine. He's the best in the field." My ex-husband, Dr. Steve Nash, was a child psychologist. He was also in love with my sister. Debbie, however, loved her husband.

"I doubt he'll have anything open for weeks."

"For you? If you called him now, on a Saturday night, he'd be here in ten minutes."

She rolled her eyes. "What an awkward situation. I'm sorry about that, too."

CHAPTER THREE

I pulled into my assigned space in the parking garage of my apartment building after ten. Jenny's pink and white polka-dot diaper bag in the backseat caught my eye as I got out. I'd thrown it there when I realized I'd neglected to give it to Bitsy at the park.

My thoughts were of Jenny's children as I rode the elevator to the ninth floor. How much, if anything, had they seen? Did they hear the gunshot? I pondered that for a moment. I couldn't recall hearing it go off with all the noise we made. Or maybe the guy had a silencer.

But that made no sense. I'd never been near a real crime before, so my expertise started and ended with the TV. And on television, they used a silencer when they *knew* they were going to kill somebody. I tried to recall what the gun looked like. Did it have one of those really long front sections?

The ride up seemed to take forever. I noticed a long scratch on one of the brand-new fake-marble laminate wall panels of the elevator. Mr. Ng, our building super, would go nuts when he saw it. Then, on the floor in the corner, I spotted a roach clip holding about an inch of a joint. Something like that could send hyper Mr. Ng into coronary land. I liked our persnickety super, but worried over his self-inflicted stress level, so I picked it up and slipped it in my purse to throw away later. Seeing my cell in there, I switched it off.

Temptation to smoke the joint lasted all of two seconds. I'd tried Hawaiian pakalolo when I first arrived in the islands and decided pot wasn't for me. Too strong. Although reaching oblivion seemed a great option just then.

My home phone rang as I placed the key in the deadbolt and realized it wasn't locked. I'd forgotten to do it again. I switched keys and undid the handle lock, opened the door, and tossed my purse onto the kitchen counter, then dove for the phone.

It was my mom in Florida.

"I just heard," Mom said. "Debbie called me. What happened? Are you all right?"

"I'm okay. In shock, I think. I can't believe it's real. I would've called you tomorrow. Debbie shouldn't have called you in the middle of the night."

"I'm just thanking God it wasn't you. This wouldn't have occurred if you were with Steve."

"What?"

"You need a man to protect you. Who's going to attack a woman with a big man standing near?"

"I didn't get attacked."

"Well," she said, "Jenny sure did. Why did the man shoot her?"

"My van looks pretty ordinary next to Jenny's Sequoia. I guess if I was going to break into a car, I'd pick hers, too."

"That's what it was? A burglary? Then why did she get shot?"

"Heck. I don't know. Maybe she interrupted the burglary? I'm not sure what happened, to be honest."

"I thought Debbie said you were there."

"Mom, I'm not thinking well at this point. How's Dad's hip? Is he still on a walker?"

"He's making good progress. They'll switch him to a cane soon."

"Great. Give him a hug for me. I'll call you tomorrow."

"Oh. Sure. Yes, you do that. You know Dad and I are here if you need us. And honey? I'm sorry about Jenny."

"Thanks, Mom." I hung up and sighed. Mom meant well. My parents lived in a retirement community in Boca Raton. Not much anyone can do to help from six thousand miles away.

I went into the hall and opened my bedroom door. The handle felt sticky. The lamp on my nightstand was on, and the Disney Channel babbled forth from the TV. Right. I'd had Quinn stay overnight. Along with leaving things on and scattered, he excelled at getting peanut butter on everything.

I buried my thoughts by busying myself stripping the sheets from the guest room bed and stuffing them into the washer. With a clean sponge, I hunted for peanut butter smears on the light switches, handles, and remotes. When I went into the third bedroom—my office—the phone rang again.

"I just got off the phone with Debbie. My God. How are you?" Steve, my ex, said. "Do you want me to come over?"

"I'm functioning. Trying not to think about it. And no, don't come over. Did you talk to Debbie about Quinn? How is he? He was sleeping when I left."

"Well, he hasn't woken up screaming."

"I guess that's a good sign. I'm not sure how much Jenny's kids know. And I was too much of a chickenshit to ask them. They think she went to the hospital. I feel awful, but I couldn't bring myself to tell them their mom was dead."

"Understandable. Don't be too hard on yourself. If you want, I'll tell them. They're at Bitsy's? How'd you pull that off?"

"James wasn't answering his phones, and Bitsy's the next relative. It wasn't up to me, you know. CPS was there."

"You called James?"

"No, the detective did."

Steve's voice did a subtle change into his *understanding counselor* mode that drove me nuts during our short marriage. "Tell me how you're feeling about this. It's a harsh and traumatic act you've witnessed."

"I just told you. I don't want to think about it now."

"So you'll think about it tomorrow, Scarlett? Come on Bess, you know denial isn't healthy."

"Neither is being harassed." I controlled my caustic reaction and didn't snap at him. "I have to see Detective Chang early tomorrow. Maybe I'll feel more like *sharing* after that."

"Ah. Bitterness towards the ones closest to you is better than no emotion. All right, I'll call you tomorrow. I love you."

"Sure." I hung up on him, then went into the bathroom and started the hot water in the tub. I needed comforting and wished my ex really did love me.

Steve denied his attraction to Debbie. He surfaced into my life every few months and tried to convince me he wanted me back. But the look on his face whenever he saw Debbie gave him away. She was taller, thinner, and prettier. He'd never stared at me that way. It was the reason I left. At least my sister believed me. My mother thought I was paranoid and somehow, that it was her fault.

Sliding into the tub, the steaming water made me yelp, but the sting almost felt good. I'm sure Steve had a touchy-feely explanation for that, too. The armor that I'd coated my raw emotions with that afternoon melted away, and the tears let loose. I curled into a fetal position and so wanted someone to hold me and rock me, and tell me it was all a terrible dream.

By the time I had the energy to lift myself out, the water had cooled, and chills tingled my limbs. Wrapped in a towel, I padded into the bedroom. When I opened the white louvered closet door to get my bathrobe, my photo boxes fell from the top shelf. I jumped back to avoid being hit on the head, but the sharp corner of one of the boxes made a direct hit on top of my right foot.

"Youch," I yelled. I sat on the bed and rubbed the red dent in my foot. How had that happened? I kept the boxes shoved to the back of the shelf. Going through them with the possibility of seeing pictures of Steve and me happy together made me want them out of sight. Maybe the constant vibration of traffic going by inched them forward over time.

I nudged the photo mess aside with my good foot and took my fluffy white spa robe off the hangar. And the tears started again. The robe brought memories of a spa weekend on Maui with Jenny years before. She'd bought it for me as a birthday present.

While double-checking locks and turning off lights, I saw the green flashing of my message machine. I hit the button, and heard Bitsy's voice telling me she was already at nervous breakdown level. I erased it. Too bad. She could manage until morning.

I laid in bed the rest of the night weathering crying jags, trying to relax. Sleep seemed impossible. Through the hours, I tried my best to keep the image of Jenny's dead body from reappearing in my mind, with no luck. Her vacant eyes wide open. Why did that man have to shoot her?

I thought about Jenny and James' wedding day. They both looked so happy. The birth of each of her children. The beaming smile she greeted them with when they stepped off the school bus, homemade cookies waiting for them at home. She was a loving, dedicated mom.

When they married, James couldn't keep his hands off her. As multiple pregnancies and the responsibilities of motherhood became

Jenny's life, James lost interest in her. He criticized her weight gain and expressed open disgust at the stretch marks on her stomach and breasts. Jenny told me the last time they'd made love was when they conceived Sammy. He was drunk that night, and he called her Cindy at the height of things. Jenny found out soon afterward who that was. James moved in with Cindy Yamaguchi two weeks later.

James had started the affair with then nineteen-year-old Cindy when Mikey was born, five years earlier. Six months after Sammy was born, Cindy called Jenny and actually apologized to her. Turned out James was cheating on Cindy, with at least two other women, and Cindy was outraged. Jenny and I had a good laugh over that.

James played with some additional aspiring young models, then moved in with Tiffanie, who was all of 21. James was 42. We didn't know for sure, of course, but Jenny and I figured that as soon as any of these young ladies mentioned a commitment, as in marriage and babies, James looked elsewhere.

I glanced at the clock on my nightstand. Five o'clock in the morning. Soon the sun would rise. I decided to get up, take a shower, and make coffee.

I looked at myself in the bathroom mirror. That was a big mistake. Whenever I cry, my eyes swell. Not just a little, they become monster sized. There isn't enough makeup in the world to hide those big, puffy sacks. I had been crying off and on for fourteen hours. Hideous doesn't begin to describe my appearance. Not that I much cared. Nobody ever expected me to look hot, anyway. I just didn't want to scare people.

After my shower and a strong cup of coffee, I almost felt awake. From my lanai, I could see the sun rising over the Koolau mountains, another beautiful Sunday morning in paradise. The world and Honolulu were going on with life. Timed streetlights dimmed, then went out. Cars traversed Beretania and King Streets, many of them probably headed to King's bakery where fresh steamed or baked manapua awaited. People would bring home the goodies, and they and their families would gobble them up while reading the paper, the kids fighting over the comics.

I wanted to scream. Life is rarely, if ever, fair. I had thought about the concept a lot. The sooner each of us plebeian humans understood that, the better we could manage our lives. I was the third of six children. Fairness had never been a factor in my world, and I was always amazed that some folks, even way into their twilight years, fought and even sued to achieve some semblance of it.

But Jenny murdered? Leaving those four great kids? How scarred were they going to be? Their mom dead. Their father couldn't be bothered, and Bitsy didn't want them either. How could anyone make it up to these children?

I drained the last of my coffee and decided that, no matter what, I'd be their advocate and find them someone who'd care.

CHAPTER 4

I placed my mug in the dishwasher, then glanced at the retro-style chrome clock on the kitchen wall. It looked like it belonged to Lucy or Ethel. Jenny made me buy it. Another reminder of her. It was seven-thirty. The phone rang.

"Bess," Bitsy shouted. "You've got to help me here. I'm not cut out for this. The boys were awake crying half the night, and the baby has some weird rash on her behind. I don't know what to do with them."

"You have to handle it." I used my quiet, everything's okay voice. "Put the three boys into the bathtub. That always calms them down. Go buy some Desitin for Sammy's bottom."

"What's that?"

"It's an ointment that comes in a big white tube. Helps to heal diaper rash."

"Oh. Another trip to the store. Can I leave them with Paul in charge while I go?"

"Hell no. He's nine. Are you remembering to feed them?" I regretted the words as soon as they left my mouth.

"There's no need to be sarcastic."

Bitsy, a skinny little thing her whole life—hence the childhood moniker—weighed one hundred pounds soaking wet. I hadn't ever had any genuine food at her house. Lots of wine or drinks, a platter of cheese and crackers maybe, but that was it.

Jenny's bitter resentment of her estranged sister had seeped its way into my psyche. Remember she's trying, I thought.

"I'm sorry," I said. "Did you buy whole milk for them? Richard's favorite food is peanut butter and grape jelly. Paul will eat any kind of frozen pizza. Mikey loves everything, and Sammy eats small bites of whatever Mikey's having. That's easy enough, isn't it?" I could tell by the following silence that she knew none of those things about her charges. I bet she'd offered them Camembert on water wafers.

"The CPS caseworker gave me a list, and I bought what was on that. The kids didn't seem to like any of it. How in the world did Jenny make it through a grocery store with the four of them? Do you know how hard that is? It's lunacy. And I have no clothing for them. They're wearing their dirty play clothes from yesterday. Can you go by Jenny's and pick up some essentials for me?"

"I have to meet with Detective Chang first, then I'll stop and get what you'll need from the house. Did you call Steve yet?"

"No, I was too tired last night. I'll do it this morning." She sounded annoyed. "He is going to drive out here, isn't he? I can't do another long car ride with the four of them."

"He'll accommodate you. Just be sure to call him and set up the appointment pronto. Those poor kids need his help. The sooner they start with him, the better. Hang in there, girl. You can do it." Despite her whining, I did feel for her. What awful alternatives—an inept auntie who didn't really like kids or a philandering father who didn't want the responsibility.

I hung up, gathered my things, and realized monster eyes required sunglasses. Rummaging through my top dresser drawer, I found a pair with dark lenses in the rear. They were huge and perfect for the day. I wondered why they were in the back instead of right in front where I kept them. Quinn never went into my drawers before, but he was only six. I decided to talk to him about what was private and what wasn't after this upset settled down.

While locking up, my next-door neighbor and friend, Tom Hanegawa, leaned from his doorway to pick up his newspaper. His Old Spice cologne masked the faint scent of mildew that often wafted from his apartment.

"Morning, Bess. You okay?" He stepped into the carpeted hallway. He was a hulk of a man, with shaggy black hair that reached past his shoulder blades. Tom was of mixed heritage and his

Okinawan ancestry showed in the wild thicket of more black hair on his forearms. He'd tied his red, green, and blue striped terrycloth bathrobe with a length of thin rope. "I saw about Jenny on the news. I'm sorry."

"Thanks. I'm surviving." I tried to sound strong.

"Well, if you need me to do anything, let me know."

"Thanks. I will. I hope you'll excuse me though. Right now, I can't talk about her."

He nodded, stepped closer, and encircled me in a big hug, giving me a closer view of his chest hair. Then a light punch in the arm. "You're a tough babe. You can handle anything."

***

I pulled off Hotel Street and found a rare space in the HPD parking garage. I had never been inside the main police building before, or in any police department, for that matter. This station was on my route to elsewhere countless times, and I never gave it a second glance.

Afraid to go in, I sat for a moment in silence, praying for strength. Rehashing the *incident* one more time with homicide was not something to look forward to. I'd told them all I could recall. It hurt to think about it again.

Detective Chang's office was on the second floor. Compared to other government buildings I'd been in, this one was not so bad. The commercial grade carpet was of good quality and the walls were beige, not institutional green. I followed a clerkish person into a corner conference room with a view of downtown. In the distance, between buildings, I glimpsed the Aloha Tower. A cute young woman, her badge hanging on a cord around her neck, came in smiling.

"Would you care for coffee?" she asked.

"No. Thank you." She seemed familiar, but I couldn't say why.

She nodded and left the room as my cell phone rang. Bitsy again.

"It just dawned on me that we've got to place an obituary," Bitsy said. "Would you write it? I simply can't. I'm beyond coping with it now."

"Um, sure." She caught me off guard. "I'll help you with the funeral details, too, if you like."

"You're a peach. I think the Honolulu Advertiser will do."

"What about the San Francisco papers? And Sacramento?"

"No one from there knows her anymore. Don't waste the money. What day can we plan on the wake and service? I hope I can get her into Fujimura's Funeral Home."

"You're too far ahead of me. We don't even know when they'll release her body. I'm at the police station. I'll ask Detective Chang when we can expect to claim Jenny. Just take care of those kids. Tell them I'll be there in a few hours."

I placed my phone in my purse and sat on the chair closest to the window. Cold. Pre-formed orange plastic. Charming. My head sank into my palms, and then my elbows slid down the sides of my thighs. I closed my eyes and let my chin rest on my knees.

"Ms. Blinke."

I straightened and opened my eyes. It was Detective Chang. "Morning, Detective."

"You look terrible. No sleep, huh?"

"No."

He pulled a chair closer to mine and sat. "Do you want coffee?" I saw kindness in his eyes. He had a great face—high cheekbones and a strong chin. Not GQ material, but very pleasant.

"Thanks, but no." I wanted to get it over with. "So, what else can I tell you?"

"It's very common for people who have witnessed a crime such as this, to block out certain details. Sometimes, hours or days later, they'll remember other pieces of what happened."

"You want to run through it one more time."

"Yes, if you'll please indulge me."

"Sure, go ahead." I took a deep breath, and counted to ten while I exhaled.

He asked about the minutes before the shooting, and I described my ride with the boys on the whirligig.

"What did you see as you were going around and around?"

"Not much, the circling made me a bit nauseous, so I concentrated on my knee."

"But before you looked down, as you circled, what flashed by? Take your time and try to see the scene again."

I thought about that, and commanded my brain to show me the picture. "The coconut palms, the back of Diamond Head, the mountains, and Jenny seated on the bench."

"Was any part of the parking lot visible to you?"

"I don't . . . wait a minute. It should have been, shouldn't it? The whirligig is on the highest level of the playground. Higher than where the bench is."

"After you left yesterday, I sat on the platform and did some slow spinning myself. I had a view of the parking lot where Mrs. Dobbins backed her car in." He leaned against his chair as he waited for me to consider this.

"Then I must have seen something, however fast the image went by, right?"

"That's what I'm hoping."

I tended to frown when deep in thought and must have done so.

"I'll try to get you out of here as soon as I can," he said. "You're an interior designer. It makes sense that, by nature, you notice things others wouldn't. I bet you can tell me what each of the children wore yesterday."

An instant picture formed in my mind of the boys in the park. He'd pegged me. "I see your point."

I concentrated harder. The trees, the crater, the mountains, the clouds over the mountains, and Jenny sitting. I went over the scene several times, each time adding more detail. The coconuts needed trimming. Cars looking like Matchbox toys parked in the Diamond Head Crater lot. Ohia Lehua trees in vibrant red-orange bloom in the distance, with the big white clouds over the mountains, and then—yes. The parking lot. And then Jenny. I kept spinning mentally until at last, I saw him.

"He was pulling everything out of her car," I said. "She didn't do it, he did."

"Who was?"

"A guy wearing faded red surf trunks."

"Describe him."

"Tall, about six foot two? Black ski mask over his head, but his hair hung out the back. He was thin, skinny. A white T-shirt."

"Could you guess at his race?"

I knew what Chang meant. In Hawaii, the races have intermarried for so long that unless you'd lived there for many years, it was tough to figure out someone's heritage. For example, I knew without asking that Clifford Chang was Filipino-Chinese.

"His face wasn't toward me, although with the mask on, it doesn't matter," I answered. "But, his coloring was medium brown. His arms were much darker than his legs."

"Good. What about the hair hanging out from beneath the hat?"

"Brown, light brown. But with long hair, his ends could have been a different color than what was on the top of his head."

"What about hair on his legs and arms, did he have much?"

I closed my eyes. "No, I don't think so. Not on his arms, anyway. Because of the parking lot being uphill from where I was, I only saw him from the knees up. Something bright green and red on his arm. A tattoo?" My throat felt dry. "Could I have a glass of water?"

"Sure." He left the room and returned a minute later.

"Here you go." He handed me a cold bottle of water. "It's from my personal stash."

I had been expecting a thin paper cone with an ounce and a half of tap water in it. "Thank you," I said. The water tasted clean, fresh and wonderful. "I'm sorry, I don't think the visualization worked that well. I've only confused things."

"On the contrary, it was very helpful." He smiled.

"How?"

"Allow me to read back the description you gave us yesterday, of the man who may have shot Jenny Dobbins." A manila file folder lay on the table next to him. He retrieved it and removed a legal pad I recognized from the day before. "Five foot ten, maybe eleven." He cocked an eyebrow. "Caucasian male, wearing blue jeans, black t-shirt, and a black ski mask. Excessive reddish blonde hair on arms."

"See? How can that be?" Had I lost my grip on reality? "I'm sorry, Detective, maybe I'm too stressed to be reliable right now."

"You are burdened. No question. Losing your best friend. Worrying about her children. No sleep on top of it. I'm not fazed by this."

"Does this mean you can't use either description? And where in the world did I cook this up from?"

"I plan to use both." He stretched his arms and stood.

Judging from the armpit stains and wrinkles in his shirt, he must have slept at his desk.

"I suspected from evidence at the scene yesterday that there might have been two of them. Now, I think I was right."

"No," I said. "I know for a fact, there is no question, there was one man there when I found Jenny's body." I was never surer about anything. "You can say I'm nuts if you want, but one man ran away, not two. And that same man almost shot at me."

"Calm down. I'm not calling you crazy. Exhausted, yes. I believe the second man left before the shooting. Let's go back to what you heard." He checked his notes again. "When you stopped the ride and got off, you heard a man's voice."

"Yes, but I couldn't make out any words."

"Then you saw no one."

"Until I got into the bushes on the other side."

"And he didn't say anything."

"No. He was talking on a cell phone. He said, 'I'm telling you, she didn't have it with her.'"

"You didn't tell me that yesterday. Didn't have what? Do you know what he wanted?"

I wondered which one of us was crazy. "Sure I told you that. Then he said, 'I'm getting out of here now.' I don't have any idea what the *it* was."

"I'm sure you think you told me, but it doesn't matter. None of this is surprising. You need to go home and get some sleep."

"Can the shock of something like this really do that to your brain?"

"I've seen it before." He rose, then walked to the door and back. "Do you know if James Dobbins ever threatened his wife?"

"Sure, Jenny said he wanted to take away everything he could."

"I mean, did he ever threaten to hurt her physically?"

"Oh. No. Not that I know of."

"What about you and Jenny?" Chang looked out the window. "Did you two ever fight?"

"Once, maybe twice." I didn't like where he seemed to be going with that question.

"How long ago? What about? Were you upset she couldn't repay the money you lent her?"

"Wait a minute." Maybe he wasn't so nice, after all. "Are you trying to say I hired someone to kill my best friend?" The idea brought tears, and I wiped them with the back of my hand.

He waited while I regained control.

"How did you and James Dobbins get along?" he asked.

"We didn't."

"You never liked him."

"Well, no. I mean, yes. When Jenny first met him, I liked him fine. He seemed to love her very much."

He lifted his yellow pad and flipped a page back. "Yesterday, you said you found him attractive. 'Extremely handsome.' And he's rich. Very rich."

I stared at him, not wanting to believe what he suggested. "You have to be kidding. Now you think James, or James and I, hired some thug to kill Jenny? Do I need a lawyer?"

He stared back. "I can't share what I think. But it's my job to consider all possibilities. You're entitled to have a lawyer present if you think you need one."

Something in his eyes told me I didn't. "You can eliminate the best friend angle. But the husband is always the first suspect, right? Or, the spouse. Whatever." Could James be that evil? "He could afford to hire someone to do it. And their fights were pretty awful. But he knows he can't cope with the kids. He almost never sees them now. It doesn't make sense to me. I don't think he did that."

"You said you were divorced. Tell me about your ex-husband."

I told him the basics about Steve and how we used to socialize with Jenny and James, but left out the in-love-with-my-sister part.

"Okay. One last question. Do you think you would recognize the man's voice from the park again?"

I replayed my mental tape. "Probably?"

CHAPTER FIVE

The Kahala mansion James built for Jenny when they married made the others on Aukai Place look like fishing shacks. Their home, two blocks in from the beach, started out in the late forties as a concrete block weekend retreat on a large, sandy lot. James bought it as an investment property in 1990 and did the necessary repairs to turn it into a rental.

I remembered the excitement in Jenny's voice the morning after James drove her to his *beach house*.

"I think he's trying to impress me," she said. "Like I wasn't already. He's got big plans for that little place. And he hinted about maybe the two of us living there together."

The bungalow had been one of the last of its kind in the neighborhood. One by one, the simple World War II era cottages disappeared, replaced with mini and mega mansions.

James proposed on the beach near the house. They made plans for a home there, with lots of bedrooms for the children they looked forward to having.

Six months after their wedding, they moved in. James made a big show of giving her the keys in a black velvet box in front of, oh, maybe thirty of us, at a lavish party he threw for the occasion. After he filed the divorce papers, he said he never intended for her to believe it was *her* house, that Jenny had misunderstood him. I'd looked forward to testifying about it at their trial. I wanted the judge to know what a rat he was.

I pulled into the circular sandstone driveway rimmed with alocasia, crimson powder puff lilies, and bird of paradise. The third garage door was open, and I saw James' yellow Ferrari inside. Scooting past his other two cars, an Audi R8 GT and an antique MG, I knocked, then let myself in through the kitchen door.

"James?" I called. "Are you here?" I navigated through toys on the family room floor and peered out the French doors. James' current girlfriend, Tiffanie, lay on a chaise by the pool. Except for a patch of a gold lamé thong, she was naked. Headphones on, she mouthed the words to whatever song played on her iPod.

She had the worst boob job I'd ever seen. Not that I'd seen a lot of women naked, but you can always tell when somebody's ta-tas are not a natural shape. Even under clothing. They don't move right. Tiffanie's stood straight up on top of her chest, even though she lay on her back. Plus, they were enormous for a girl of her tiny stature. The effect was freakish.

There were two Louis Vuitton suitcases in the front hall. Jeez, his wife wasn't dead for 24 hours, and the man moved himself and his girlfriend into the house. Did he have Jenny killed? Could he? Somehow, I didn't believe that. "James?" I called again. I started up the staircase when I heard him talking.

"I never said to use that. What do you mean you didn't find it yet?" James said. His voice seemed to be coming from Mikey's room. "Yes. I've checked all of them. What about the apartment?"

At the top of the stairs, as I rounded the corner, I ran into him. He wore surf trunks and his dark hair looked damp.

"Christ almighty," he yelled. "What are you doing here? I'll have to call you back," he said into his phone. He switched it off and placed it in a pocket. "What are you doing in my house?"

"You look like you're taking Jenny's death real hard." I scooted by him and walked down the hall toward the kids' rooms. On the way, I passed the master bedroom. More suitcases sat by the door. The sheets were a tangled mess at the bottom of the bed. "Oh, my God. James, you are disgusting. You and the tartlet out there already did it in Jenny's bed?"

"It's my damn house. I'll do whatever I want here. Now what the hell do you want?"

"It's not just your house. Jenny's name is on the deed, too, remember?"

He followed me into Mikey's room. "How did you get in?"

"You left the garage and kitchen doors open." He didn't need to know I had a key. "I called and knocked, but nobody answered. Bitsy asked me to get some clothes for the kids. You know, your four children? The ones you couldn't wait to have with your beloved wife? I think that's about how your speech went."

"Shut up. I spoke to Bitsy about an hour ago. She didn't say she needed anything."

"Because she knows you wouldn't have a clue what to bring for them. Do you even know which boy lives in which room?"

"Why are you such a bitch?" He flung his arms wide. "I don't how Jenny could stand you."

"Maybe I'm angry. Maybe I'm hurt on my best friend's behalf. Maybe she deserved better. Maybe your kids do, too. Did you ever think of that?"

He didn't answer.

The bedroom was a mess. Mikey's toy box, painted like a circus tent, lay on its side, the contents scattered on the floor. "What happened in here?" I stepped around them, grabbed a suitcase from the closet shelf, and laid it open on the red race-car bed.

"Jenny didn't pay the maid? How should I know?"

"She couldn't afford help, not on what you gave her a month. She let the maid go the day after you moved out. I was here two days ago. It didn't look like this, and furthermore, Jenny kept the place immaculate on her own."

"The police were here when I arrived last night. Maybe they did it."

I gathered Mikey's clothes and carried them to the suitcase. My sunglasses fell off and into the clothes.

"Christ. Bess, you look like shit."

"Was up crying all night." I glared at him. "At least one of us loved Jenny."

"I loved her . . . when I married her."

"Yeah, what happened with that?" I sat next to the suitcase. "And why aren't you grieving? She was the mother of your children. Your *soul mate*, as you told us eight million times. You swore you'd love her forever, that she was a part of you. I don't get it. I just don't." Tears dripped down my cheeks.

The irritated look on his face relaxed, and he sat on the carpet in front of me, massaging his temples with his fingers. "I didn't want her to die, okay? I'll miss her, but I don't cry for anybody. She was a good person." His voice softened, reminding me of the *old* James, the one I liked. "People make mistakes . . . I made a mistake. I'm not cut out to be a married man. Only I didn't know it until Paul was born."

"You kept having babies with her. Why?"

"I did what I thought I was supposed to do. Went through the motions. Isn't that what everyone expected of me? And she kept getting pregnant, even though she was on the pill. It shocked her as much as it did me. I swear, that was the most fertile woman." He shook his head. "At least I didn't bail out in the first year like Steve did to you."

"Steve didn't bail. I did. And my situation was different."

"So you say. Sooner or later we all leave, if we're not happy."

I couldn't argue with that, as much as I wanted to. Paul's, Richard's, and Sammy's rooms were in the same disarray. I managed to find clean clothes and some favorite toys to take with me, while James stood, looking pensive, in each doorway. I don't know what he thought I'd take if he didn't stand guard. He followed me down the stairs and seemed to be in a friendlier state of mind, so I decided to ask him about something he said that bothered me. "I'm surprised you called Bitsy. You two don't get along."

"She called me."

"Did you talk to the boys? How did they sound?"

"I didn't talk to them." He frowned. "I didn't know what to say. Bitsy wanted to know if I could come get them soon."

"What did you tell her?"

"That I think they are better off with her for now." He sighed. "I don't think . . . hell, I *know* I can't deal with the lot of them. We'll work something out."

We reached the bottom of the stairs as Tiffanie came bouncing in from the sun in all her topless glory. Her tiny body with the smooth dark tan made me feel like a lumbering albino behemoth.

"Ooh," she said. "Are we having company already, sweetie?" She did a hair toss over her right shoulder. Amazing that the auburn hair extensions stayed put. She marched over to me and offered her hand. "I'm Tiffanie, Jamey's fiancée."

"For God's sake. Put on a robe." Ignoring her hand, I carried the suitcase toward the kitchen. "We've met. Remember? I'm wifey number one's best friend. The one who died? Yesterday?" I stepped out the door and flashed a look of disgust at James. "Not cut out to be married, huh? Oh, and by the way, Tiff? Your nipples don't line up. They're crooked. Maybe you should ask for a refund."

CHAPTER SIX

To think I felt an iota of compassion for James. Wow, that pissed me off. I drove up the H-1 entrance ramp, headed for the H-2 freeway and the North Shore, fuming all the way.

I was mad at Bitsy for being so incapable. I hated James for, well, just for being such an ass. He planned to marry that ditz-bomb Tiffanie? At least it was a small mercy Jenny would never know. I resented Chang for the mere suggestion I would harm Jenny. And I was mad at God for letting it happen.

The H-2 ends in the town of Wahiawa, in the middle of Oahu. From there, the rest of the journey to the North Shore is a two-lane road, Kamehameha Highway, that bisects miles and miles of pineapple fields. It was once half sugar cane, but Oahu Sugar closed. Both industries burned the fields before or after the harvest though, and one of my favorite experiences in Hawaii was a drive through that area when they did their controlled burns. The tantalizing aroma made it seem as though the entire populace decided to bake a pineapple upside down cake at the same time.

Alas, no cake smells to distract me that day. Was James monstrous enough to have Jenny killed? Why? Because of money? He had tons of the green stuff. And he was an only child, so when his parents died, he'd get everything. Jenny had guessed they were worth hundreds of millions. No matter what he had to pay her in the divorce, it wouldn't make a dent in his lifestyle. He sure as heck didn't want his kids. I reasoned that as nasty as he could be, it still didn't make sense for him to kill her.

What James said about Jenny's pregnancies bothered me. Jenny had acknowledged that after Paul, the kids were all *accidents*, but she'd seemed pretty darned jazzed each time she found herself pregnant. Hers and James' versions didn't line up. I would have asked him why he didn't use condoms with Miss Fertility, but I was sure I knew that answer already.

Bitsy lived on top of Pupukea, a mountain at the north end of the Koolau range. Her house overlooked the shoreline, 3000 feet below, and the tiny quaint towns of Waialua and Haleiwa. The narrow Pupukea Road up the hill twisted back on itself several times. I dreaded it. A flimsy, two foot-high metal guard rail was all that stood between me and a spectacular tumble down the cliff side. A lot of families lived up there, many with driving teenagers. I didn't know how they could stand the worry. I navigated the hairpin turns and soon arrived at Bitsy's house.

"Auntie Bess! Auntie Bess!"

I heard the boys before I saw the front door fly open. They were on me in seconds. We did a huge group hug, and I kissed them on their fuzzy little crew-cut heads.

"Did you bring us some real food?" Richard asked.

"Where's my blanket?" Mikey wanted to know.

"Did you bring my Nintendo DS?" Paul asked.

"Yes, to the blanket and the DS. Your Aunt Bitsy told me this morning that she'd go buy some *real* food."

"We didn't go yet. I'm hungry," Richard said. "I don't like the food she fixed us. It had green peppers. Then she gave us crackers with weird stuff in them."

Bitsy appeared in the front doorway, holding a crying Sammy on her hip. "Thank Mary and Joseph, you're here." She waited for me to climb the painted lanai steps, then handed over the baby. "I have got to get cleaned up. Steve's coming in half an hour. I'll be out in a bit." She went inside, calling behind her, "Make yourself at home."

Paul tugged at my shirt, and I turned to acknowledge him.

"When can we see Mommy? Is she still in the hospital?"

"The hospital?" I asked.

"Auntie Bitsy said the man hurt Mommy really bad and she was in the hospital. I want to go see her."

"Oh. Right." My heart sank. I opened the door. "Let's go inside. We'll talk about this when Dr. Steve comes."

I got the boys changed into clean clothes, and they played with the Ninja Turtle action figures I brought. Sammy calmed down and fell asleep on my shoulder while I sat on the sofa. I caught Steve on his cell before he chugged up the hill and asked him to please pick up milk, hot dogs, macaroni and cheese, eggs, apples, and lots of frozen pizza. And Desitin. I nestled into the cushions and moved Sammy so she lay on my chest.

***

The back door shut, jarring me awake.

"Where is everybody?" Steve called.

Not wanting to disturb Sammy by shouting an answer to him, I waited until he entered the family room. I waved and pointed to the sweaty baby.

"Ahh." He knelt in front of the sofa. "You look God awful."

I yawned. "Yeah, everybody keeps telling me. Thanks." He, on the other hand, looked perfect, as always. The windswept blonde hair, his tanned muscular chest and arms showcased in a bright white polo shirt.

"Hi, boys," Steve said. "Ninja Turtles, eh? One of my all-time favorites."

Paul and Richard greeted him with blank expressions. Mikey slept on the carpet.

"Guys, you remember Dr. Steve, don't you?" I asked.

"I guess." Paul seemed puzzled. "Are you the one Auntie Bess married?"

"Yes, I am," Steve said.

One side of Richard's face screwed upward. "How come you're not married anymore? Do you have a new girlfriend, too? Like my dad?"

"I'm never getting married," Paul said.

"Ohh-kayy." Steve stood. "Bess, can you put her down? I'd like to talk to you."

"I can try." Rising from the sofa with Sammy's dead weight wasn't easy. I teetered backward, and Steve's strong arm was at my back in an instant, supporting me. I ignored the shivery sensation that caused, and lay Sammy on the cushion.

"Where's Bitsy?" Steve asked.

"She went to take a shower at least an hour ago." I stretched my back and arms. "I'll bet she fell asleep instead. No one's had much rest." The entire right shoulder of my tee shirt was soaked with Sammy's drool. I bent down and pulled away the golden curls plastered to her face.

"She's grown a lot since I last saw her," Steve said.

"That was over a year and twelve pounds ago. Did you get the food?"

"In the car."

"Come on, I'll help you. Paul, we'll be right back. Watch Sammy. We're getting the groceries from the car."

Outside, Steve was one step below me when he turned. I stood on the landing, and the elevation difference put his face in front of mine. His big blue eyes had flecks of amber and olive on the outer edges of the iris in quartz-like formations. They had the power to mesmerize me.

"Bess."

He placed his hands on my waist. I would have torn them off me, but it felt darned good.

"I'm worried about you. Debbie is, too."

Pop. Bubble broken. I removed his hands, then slipped past him down the stairs. "I'll be fine," I called over my shoulder.

"I'm serious." He caught up with me and opened the car door.

"So am I." I grabbed two bags and retreated to the house.

"How is Quinn? What did he see yesterday?" I asked him when he set his bags on the counter. I'd already emptied mine, and I started on his.

"He saw the man running away," he spoke in a hushed tone. "Nothing else."

"Thank God."

"I'm not so happy you were almost shot at. I love you."

"Please, not now."

"You've got to get over the notion I'm attracted to your sister. You need me to take care of you. Your mother called me. She's worried."

"I don't want to talk about it. Not now. I'll find Bitsy." I lowered my voice to a whisper. "They don't know she's dead. I assume that means they didn't hear anything either." I put a frozen cheese pizza into the cavernous top of the stainless double oven, then passed through the family room to Bitsy's bedroom.

Behind me, I heard Steve talking to the kids. I knocked on the bedroom door. It was ajar. I pushed it open.

"Bitsy?" I expected to see her sacked out on the bed, but the silk embroidered coverlet was empty. I went to the bathroom door and was about to knock, when I heard her speak.

"Sweetcakes, I told you. That's not what it was about. We had a strange childhood, okay? Leave it alone. It was what it was. What I want to know is—when are you going to come and get *your* children?"

James? Sweetcakes? But then, that didn't necessarily mean much. Bitsy called everybody sugar or honey, when she wanted something.

"And how soon are they coming? . . . Uh-huh. Fine. Listen, I've got to go. Steve's coming to counsel the kids. You should be here, you know."

I ran back to the bedroom door and knocked as she opened the bathroom door.

"Bitsy?" I called. "Are you in there?"

"Coming," she said. "Is Steve here?"

Wearing what had to be size zero tight jeans, a clingy black tank top, and high-heeled sandals, she emerged. Her natural red hair gleamed with caramel highlights. The controlled, soft waves fluttered about her face and past her shoulders. Her make up was perfect. She looked every bit the petites model she used to be.

The scent of Chanel Number Five hit me. All I could do was say, "Yes, he's here." I wished that once, just once, I could appear so sexy.

She breezed by me, sashayed her way to Steve, and threw her arms around him. "Thank you for coming. You're a lifesaver. Isn't it awful? I don't know what I'd do if I had to deal with this alone."

He stared at me over her shoulder with a how-did-I-get-elected look.

"Glad to be able to help." He unwrapped her arms and took a step back. "Why don't the three of us talk in the kitchen?" He whispered, "I'd like to discuss how to break the news to the boys."

We followed him to the kitchen table. I realized with my larger-sized body obscured further by a loose wrinkled T-shirt and baggy jeans, plus my unadorned face, I was no match for Bitsy's radiance.

Well, he did say I looked awful. I told myself I was too weary to care anyway.

CHAPTER SEVEN

We had everyone ready when Steve's phone rang. He took the call outside. The boys and I shared the sofa while we waited.

Sammy sat on Bitsy's cloth-diaper layered lap chewing on a Ninja Turtle. Bitsy stared out the window. I couldn't read her expression.

I picked up Paul's left hand with my right and held it, fingering the precise joints. How did God manage to make children so perfect? Paul had more freckles than the others, and I studied the pattern of them as they increased closer to his elbow. Downy white hair covered his soft arms.

"I'm tired," Richard said. "Why do we have to sit here?"

"We're going to talk about your mom," I said. "Dr. Steve wants to help." I observed what I could of their faces.

Before Mom died. After Mom died. Soon to be the definition for everything that entered their lives. These were the final precious moments of their innocence.

Steve came in holding a box of tissues and sat in the leather chair opposite us.

"It's about time." Bitsy turned her gaze back into the room. "Kids, listen up."

Steve shot her a look, then did an eye raise toward me. "Guys, I need you to look at me."

I nudged them.

"Your mom's injury was bad," Steve said. "Sometimes, even though we want them to, the people we love don't get better."

"I want to see her," Richard said.

"I want to go home," Mikey said. "I hate it here."

"Sometimes, the doctors do the very best they know how, but their patients don't make it. Your mom had the very best doctors," Steve said.

"Our mom's dead, isn't she," Paul said. It was a statement, not a question.

"Mommy's dead?" Richard asked.

"Yes," Steve said.

A hiccoughing sound escaped Paul's lips, followed by a low wail that gained strength at a gut-seizing pace.

Richard chimed in, joined by Mikey. Paul buried his face in my T-shirt sleeve and clutched my arm. I stoked his head and hugged Mikey tighter with my other arm. Sammy began to whimper. My tears resumed, and Steve got on his knees in front of us.

He rubbed Richard's shoulders, then pulled a tissue and wiped the child's tears.

It took about a half an hour, but we managed to calm them.

"Try to think of your mom as a beautiful angel who helps God now," Steve said. "The prettiest one he's got, I'll bet."

"You boys have so many people who love you," Bitsy said. She'd kept silent until then. Her eyes were dry, make-up perfect. "You have your dad," she said.

"Our dad doesn't even *like* us anymore," Paul said.

"Yes, he does," Steve said. "And Auntie Bitsy loves you, your grandparents love you, and Auntie Bess loves you."

"I don't know some of those people," Paul said.

"Don't be silly, sweetheart," Bitsy said. "You know us."

"My dad only loves Tiffanie now," Richard sobbed. "He doesn't want us. We heard him tell Mom, didn't we, Paul?"

I wondered what else they'd heard.

"Grandma and Grandpa Dobbins are coming tomorrow," Bitsy said. "Won't that be great? They'll be staying with you at your house."

"They are?" Steve asked.

"Oh." Her fake smile faded. "Sure. I thought it would help if they knew."

"You might have told us first," I said. The kids had met James' parents twice. I was there for both occasions. They were not warm and fuzzy grandparents.

"Those are the people we don't know," Paul said. "Is our dad gonna be there?"

"Well . . ." Bitsy said.

"We're working out the details," Steve said. "This is better though, isn't it? You wanted to go home to your house and now you can." He cast a wary glance at me. "Tomorrow, Auntie Bitsy will drive you home and—"

"Uh. Can't do that, Steve," Bitsy said. "I've got so much to do. It'd be easier if you or Bess could do it." She placed Sammy on the floor, peeled away the sweat-damp cloth diapers from her lap, and stood.

"I'll come back and get them tomorrow." I wondered why she seemed so abrupt and detached. Did it have to do with her conversation with James I overheard? What else did she know that I didn't? "What time are William and Vivian coming in?"

"James said their flight lands at ten AM."

"So, they should be in the house by noon at the latest, right?" I asked. "I'll be here at eleven-thirty. That way we'll get to Kahala about twelve-thirty. By the way, does the CPS lady know about the grandparent thing?"

"I left that to James," Bitsy said. "He should be doing something."

"I don't want to sleep here tonight," Richard said.

"Me, neither," Mikey said. "I want to go home now."

"One more night, okay? Then I'll come back tomorrow—"

"Don't go. You can't leave us here alone, Auntie Bess," Paul said. "Stay with us."

"I want you to, too," Richard said.

Mikey made a whimpering sound and nuzzled deeper into my chest.

Steve spent another hour with the kids. They were in decent shape when he left, and he told me he'd check on them at the Kahala house the next day, Monday.

I would stay overnight at Bitsy's. By eight, I had the baby settled in the playpen in the second bedroom.

While the boys took turns brushing teeth, Bitsy pulled pillows and sheets from the hall linen closet and handed them to me.

"Guess I'll set up a makeshift bed on the den carpet," I said. "Who buys a two-bedroom house, anyway?"

"Couples with no children," she said. "We hardly needed the second one as it was."

I withheld a snarky comment regarding her lack of hostessing charm and carried the bedding into the den.

"I'm going to bed," Bitsy said. "I've got an early morning ahead of me."

I heard her door shut. I spread out one king flat sheet, placed the pillows on it, and turned the TV on to the cartoon channel.

The boys wandered in from the bathroom and cozied next to me. We watched a few road-runner and coyote classics, then hit the sack.

***

I awoke feeling like I'd been turned into a pretzel overnight. Bent at the waist, I stared at Richard's face. Paul's knobby knees pressed against the small of my back. Mikey's foot lay on Richard's head, his big toe about an inch from my eye.

Sammy's crying from down the hall got my attention, and I extracted myself from the jungle of little boy limbs. I glanced at my watch on the way. It was already nine. Bitsy's door was closed. So much for her so-called early morning.

I bathed the kids and had them in clean clothes sitting at the kitchen table by the time Bitsy emerged dressed for success.

She eyed the eggs I broke into a bowl with detached interest. "I didn't know you could cook."

"Do you want some?" I added milk and whisked the mixture until it was frothy.

She peered at the gleaming stainless frying pan on the cooktop and winced at the sight of a quarter-stick of butter melting in it. "No," she said. "That's going right to your hips, you know."

I poured the eggs in. A loud satisfying sizzle drowned out whatever else she had to say about my hips. With a fork, I whirled the eggs around the pan until they were soft and fluffy.

"This is great cookware you've got." I portioned out the scrambled eggs and placed a piece of buttered toast on each plate.

"I wouldn't know," she said. "Saturday night was the first time I used any of it. Cooking was Henry's thing, not mine."

"Didn't realize that." Henry Zeller was Bitsy's husband. A heart attack took him out at age fifty-three, four years previous. She was thirty-five at the time. Wealthy widowhood seemed to agree with her.

"Do you miss him?" I asked.

She looked at me like I'd sprouted wings. "You're joking, right?"

"Don't think I was, no." I carried the plates to the table.

"Yes. Real food," Richard said.

"Ono awesome," Paul said.

The kids dug in, and I returned to the island where Bitsy added items to a list.

"I thought you loved him," I said.

"Who?" She answered without looking up.

"Your husband."

She snorted. "You're such a hopeless romantic."

"I am not."

"Please. You packed and left Dr. Wonderful because he glanced at your sister."

"That's not true. He had, still *has*, the major league hots for her. Nobody wants a husband who's in love with someone else."

"Everything's got to be perfect with you. I learned very young that life isn't that way. Henry and I had some fun and some problems, but we both knew what our deal was."

"Your deal? It sounds so businesslike. What was your *deal?*"

She stopped writing, faced me, and lowered her voice. "Henry was short, balding, and fat. And I'm . . .well, look at me. There was only one way someone like him could get me. He was rich. Very, very rich. And happy to share it." She bent to finish her list.

"Poor Henry."

"Poor Henry, my bottom. Grow up. He got his trophy wife and the status that conveyed. I was the perfect escort for his important company dinners and parties. He got laid once a week. Every Sunday, like clockwork. For ten years of marriage. Now you tell me how many couples you know who profess to *love* each other still have regular sex? Even after five years? Believe me, I never heard a complaint out of him."

"Weren't you lonely?"

"I'm not like you, Bess." She took her list and left the room. "Neither was Jenny," she added as she disappeared down the hall.

45

The kids were done eating. I sent the boys to the den. Sammy had eggs in her hair, so I sat her on the counter next to the sink, did a wipe down, then plunked her beside her brothers in front of the television.

I thought about Bitsy's last comment as I ate my cold breakfast. Jenny wasn't a viper like her sister. I'd known her better than anyone, and she loved James. Even when he began fooling around, she loved him. As nasty as the proceedings got, if he'd changed his mind and said take him back, she would have. I decided Bitsy was one of those people who are unable to feel real emotion, and she projected that emptiness into her comprehension of her sister. Or did it have to do with what I'd heard? Had she and James slept together? Was that the cause of Jenny's intense resentment of Bitsy, and Bitsy's dispassionate attitude?

"Here are the diapers." Bitsy came in carrying the suitcase I brought and two extra-large bags of disposables. She dropped them on the floor next to the back door. "This is the alarm code." She placed a pink Post-it on the table at my elbow. "It's easy. Just press this number on the pad, then the pound key. You have sixty seconds to close the door."

"Where are you going?"

"To show a house."

In three years, I think she'd sold one house with her glorified hobby. "I thought you were so busy planning the funeral, dealing with your loss, and all that."

She sniffed and gave me a half-smile on her way out the door.

I watched her back her Mercedes out of the garage then stop by my van. Seconds later, the car seat waited for me on the grass by my van's passenger side, and a thin waft of dust rose from the pebbled driveway.

CHAPTER EIGHT

I finished loading the dishwasher, then did a final look-see for toys, toothbrushes, etc., my brain on overload as I did. Something felt wrong again. Maybe it was Bitsy seeming so chummy with James on the phone call I overheard. Jenny had told me once he moved out, Bitsy stopped speaking to him. That didn't ring true now, so maybe Jenny didn't know about the two of them. Did they have an affair? Were they still involved? Which led me to the awful possibility that Bitsy and James could have conspired to kill Jenny.

But there was another possible clue. Bitsy told him on the phone they'd had a weird childhood. James already knew that story. Why would he ask again?

I tried the handle to her bedroom. Locked. I hoped maybe I could find something explaining their newfound friendship. My phone rang, and I ran to the kitchen.

"Bess? Detective Chang."

"Hi."

"We picked up a possible suspect. Can you come by about one? I'd like you to look at a photographic line-up."

"But I didn't see their faces."

"These are pictures of bodies. With tattoos."

"Really?" I glanced at my watch. It was eleven-fifteen. I'd need an hour to deliver the kids to their grandparents, then go home and change. "Sure. It'll be close, but I think I can get there. You think you found one of the guys?"

"Don't know, but I'm hoping. A patrol car pulled him over this morning for a broken tail light. He matches your description."

"I'll be there as soon as I can."

I walked into the family room. A commercial for the governor's re-election campaign was on the TV. Though the election wasn't for nine months, the contest was already predicted to be a landslide for the governor.

I liked Governor Samuels. He seemed like a good guy. I met his wife, Emily, at a fund-raiser once, and she was very gracious. He created a compromise bill for the Hawaiian Sovereignty Movement, which would grant Native Hawaiians the same rights as Native Americans and lots more, but not enough to upset the balance of life in the state. He was part-Hawaiian, a lawyer with a degree from the prestigious Camorra University in San Francisco, and the local people loved him.

Switching off the television, I announced our imminent departure.

The boys scrambled into high gear and ran to the van.

"Guys?" I called after them. "Get back here and help carry things, please. And do a bathroom check, too. It's a long drive to town."

The trip lulled the kids to sleep. I left the radio off and appreciated the quiet. Hawaiian *snow* touched, then danced across my windshield as we passed the pineapple fields. A controlled burn was under way several fields in from the highway. The wispy black cinders and the delicious cake smell traveled with us for miles.

A black Lincoln Navigator blocked one end of Jenny's driveway. I parked on the other side. Carrying Sammy on my left hip, with the sleepy boys in tow, I knocked at the kitchen door in the garage. I didn't see any of James' three cars.

"Well, well." Vivian Dobbins opened the door with a planted smile. "Look who's here."

She smelled of Shalimar. She wore lime-green linen slacks topped by a Lilly Pulitzer pink and green blouse. Her polished toenails peeked from matching lime sandals. Grayer than when I'd last seen it, her hair was swept into a chignon. It gave her a casual, easy elegance. A silver cross on a chain hung from her neck.

I let the boys go in first, then stepped inside with Sammy. "Hello, Vivian. I'm Bess. Do you remember me?"

"Of course I do. How are you? You've dyed your hair another color. Look at these children. How they've grown." She dipped into a squat and opened her arms, silver bangle bracelets jangling. "Give me a hug."

Paul shot me a *do I have to* look, and I mouthed the words, *do it.*

Richard ventured toward her first, followed by Mikey, then Paul. None of them put much effort into a return hug. They charged toward the stairs.

If Vivian was put off by their lack of enthusiasm, she didn't let it show. What could she expect anyway? She hadn't seen them in two years.

She stood and gestured for Sammy.

"Go to Grandma," I said.

Vivian winced.

I handed the baby over. "I'll get their things from the car. Be back in flash, then I'll change her for you."

I removed the car seat, placed it on the garage floor, and went back for the suitcase and diapers. When I re-entered the kitchen, they were gone. I set my load down, grabbed a diaper and the box of wipes, and hearing voices out by the pool, headed there.

William sat on a chaise with Sammy on his lap, the boys and Vivian standing near. He was stealing Paul's nose, a game the kid outgrew at four. William got an exasperated eye-roll for his trouble.

"He's too old for that nonsense," Vivian said.

I was struck, again, by what a handsome man James' father was. He had classic features. Silver-gray hair, structured cheek bones, wide shoulders, a strong chin.

"Hello, William." I walked around the pool toward him. "How are you?"

He stared at me with a puzzled expression. He knew I was supposed to drop off the kids, didn't he?

"This is Bess, honey," Vivian said. "*Jenny's* friend. You met her the last time we were here. She's gained some weight and changed her hair color, but you remember, don't you?"

Witch. The way she said Jenny's name was strange, kind of mocking-toned. Not to mention putting me down. And we'd met twice before, not once.

"Sure. How are you? Thank you for driving the children," he said.

William didn't sound one bit sure.

"Yes. I forgot to thank you," Vivian jumped in. "Bitsy sounded so upset on the phone. Poor thing, it must have been difficult for her to handle the children on top of everything else she's going through."

"Yeah, she's a real trooper." Restraining my natural sarcasm wasn't easy. "Bringing them was my pleasure. I love these kids. If you'll give me Sammy, I'll clean her up."

William passed her to me, and I retreated into the house. I didn't want to ask in front of the boys, but where was James? I carted Sammy up the stairs toward her nursery and stopped at the door to Jenny's bedroom. The room looked antiseptic clean, with different Louis Vuitton luggage piled in one corner. James and Tiffanie must have decided to vacate since the grandparents had volunteered to come.

Venturing into the room, I realized an odd fact. No trace of Jenny remained. Every personal item of hers—the framed photos, jewelry box, blue silk scarf tied around the lamp—gone. I peeked inside her closet. Emptied. Her sink counter in the master bath was cleared off. I checked the vanity drawers. Emptied also. Anger rose in me. The woman hadn't been dead for forty-eight hours, and it was like she'd never been there.

"Mama," Sammy said.

"Yes. Mama," I answered. "Even you know something stinks here. Come on, let's get you changed."

When we returned downstairs, Vivian stood in front of the fridge.

"What do you think of your only granddaughter?" I'd put Sammy into a pink cotton sundress with matching ruffled shorts, washed her face, and combed her curls. "Can you believe how beautiful she is?"

"She is precious." Vivian glanced up from the deli drawer. "She looks much better now. Would you like to stay for lunch? We're making sandwiches."

I'd have taken any bet she'd never done that before. I sent up a silent prayer of thanks my mother took an avid interest in her grandkids. Vivian had never laid eyes on this child, and her interest seemed marginal at best. No wonder James was screwed up.

"Thanks," I said. "But I can't stay. I'm supposed to be somewhere at one. If it's all right with you, I'll come back later to see them. Do you know if James will be here?"

"That's fine. I don't know anything about James' schedule." She looked at her watch. "You'd better hurry. It's twenty minutes to one." She pulled a few packages out and placed them on the counter.

I went to the family room and, with my free hand, dragged the playpen back with me into the kitchen. "I'll leave her here, in the playpen." I kissed Sammy on the cheek, set her down, and started to walk out of the room, then stopped. Vivian hadn't acknowledged me. "Sammy's in here, okay?"

"Mmhm."

Out on the pool terrace, the boys and William sat around the umbrella-shaded table. William fanned a deck of cards, looking like he'd show them a few tricks. It made me feel better to know he cared enough to try. I had serious concerns about leaving the kids with their grandparents, but there were no other choices.

"Hey guys?" I said. "I have to go now."

Paul's eyebrows raised in alarm. "No."

"I don't want you to go," Richard said.

Nothing came out of Mikey's mouth, but his sad eyes said it all.

It made me tear up again. I went one by one around the table, giving them big hugs. "I'll be back later to see you. I promise."

There was no time to go home and change, much less shower. I headed straight to the police station, feeling awful. All the spaces in the garage were taken, so I parked in the hot sun on the street. I rummaged around the back of the van, knowing under the wallpaper books and fabric samples, there was a silver windshield sunscreen. I came across the pink and white polka-dot diaper bag again. I'd thrown it into the way back when I got the kids into the van at Bitsy's. And forgotten it, again.

It was a good thing I was between projects at work. I'd have been dangerous if left to make crucial decisions in my state. Most of my schedule for the week entailed follow-up calls and punch lists.

As though one of my clients tapped into my thoughts, my new ring tone, an embarrassing oldie of Frankie Lymon's—*Goody Goody*, sang to life. I recognized the number.

"Mrs. Plimpton. Good morning. Um. Afternoon."

"Bess? Jocelyn Plimpton here."

Yes, I got that. The woman always began a conversation the same way. "Yes. What can I do for you?"

"Have you forgotten me? It's five after."

Crud. We were supposed to meet at the wholesale lighting store at one. "I'm so sorry. I should have called you. We need to reschedule. There's been an emergency situation. May I call you later?"

"Well. I am very busy. I don't appreciate this. I drove from Kahala to Iwalei for nothing."

"Again, I am so sorry. Please forgive me."

"What happened? This isn't like you."

52

"My best friend was killed on Saturday."

"Dear Lord. Killed? Wait. You don't mean the one on the news, James Dobbins' wife?"

"Yes. Her name was Jenny."

"My condolences, dear. I wasn't aware you knew her. You know, I used to date her father-in-law, back in college."

"You knew William? Dated him? Really."

"It's a small island. Hard not to know certain people."

"What college was that?"

"Camorra University. For a time there, it was a popular choice for Oahu's high-school grads. Especially Punahou."

"Camorra. The same one as the governor?"

"Yes. And William Dobbins. He and I were quite the pair until a certain socialite's parents interfered."

"You mean Vivian." My brain refused to see that love triangle.

"Ah. Stories for another day. Ancient history. Tell me, do you know anything about a service? There's been nothing in the paper."

"No. They haven't released her body yet. Can't make plans 'til they do. I'm outside the police station right now. I'm due inside. Can I call you later? I'll let you know about a service, and maybe we can postpone the lighting selection until next week."

"Of course. You take your time."

I closed the phone, finished placing the sunshield, and locked the van. Jocelyn Plimpton dated William? Hard to imagine. Tall, reserved, perfect William stood out as a distinguished figure in any crowd. Understated elegance defined him. A lifetime of wealth, privilege, and proper breeding did that for a person.

I knew Mrs. Plimpton was about the same age. While she too had wealth, it didn't appear to be anywhere near the Dobbins' fortune. She looked ten years older, weighed at least seventy-five pounds too much, and was prone to passing juicy gossip and name dropping. Both of which were Dobbins family no-nos. She was a lot more like me than anybody with any business marrying into the Dobbins family. I could see why the parents interfered. She didn't belong to their world any more than I did. Which made me think.

How the hell had Jenny and James' marriage happened? Jenny had no money. No pedigree. Her father left them when Jenny was a baby, and her mother drank her waitressing life away. I guess when you're as drop-dead gorgeous as Jenny was, you can pretty much do anything. I entered the building.

"You look much better." Cliff Chang stood in the doorway of a large conference room.

I walked inside.

Chang shut the door and sat at a desk at the far end. "Get some sleep?

"Thanks. Yes. I feel more able to deal with this today, too." I sat in a chair at a rectangular fake-wood table. "I'm guessing I'm not the only one. You changed your shirt. Doesn't your wife get upset if you stay at the office all night?"

"I'm divorced. And speaking of changing clothes, um . . ." He gestured toward me.

I felt a blush warm my cheeks as I remembered I'd slept in my clothes and now appeared before him in the same T-shirt and jeans as the day before.

"How embarrassing," I said. "I had to go to Bitsy's, and the kids didn't want me to leave, and so I spent the night, and then I had to . . ."

A bemused look greeted me from across the desk.

"Never mind," I said. "I'm sorry about your divorce. My marriage broke up, too. It sucks."

"I'm not sorry. Let's just say she found something to do on those nights I had to work."

"Like bingo?"

"His name was Frank."

"Oh."

His grin blossomed into a smile.

I decided he was quite handsome. "Not that it's any of my business, but you seem happy about it."

"Took me about three months to realize I liked my life better without her in it. I also got an unforeseen bonus. My wretched shrew of a mother-in-law stopped speaking to me."

A loud, impatient knock sounded on the door.

"Come in," Chang said.

I turned to see James stride to the desk. He wore that *why the hell are you messing with me* expression I'd seen more than a few times. His imposing six-foot frame hovered above the seated Chang.

"Why do I need to do this again?" James demanded. "You people are driving me nuts. I have other things to do, you know. Wasn't three hours of questioning Saturday night enough?" He swiveled his head and stared at me. "Bess? What're you doing here?"

"Hi, James," I said.

He sneered at me. His mellowed attitude toward me from the day before must have expired at midnight.

"Mr. Dobbins," Chang said, "thank you for coming. In light of your busy schedule, I do appreciate it."

Chang didn't seem intimidated in the least by James' size or his blustering.

"Please, have a seat. Would you like coffee?" Chang said.

"No. I do not want coffee. Do you have any idea how many powerful people my family knows in this state? This better be about finding Jenny's killer."

I couldn't imagine what else it would be about. What did he think? Parking tickets?

"There's been a development," Chang said. "That's why I need to speak with you again. I apologize if they didn't tell you on the phone. Until this case is solved, I'll need your cooperation. The fact you're so anxious for us to find the assailant tells me I have your full support. Am I correct?"

James didn't answer.

Unflappable Chang. I liked him more every minute.

"Mr. Dobbins, I'll be with you in a moment. Would you mind having a seat? Just bring one over here to the desk from against the wall there." He pointed to the three orange plastic chairs next to the window.

Watching James carry a chair and settle himself, he reminded me of a spoiled eight-year-old.

"Now, Ms. Blinke," Chang said, "they'll be ready for us soon. What I'd like you to do is wait for me in the hall. While you're waiting, conjure up once again the images we went over yesterday."

"The ones of the—"

He put a finger to his lips.

"Gotcha." I rose and made my way to the door. "Say hi to your fiancée, *Jamey*."

"Fiancée?" Chang's brows furrowed.

"Didn't he tell you? He and Tiffanie are getting married." I loved being helpful.

"*There's* a detail you left out the other day," Chang said.

"That's because I'm *not* getting married." James glared at me. "I just let her think that. You didn't see a ring on her finger, did you?"

As a matter of fact, I hadn't. "That's even lower. And in case you had any interest, your children are doing remarkably well considering their lives are turned upside-down. Not that you asked." I closed the door behind me.

CHAPTER NINE

I loved Chang's subtle method of establishing dominance over James.

The conference room door opened five minutes later. Chang and James walked into the hall.

"Thank you, Detective." James extended his right hand.

Thank you and a handshake? What went on in there?

Chang shook with him. "I'll let you know as soon as I can."

"Vivian said you're going to the house later?" James said to me. He sounded civil again.

"I promised the kids I would. Are you and Tiff going to be there?"

"I will. Don't think William and Vivian are ready for Tiffanie." He started down the hall, then turned. "For God's sake, don't tell them about any supposed engagement."

"*Nobody's* ready for Tiffanie," I said to Chang.

He smiled at me. "Thanks for waiting. Come in, Detective Smalley's on her way with the photo file. It won't take long. You must be anxious to get home."

"I smell that good, huh?"

He laughed. "I wouldn't know. I have the remnants of a cold." His eyes focused on mine a moment too long.

I stole fleeting glances as he studied his file on the table in front of him. Long black lashes any woman would kill for framed his dark eyes. Were they brown? I sat and placed my purse on the floor beside my chair, feeling guilty for having a romantic reaction to him at an inappropriate time.

Any further flirtatious thoughts galloped away when Detective Kelly Smalley entered the room. Her smile gave the sunlight, flooding in from the western exposure windows, some stiff competition. Though her smile was clearly meant for Chang, even I got caught up in it. She was Hawaiian-Japanese, I guessed. But then, where'd the Smalley moniker derive from? Had to be an English ancestor in there somewhere. Was it from one of those pesky missionaries in the seventeen-hundreds? Then again, it could have been her husband's. Or an ex, since her ring finger was bare.

"Hello, Ms. Blinke," she said. "Do you remember me now? You seemed a little fuzzy yesterday." She sat to my right.

Great gobs, she was adorable. Tiny and thin, yet with a woman's figure, and a beautiful face. If Chang had any brains in his head, he would grab her, and quick. Anyone could see she desired him.

Yes. I remembered her. Now. She was the one who occupied the kids on Saturday while I spoke to Chang. Stress can be weird, I discovered. "I'm sorry I didn't recognize you. You're right, I was fuzzy. Good word."

Chang let loose a loud sneeze. "Excuse me. Had no warning on that one." He glanced around the room.

"Bless you," Smalley said.

"I have tissues." I grabbed up my purse, then pulled out my wallet, keys, phone, sunglasses, and daily planner.

"That's okay. I've got a box in my office." Chang rose.

"No. They're right here." I found the stash of tissues, yanked them out and onto the table, smiling and feeling useful.

Smalley and Chang exchanged hesitant looks, then both stared at me.

"What?" I asked, my smile fading.

Chang nodded toward the pile.

"They're clean," I said. "Unused. I promise. I know they're not neat and folded because they've been at the bottom of my purse, but—"

"That's not it." Chang pulled the top tissue away from the rest revealing a joint in a roach clip.

"It's not mine." I felt the blood rush to my face.

He leveled an *oh, please* look at me.

"No, really. It's not." I tried not to sound as panicky as I felt. "I don't smoke anything, ever. Well, not *ever*, because I did try some Maui Wowie when I first moved here, but it was so strong. I didn't like it." My heart pounded. "I found this on the floor of the elevator in my building and picked it up because I didn't want my super to see it. He's got a heart condition. Gets stressed out way too fast, and I meant to throw it away but I forgot and—"

"Stop," Chang said, his voice stern.

I blinked back tears.

Using one of the tissues, he picked up the roach, stood, and walked to a counter at the far end of the room. He took a plastic bag from a drawer and dropped the joint into it.

"You can test it for DNA, if you want. I'll swab my cheek, and you can compare. That thing never touched my lips." I looked at Smalley. "I mean, when you said I was fuzzy and I agreed, I didn't mean *that kind* of fuzzy."

"It's okay." Chang placed the bag in his briefcase and sat. "I believe you."

"You do?"

"Yes. This never happened. Right?" He looked at Smalley.

"What never happened?" Smalley grinned. "I believe you, too. Relax."

"Thank you." I exhaled. "Thank you so much." I willed my pulse to return to normal.

A haole man knocked at the open door and entered. He placed his briefcase on the table next to Chang. "Are you Ms. Blinke?"

"Yes."

"I'm Lawrence Talbot. I'm a Public Defender for the city and county of Honolulu."

I looked at Chang. "Do I need a defense attorney?"

"No. He's here to make sure we don't tell you which of these guys we picked up this morning. He represents that guy downstairs."

Talbot pulled over another chair and sat to Chang's right, opposite me.

Smalley opened her file. "There are six men featured here. On each page are five shots of each man. We're hoping you might recognize the man you saw on Saturday." She passed them to me.

The men wore shorts and T-shirts. Solid black squares blocked their heads. All stood against a backdrop wall with horizontal height markings. I studied the first one. They had photographed him from the front, both sides, the back, and a close-up of his tattoo. Not just skinny, this guy was emaciated.

"He's too thin," I said. "And his arms aren't as dark. The hair's the same length, though." I pointed to the hair extending below the black square. "I don't think that's the right tattoo." I closed my eyes and recalled the flashing image. A long green stain on his arm. "You know, it could have been a snake."

Number two had a finger missing from his left hand. I didn't recall seeing that on the guy. He also looked a bit heavier set.

Three seemed the right height and build, but his skin color made midnight look pale. "He's way too dark."

The fourth had possibilities. Then I noticed the profuse amount of hair on his legs. "Too hairy." I tossed that one back onto the file.

Five scared me. Horrible red slash scars covered his arms and legs. "What happened to him? You have to deal with this sort of creep?" I asked Smalley. "I bet your mother can't stand it."

"You're right. She hates my being a cop." Smalley winked. "Maybe that's why I love what I do."

Both Chang and Talbot chuckled.

"Don't let her petite and delicate exterior fool you," Chang said. "She's tougher than any of us. Never loses it at a crime scene."

I turned my attention to Mr. Six. "It was a snake." I held the photo up to show Chang. "This looks like the tattoo. I remember a deep emerald color. It was elongated. The bright cherry-red at one end." I studied the rest of number six's pictures. His body type matched, his arms were darker than his legs, and he had very little body hair.

"This is the guy I saw pulling the stuff from Jenny's car. Put him in red surf trunks and you're done." I gave Chang the picture sheet.

"In truth, what you know is the man in that photo has a similar body and tattoo like the one you remember." Chang passed the photo to Talbot.

"I'll get the process moving on my end." Talbot stood and went to the door.

"You might want to wait a while," Smalley said. "I don't know if he's sober yet. He vomited on the men trying to get him photographed earlier."

***

Chang insisted on walking me outside. I stopped midway to my van, in the blissful shade of a kiawe tree.

"I'm embarrassed about the joint," I said. "I really don't smoke. Thank you for believing me."

"You can thank Detective Smalley," Chang said. "She's got a nose like a bloodhound, and if you did smoke any pakalolo over the last few days, she'd have smelled it and nailed you."

"What happens now with the tattoo guy?"

"We encourage the man to tell us who his partner is. And what they were looking for. And why it's important enough to them to justify shooting Mrs. Dobbins."

"Do you think they maybe got her mixed-up with somebody else? When the guy said he didn't find *it*, could it be a drug stash?"

"We're considering that and other ideas. Smalley and I imagined at least a dozen scenarios. We'll figure it out."

"Speaking of Detective Smalley," I said, "I think she wants you to ask her out. Not that it's any of my business, but she's a real cutie-pie."

"I'll take that under consideration." His voice was flat.

"Oops. Sorry again. None of my business."

His face reddened. "No problem."

"Probably against some police rule, anyway, huh?"

"Moving on." He glanced up into the tree. "Is there a man in your life?"

"What?" Then I understood. "Just my ex trying to get back into my life, but there's no way he had anything to do with Jenny's death."

He stared at me, a crooked grin on the left side of his mouth.

As a detective, there was no way he wouldn't discover my lack of a love life, so I confessed. "I don't have a boyfriend or even a casual fling guy who could be mixed into this mess." I sighed. "Truth is, I don't get asked out much."

He placed a hand on my arm. "Come on. Where's your car?"

An electrical charge zoomed through me. He had my full attention. His eyes, by the way, were brown. Dark, deep, velvety-sable brown.

"Over there." I pointed, wondering if he felt a corresponding *zoom*.

We started in that direction.

"Just for the record," he said. "I'd ask you out."

For one of the rare times in my life, I couldn't cough up a word.

"If," he said, "you know, this crime wasn't the way we'd met. And if it turned out you really had no part in Mrs. Dobbins' death."

"I didn't. You'll see. But I'm so—" I came close to saying *dumpy*. "I'm so *not* a tiny, cute person. Like Detective Smalley."

"Tiny and cute can be overrated. I find you attractive, albeit larger than most the local girls, and I can't believe I just said that." He dropped his head. "I'm sorry."

"It's okay. I know what I look like."

"You're smart and funny—and beautiful. Don't let anyone tell you otherwise."

Not knowing if he was simply attempting to make me feel better about myself or whether he meant it, I managed a smile. "That's very kind of you."

He shook his head. "You always this hard to compliment?"

"Yes." We'd reached the van. I found my keys, then saw him gazing at me again, with an intensity I'd never forget. I felt a shiver, the good and lusty kind. "There's no rule against our meeting for coffee to discuss the case, is there?"

"As long as I don't tell you anything I'm not supposed to, we could do that."

"Great. Tomorrow morning at seven. The Starbucks at Ala Moana." I walked away with the stupid thought that if we ever did go out, I wouldn't let him meet my sister.

***

I fell across my bed with every intention of lying there for a minute, then hitting the shower. A banging on my door woke me. I glanced at the clock. Three hours gone. It was five-thirty.

Steve's voice shouted at me. "Bess. Open the door. Are you alright? Bess?"

Bleary-eyed, I undid the deadbolt and let him in. "I'm fine. Come in." I waved him onward toward my living room, then made a stop in the bathroom. A cool splash of water revived me. I brushed my teeth. Running a brush through my hair, I heard my cell ringing and bolted to the kitchen where I left my purse.

"Where are you?" Vivian asked from the other end. "You said you were coming to see the children this afternoon, so I made reservations."

"Hello, Vivian. Reservations for what?" Were she and William taking all four kids to dinner? Steve came in the kitchen with an expectant look.

"We're going to Montrachet," Vivian said. "Our table is set for seven o'clock."

Montrachet, the fussed-over new restaurant at the far end of Waikiki. *Everybody* who was *anybody* went there while in town. Situated on the beach near Diamond Head and the Outrigger Canoe Club, I knew for a fact most people had to wait months for a reservation. The Dobbins weren't *most* people.

"I hear it's wonderful," I said, "but I doubt there's a children's menu."

"What?"

"You know. Chicken fingers, kid-size pizza?"

"Goodness, why would we want that?"

"Trust me, your grandchildren are not going to eat anything on the regular menu." It frightened me how clueless she was. "I suppose I could be at Jenny's house by six-thirty, if I hustle. Why don't we go to MacDougal's Steakhouse instead? The guys love the macaroni and cheese there."

"We? Oh, no-no. William and I are taking James to Montrachet. He needs some distraction from this awful murder investigation. We naturally assumed you'd want to watch the little ones."

"I'll call you back." I slammed the phone on the counter.

"You're going to dinner with them?" Steve asked.

"No. I'm not." I pushed past him to the living room and plopped into my comfy microfiber chair-and-a-half. "They want me to babysit. Unbelievable. Not that I'd go with them even if they invited me." I shook off my indignant feelings. "What are you doing here? I haven't spoken to Debbie yet today. How's Quinn?"

"He's fine, considering." He sat on the end of the sofa closest to my chair.

"Careful," I said, "I haven't showered in two days. Don't stand downwind."

"I'm worried about you. Left three messages. One on the home phone, and two on your cell."

"I must have slept through them. Sorry." My thigh nudged the TV remote, and I dug it out from the side of the cushion and turned on CNN.

"Can we talk please?" he said.

"Sure. About what?" I stared at the screen, pretending interest in the latest hemlines reported by the very blonde and chesty Vera Sterling.

"About Jenny. About us. There's so much. I miss you. Turn off the tube." He reached over and lifted the remote out of my hand, clicking off Vera, then knelt on the floor next to me.

I could feel his eyes boring into me. Why was he pursuing me again like this? Before Saturday, he hadn't contacted me in over a month.

"Would you look at me?" he said.

"Fine." I turned my head toward him and tried not to let those gorgeous eyeballs get to me.

"Thank you. I love you, you know. I know how much you're hurting right now, and I want to be here for you. I think I should stay with you for a few days." His hand found his way to my thigh.

Maybe it wouldn't be such a bad idea.

"I could scrub your back for you in the shower." He leaned in close and touched his lips to mine.

I kissed him back. His lips were so soft.

His hands began to explore and for a fleeting moment, I experienced the happiness he once brought me—until. Then it hit me.

I pushed him away. "You jerk," I yelled, then walked across the room.

"What?"

"That's why you're all over me the last two days. You saw Debbie yesterday and today. You're turned on by her, but you can't have her, so you come pursue me. Your second choice. The beautiful Debbie's plainer, clunkier sister. We look enough alike for you that maybe you can pretend you're with her."

"That's crazy."

"If anybody should know, you would."

He stood and took a step. "I want *you*."

"Then how come I didn't hear word one from you for over a month? You're *so* concerned about me, but you don't call to see how I am for four—no—five weeks? Give me a break. Please leave."

"Honey, listen to me. I didn't want to bother you. But now, with Jenny's death, well, you need me. I want to be here for you."

"Leave now." I pointed to the door.

"But—"

"Now!"

CHAPTER TEN

The hot shower soothed my frayed nerves and took the sting of new tears from my eyes. I cried for two reasons. Jenny. And the frustration I felt with Steve. I knew I was right about him, no matter how he protested. Being his second choice, a *she'll have to do* person didn't work for me.

I'd experienced a confusing new situation. Intense attraction to two men at the same time. Having Cliff Chang possibly interested in me changed everything. Before my talk with Chang, Steve's sexy kiss would guarantee I'd be scrambling his eggs in the morning. No wonder he seemed shocked when I booted him out.

Toweling off, I checked the mirror. My puffy eyes had receded to almost normal and my plain brown shoulder-length hair decided to behave. I forced my way into my skinny jeans—which could serve as a tent for the likes of the Bitsy-ies of the world, then went into my office.

My unopened emails totaled fifty-three. Since Friday? I scanned through them for anyone important, and left the rest for later. I decided to record in my journal what the past three days were like, a few notes—not a long entry—that would come later.

My journal wasn't on the bookshelf where it belonged. I did a quick search through the shelves, then ran to my bedroom and checked the nightstand and its drawers. Had Quinn looked at it? He couldn't have read any of it. My illegible writing baffled me most the time, and he was six. I combed through every conceivable space I could think of. It wasn't there. Where the heck could I have left it? What was happening to me?

I shook it off, gave it up, and left for Kahala. If I had remembered two very different men as one man in front of Chang, then who knew what other goofy things I'd done.

By the time I pulled into James' driveway, Vivian and William's dinner reservations had expired. Excellent. I waltzed through the unlocked kitchen screen door.

"Hello?" I called. "Where are you guys?"

"Auntie Bess." Richard bounded in from the dining room. He grabbed my hand and yanked. "Come on. You gotta see this. Grandpa made the funniest sandwiches."

"He did?"

William sat at the head of the table, an array of lunchmeats, condiments, and a loaf of bread spread out in front of him. He wore a white paper chef's hat. White bread slices, with holes ripped from their middles, dangled from his ears. "Hi, Bess." He smiled at me.

"Hello." There was hope yet for this situation.

Paul took a tentative bite from his sandwich and grinned at me. Alarm registered in his face and he spit it onto his plate. "I don't like the barbeque sauce on it. Not with the olives."

"Told you," Richard said.

"Mine's good," Mikey said. "I invented it. Look. Ham, cheese, and potato chips."

"Very clever of you," I said, tousling his hair. "Looks delish."

Vivian rose from her seat beside Sammy's highchair. "Here. Why don't you finish doing this?" She handed me a washcloth. "It's after eight. We've missed our time at Montrachet. Where have you been?"

I took the cloth, but felt no need to explain anything to her. Sammy must have bathed in peanut butter. "She needs more than a wipe-off."

"Well," Vivian said, "I'm off to change. Come along, William. You can't go looking like that."

"Um. Vivian?" I said.

"James," Vivian called up the stairs. "Bess is here, hon. We can go now."

"Actually, no. You can't," I said.

"What?"

"I'm not staying." I lifted Sammy from the highchair, carried her to the kitchen, and sat her on the granite counter, her legs dangling in the sink.

Vivian followed me. "What do you mean?"

"I mean, I can't stay and babysit for you." I ran the faucet to bring warm water.

"Then how will we go out?"

I peeled off the baby's clothes. "Let's see. James could watch his own kids. Then you and William could go anywhere you wanted. Or you could stay here and the men could go. Or, I just thought of another option. Jenny keeps coupons in that drawer right behind you. You could order delivery."

Vivian shot me a poisonous glare. If this was her true nature revealed, it explained a lot about James. The other two times she'd visited, we didn't have much interaction. Jenny said Vivian went shopping at the mall every day by herself then, as though she couldn't stand to be near the kids. She didn't seem comfortable around children. Jenny and I guessed it was the same even with her own son. A nanny named Sylvie raised James until he left for boarding school.

Vivian said nothing further and stormed from the kitchen.

Sammy's little head of curls nodded toward her chest. Poor thing, it was a half-hour past bedtime. I finished cleaning her, got her ready for bed, and tucked into the crib.

"Good night, James," I said to the closed master bedroom door. I heard him talking in there. I assumed on the phone. "Say hi to Tiffy-tart for me."

Downstairs, Paul chomped through another rendition of his dinner. This one more palatable, judging by the way he wolfed it down.

"Good night, boys," I said. "I'll call you tomorrow and see how you're doing. If I can, I'll come over, okay?" I walked around the table and gave them hugs.

Vivian now sat to William's right with a sour expression on her face, placing lids on the various jars. She didn't look at me.

"Bye, Bess," William said. "Sure you don't want one of these *special* sandwiches? Paul's fifth try here is pretty good. Maybe he'll make one for you."

"Yeah, I can," Paul said. "It's peanut butter, mayonnaise, lettuce, and tomato."

"Sounds great. Not." I kissed his head. "Maybe next time. Be good for Grandpa, guys." I let myself out.

***

Her body is being released this afternoon." Cliff Chang opened his sixth sugar packet and poured it into his gargantuan-sized coffee. "You or Bitsy need to let them know who'll be transporting her."

"Bitsy wants Fujimura's Funeral Home," I said. "I'll call her. It's Tuesday, so I guess that means the service and burial will be on Friday. I want it to be over with. It hurts."

"I can imagine." He removed the wrapper from his second blueberry muffin.

"Everything is so screwy now, too." I sipped my black—no cream, no sugar—coffee and tried to remember the last time I'd allowed myself to eat a blueberry muffin. "My stuff is in all the wrong places at home. I can't find my journal. I'm a mess."

Chang wiped the crumbs from his mouth with a napkin.

"This is so typical," I said.

"What is?"

"You eat like a horse. Sugar and cream, muffins, and probably lots of ice cream in your life, too."

70

He nodded, then swallowed. "Dove bars."

"I bet you have trouble gaining weight, don't you?"

"Men are different than women." He shrugged.

"There's an understatement."

"Women get to be beautiful. Did I tell you that your tattoo guy made bail yesterday?"

"No. How could that happen?"

"Somebody showed up and paid the five grand."

"Why was bail only five thousand? Isn't that kind of cheap for a murder suspect?"

"He's not wanted for murder. All we have is possible robbery, from a woman's account—you—who saw him while on the playground. There's nothing to say he knew anything about the shooting. He might have left before that happened."

The sight of the Iwa birds hitting the sky that day came back to me. "Huh. Do you know how they got to and from the park?"

"Can't say. Why?"

"Because when I went looking for Jenny, something spooked a flock of birds that were in the tall grass. I thought it was a mongoose, the way the grass kept moving after the birds took off, but maybe it was the tattoo guy making his way back to their car. I wonder what's on the other side of all that brush."

"A dirt road that leads to nowhere."

"You already checked."

"Yup." He sat back and stretched. "But knowing both men ran that way does help."

"Who bailed out tattoo man?"

"Said he was a cousin. Local guy, maybe Samoan. I'm having Smalley run a check on him."

I finished my coffee and threw my crumpled napkin into the cup. "Do you really think James paid them to kill Jenny?"

"I never said that."

"Well, you put the idea into my head. I've been thinking about it more and wondering exactly how much James could've lost in a divorce. Money-wise, I mean."

"He said they had a pre-nup."

"They did. Jenny told me he made her sign it at his parents' insistence. On their first anniversary, she said he ripped it up."

Chang's eyes narrowed. He stood, returned his wallet to his back pocket, and picked up his coffee. "I'd better get to work. I want to see this pre-nup Mr. Dobbins says he has."

We walked outside.

Chang smiled at me. "Let's do it again soon."

"Yessir." I watched him get into his car. My phone rang as I unlocked mine.

"It's James."

"Yes?" Was he psychic? "Are the kids okay?"

"They're fine. What are you doing tomorrow afternoon?"

I slid into the driver's seat and started the van. "Paperwork, I guess. Gotta make funeral phone calls, too." I thought about telling him Jenny's body was ready for release, but decided to wait and see if he asked.

"You play golf, don't you?"

"Badly, but yes. Why?"

"The governor wants you to join us."

"The what? Excuse me? Governor Samuels? Why on God's green earth?"

"Dad and I went to see him last night, after you left. He and his wife Emily want to redo their Kauai condo, and I told them all about you. Emily said she recalls meeting you once."

No she didn't. My heart skipped a beat. "I can't believe that." Mrs. Plimpton told me they'd gone to the same university. I played dumb. "I didn't know you knew the governor."

"He and Dad go way back. Went to college together. Are you interested?"

"Of course, I'm interested." A huge red flag waved in my frontal lobes. "Wait a minute. Why are you being so nice to me?"

"I'm thinking that you and I should try to get along. My kids really need you. Vivian sucked at momhood, and she sucks at the grandma thing, too. When Dad and I got back last night, the boys were still up, watching a video. Vivian was on her third martini."

"On a school night?" How zombied-out were they going to be today? Then I remembered they weren't going to school that week. Bereavement pass. "Never mind. For a second, I forgot."

"Dad and I are doing what we can, but—it's hard to admit this—you're the one who knows them best. They love you."

"Fine. I'll play golf. Where and what time?" I pulled out of the lot and headed to Debbie's.

"Hawaii International Country Club. One o'clock tee time. Reservations are under Dobbins."

**

"How strange Jenny never mentioned it." Debbie closed her eyes and rolled her neck while sitting in her ergonomic chair.

We were in the third bedroom of her house, which she used as a home office for her free-lance graphic design business. "Isn't it? I'll bet Jenny didn't know they knew Samuels. She'd have told me for sure. How's Quinn?"

"He seems fine. Steve is coming back this Saturday to talk to him again, just to make sure."

"I kicked him out of my apartment last night."

"What was he doing there?"

"Trying to get me in bed while pretending he gave a damn about my mental condition."

She had a thoughtful look, then shook her head.

"What are you thinking?"

"Same thing you did, I'm sure. You do know I'd *never* encourage him. Even if I were single. Are you still coming for dinner tonight? Aden's making his fajitas."

"Sure. Do you think he'd move the larger stuff from in front of the garage door when he comes home? Then I can look for my clubs tonight."

"Your golf clubs are in there? Oh, lordie."

I yawned. "Sorry. All this is catching up with me. I need a nap. But first, I need to call Bitsy. Want to do it for me?"

"Yikes, no. That woman is a master manipulator. You're not going to plan the whole funeral, are you?"

"No. She got me at a weak moment the other day. I'll help, but it's her responsibility. I hope she's capable of giving Jenny a proper send-off."

"Doubtful. Don't let her guilt you into relenting. Jenny was *her* sister."

"Yeah. But it feels more like she was one of mine."

***

"I can't manage this," Bitsy whined.

I toyed with the magnetic paper clip holder on my desk. "Yes, you can. I notified Fujimura's yesterday that it would be soon. They're expecting your call. It's just phone calls. You're good at that, so make 'em. Let me know what time to be there on Friday. Bye."

My emails needed to be opened and dealt with, so I charged forward. Frankie Lymon sang *Goody Goody* from my cell.

"Bess? Jocelyn Plimpton here. I still haven't seen an announcement regarding the Dobbins funeral. Do you know anything?"

For crying out loud, it had been one day since she called. "It looks like the service will be on Friday at Fujimura's. Don't know about times yet, but I'll let you know."

"Oh. Fujimura's."

"What's wrong with them?"

"Nothing. Nothing, of course. I'm sure it will be a lovely service."

Wouldn't count on it. "Her sister's making the arrangements."

"I see. Not the Dobbins? Well, that explains it."

"They haven't mentioned wanting any part of the planning."

"Really. How unusual. That doesn't sound like William. Perhaps Vivian is at the root of this. She is a cold one, as I'm sure you're aware."

"You know her as well?" The disdain in her voice as she said Vivian's name surprised me. "Did she go to the same college as you and William? Say, did you know Governor Samuels back then, too?"

"Oh, yes. We were all chums at Camorra. But not Vivian. She'd gone to Wellesley. William's parents and hers pushed them together. Poor man, he didn't know what hit him. Broke my heart in the bargain, too. *She's* the one responsible for so much grief. If the family's not helpful, it's her fault."

"Maybe not. You see, they were divorcing."

"William and Vivian?"

She sounded excited. Could the woman still have a thing for William? "I mean Jenny and James. The situation verged on Shakespearean drama."

"Nasty details in the break-up?"

"Some bad behavior, yes." I forgot about her insatiable appetite for gossip. "My other line is ringing. We'll talk more soon."

"All right then. Do call me about Friday."

I set the phone on the desk and wandered into my bedroom. The fallen photos on the carpet in front of my closet beckoned me. I sat cross-legged, picked up a handful and flipped through them. Quinn's baby pictures. Grabbing more, I sorted them into piles, thinking this time I'd bag and label by category. That way, when I created the memory books I'd been planning forever, it'd be easy. Any pictures of Steve went to the shredder.

A snapshot from a Halloween party Jenny and James threw soon after their marriage caught my eye. I remembered this one because she'd sent it to her in-laws. And they sent it back, or rather, William did. Then she gave it to me.

James dressed as an outrageous pimp that year, and Jenny as his lady of the evening. His purple velvet suit and huge white hat with a magenta feather made us keel over with laughter. Jenny in her tarty black fishnets, garters, and micro-short skirt had the men drooling that night. Tasteless, but harmless.

I turned the picture over. Jenny's handwriting said, *What do you think? Don't we look like we could do this for real?* William's response, written in no-nonsense block letters, said, *I fail to see the humor in this.*

Stuffy, stuffy, stuck-up intolerant people. No matter how she tried, Jenny wouldn't have ever fit into that family. She couldn't fathom the subtleties of their social world, and wanted no part of it, anyway. She seemed to relish any opportunity to remind them of that fact.

CHAPTER ELEVEN

The aroma of grilled steak, peppers, and onions greeted me at Debbie's lanai.

"Auntie Bess." Quinn ran out the door and hugged me around my thighs.

"Hey, Tiger." I picked him up, squeezed him tight, then planted a sloppy kiss on his cheek. "You doing okay?"

"Yeah, but Mom's making me go back to school tomorrow."

We walked into the house, and I let the screen door slam behind me.

"Quinn?" Debbie's voice sounded agitated.

"It was me," I yelled. "My fault. I let it slam."

Quinn wandered back to the television in the den, and I headed to the kitchen.

Using tongs, Debbie lifted a browned flour tortilla from a cast-iron frying pan and draped it over a paper towel tube whose ends rested on two cans.

"That's clever." I gave her peck on the cheek.

"Keeps the taco shape while it cools," she said. "Don't worry, there's plenty of steamed ones too, in the oven." She threw another tortilla in the pan.

"Awesome." I glanced through the sliding glass door to the back. "Hi, Aden. Smells ono-licious, dude."

He worked the grill like a madman, turning the steak slices and scooping the peppers and onions into a bowl. "Aloha seestah." He said it using the localized pidgin-English inflection. "Almost done here. Be there in a sec."

"Anything I can do?" I asked.

"Set the table," Debbie said.

"Okee-doke." I gathered plates, silverware, and napkins, then arranged them on the blue cotton placemats already on the table.

Aden bounded in, set his bowl of savories on the table, and gave me a bear hug. "Bessy, Bessy, Bessy. How you holding up?" He released me.

I saw real sorrow in his eyes. Such a tower of strength he was. For each of us. Debbie had lucked out big time in finding him. All six-foot-four of him. Half superman, half mush. He looked one-hundred percent Hawaiian, but was part-Irish. He had smooth brown skin, almost jet-black hair, and wide-spaced expressive brown eyes that seemed to comprehend the joys and woes of life.

He embodied the Hawaiian *code* as I, after sixteen years of living in Hawaii, had come to understand it. Love. Aloha. Above all, the spirit connecting us was more powerful than anything that could try and divide us.

We ate in relative quiet, the three adults aware of six-year-old ears sitting next to us. When Quinn finished and left the room, Aden asked about Jenny. Then James and the kids.

I filled him in on the three days since the shooting.

He twisted the end of a napkin, listening to me. "I don't want to sound alarmist," he said in a quiet tone, "but it seems to me that whoever was looking for whatever it was Jenny had, thinks maybe you have it now."

I stared at him, not understanding.

"Your apartment's in disarray—"

"Well, not in disarray. Just some things are in the wrong places."

"Fine. Things are out of place, and your journal is missing," he said. "What did you think caused that?"

I flushed. "I thought Quinn might have—"

"Are you kidding me?" Debbie said. "You know I'm raising him better than that. He wouldn't dare go into anything of yours."

"Hush." Aden put his huge hand on top of hers. "Little kids can do anything. Even Quinn. But since he can't read cursive, I doubt he took your journal. Therefore, my gut tells me someone searched your apartment."

I sat back and thought. Why hadn't the idea occurred to me?

"Is Tom-next-door in town?" Aden asked.

"Yes," I said. "He's there."

"Good. I'm going to ask him to keep watch on you. That okay?"

"Sure. We're buds. I hate the idea somebody was in my apartment. I hope you're wrong."

"So do I. Now, what about this golfing with the governor business? Debbie says the Dobbins know him well?"

"Go figure, huh?" I said. "Jenny would've told me if she knew."

"Samuels has my vote for pushing hard for his Hawaiian Sovereignty Bill," Aden said.

"Me, too," Debbie said. "Except I don't know that I like the way they keep talking about separating after it's passed."

"Separating?" I said. "From the United States? Can't happen. No privately owned lands can be taken, so what would there be to secede? They'd be an isolated odd parcel of acres here and there. How could that be an independent country? I don't get it."

"Babe," Aden said to Debbie. "One of the provisions spells out that the bill does not allow Hawaii to secede. All that would change is the Office of Hawaiian Affairs and how they relate to the Interior Department. And the native Hawaiian vote."

"I find the whole issue kind of confusing," I said. "But I'd love to see some more consideration toward Native Hawaiians. They *so* got shafted."

Aden nodded and pushed back from the table. "It'll go through this time. As for your golf clubs, I moved the big things away from the garage door before dinner. You sure you don't want me to help find them?"

"No. You do dishes with Debbie. Your son said he'd attack the garage with me."

I collected Quinn, and we headed to the two-car garage. The fragrant smell of night-blooming jasmine greeted us. The garage was a separate building from the house, set to the left, about thirty feet behind it. An oak dresser, a rattan sofa, and a papa-san chair sat before it in the driveway.

I hoisted the double door and sighed. A mountain of junk faced us. "Holey moley, kiddo."

"Yeah." Quinn ducked under a window frame whose paint had alligatored and through a narrow space between two tall and dusty stereo speakers.

"I don't know where to start. Where'd you go?"

"Back here."

I could hear him, but towers of cardboard moving-boxes, a ratty brocade chair, and a pile of ancient sports equipment blocked any view. "Honey, I can't see you. Which side are you on?"

"The window side. Hey, I found my old bike. Cool."

"What about golf clubs?"

"I see Dad's. They're on top of the workbench."

Aden enjoyed golf about as much as I did. "That's good. Mine are in a dark-blue bag. They must be nearby."

"I see them. They're on the floor, under rolls of carpet."

"Don't touch the carpets. There could be scorpions hiding in them."

"If we find one, can I have it?"

"What for? Come out of there now, you're making me nervous. Something could fall on you."

"'kay." Thirty seconds later, he emerged, sneezed, and brushed cobwebs from his hair. "Dad said he and his brothers used to put a scorpion and a centipede in a bucket and make 'em have a war."

"Oh, goody. Take it up with your father. Let's stack this stuff on the driveway."

We moved boxes, broken and peeling surfboards, and a salt encrusted fifty-gallon aquarium. Amongst the junk, we came to a clearing. Candy wrappers, potato chip bags, and soda cans littered the four-foot by four-foot area.

"Where did this garbage come from?" I asked. "You might have rats in here."

Quinn looked sheepish. "Mikey and I made it our secret clubhouse."

We freed my golf bag. Black mold spotted the ridiculous pink pom-poms covering my woods. I removed the covers and tossed them into the trash pile. I hated them. Anyone who knew me, knew I wasn't a pink pom-pom kind of girl. Steve bought the pom-poms for me. Debbie, on the other hand, loved pink and all kinds of frillies. Hmmm.

It was full-dark by the time we swept and began restacking. The trade winds continued their gentle flow, keeping the notorious mosquitoes at bay while we finished. We decided to keep the clubhouse area intact for Mikey and Quinn. I made sure there was nothing around it that could get jostled and fall on them. Quinn promised to clean up their trash in the future.

***

Wednesday morning brought good news. Dr. Donald Farrington hired me for the renovation of his two-story penthouse at the Moanalua, a ritzy condominium at the edge of Waikiki. The presentation took me weeks to prepare and my competition was a large design firm whose designers' work often appeared in *Architectural Digest.* Farrington set the budget at two-hundred thousand, not including my fee.

With Governor Samuels and his wife now considering me, I felt I might at last be entering the big leagues of residential design. Maybe moving to a real office space was the next prudent step. It also occurred to me what a blessing having to think about work—that ever-present necessity of supporting myself—was. If I wanted continued occupation in a building with a roof and indoor plumbing, clothing, and food, then as much as I felt like cowering in a corner and crying over my best friend's death, I simply couldn't. It made the guilt of going forward easier to handle.

I mulled this over as I laid clothing on the bed. I didn't own genuine golf togs, and hadn't played since before Steve and I split. The forecast was for a sunny, eighty-two degree afternoon, typical for February on Oahu. I decided on a pair of long khakis, white Polo shirt, and a white terry-cloth visor.

Driving up the Pali Highway to the country club, I rehearsed my best design catch-phrases and responses to the usual array of questions from prospective clients. I wanted to make a good impression. My nervousness grew as I parked the van. William's rented Navigator was already in the lot. I'd hoped for a little extra time to settle myself, but there they were by the entrance, waving me over.

"Any problem finding the place?" William opened the glass door to the clubhouse for me. Its etched design featured hibiscus and protea.

"No. I've been here before." I nodded at James, who nodded back. He, Jenny, Steve, and I once played here as a foursome. Jenny and I quit after nine holes and fled to the bar for margaritas. The competitive, macho idiocy of the men made us crazy. They bet on every shot, then argued the results. Steve won a hundred dollars from James that day. We were never invited back.

Governor Samuels met us in the expansive, glass-walled lobby. "You must be Bess Blinke." He extended his hand and smiled.

His was a friendly smile, and I couldn't help but return it. I was more at ease at once. "Thank you for inviting me today, sir. I hope the Dobbins' warned you that I'm not much of a golfer."

"Neither am I. Please, call me Lewis."

His smile broadened, and the crinkles around his eyes deepened. He had a dark tan, and that, combined with a thick head of salt and pepper hair plus a trim athletic build, made him a most attractive older man. No wonder he had zero problems with fund-raising. I could see every sixty-plus woman in the state throwing money at him.

We proceeded to our carts. I'd thought by arriving fifteen minutes early, I'd have time for some warm-up shots. Samuels gestured for me to join him in his cart. We drove past the practice green and chipping area, straight to the first tee. It was twelve-fifty. I guess when you're the governor, you can start whenever you want, tee-off time be damned.

"Bess, you want to kick us off?" Samuels asked.

"I'd rather go last, if you don't mind." I got out of the cart and pulled my three-wood from my bag. "I'm going to hang back here a bit and get a few swings in. Haven't touched a club in a while."

The country club sat far back in a wide valley, about fifteen-hundred feet above sea level. The spectacular view from the first tee took my breath away. The deep forests growing on the steep sides of the Koolaus gave the impression of an undulating thick green carpet. In the distance, I saw a narrow waterfall in the cleft of a small side valley, the sunlight sending sparkling gems off the water. Scenes like that stirred something primal in me. Feelings of being where time began. Like at any moment, aborigines might come screaming out of the forest brandishing crude spears.

The three men took their shots, all hitting a respectable distance into the middle of the fairway. It was my turn. Embarrassed, I set a pink Titleist—yes, Steve bought those too—on the women's tee and took another practice swing. Then I steeled myself, remembered to *be the ball*, and swung. My ball landed twenty-five yards back from theirs, but it thrilled me. I'd taken my first shot without hitting it into the rough or looking like a dork.

Samuels and I made polite small talk as we played. He asked about my family and upbringing. I knew to let him initiate talk about the design job for his condo, so I inquired as to the health of his wife, kids, and grandchildren.

Afterward, at the bar outside the clubhouse, the four of us sat at an aqua and white striped umbrella covered table. The men ordered beer. I had a Diet Pepsi. My score for the day was one-hundred six. Par was seventy-two. Without the gimmees they allowed me on the five toughest holes, my number would've been way higher. I'd lost two balls in the rough, and three in the water. I was tired, and my new BFF Lewis still hadn't mentioned the design job.

"Will you and Vivian be staying in town long enough to attend the Policemans' Benefit Bash?" Samuels asked William. "Emily's worked real hard on it this year, along with Paula Ortiz."

"Ed's new wife?" William said.

Ed Ortiz. I knew that name. The current Honolulu Police Chief, whose very public affair resulted in a divorce and marriage to a twenty-something nymphet last year.

James laughed. "Wonder if he knows I dated Paula first."

"I wouldn't mention it if you see him," William said. "Not if you value patrolmen overlooking your parking indiscretions. From what I hear, there's a bundle of 'em." He smiled.

I must have looked puzzled, because James nudged me.

"Dad and Lewis contribute a lot to the Policeman's Benefit Fund," he said. "I don't think I really have to worry about tickets."

William shook his head. "Don't push it, James. Ed's territorial. Money or no money, I guarantee he'd rather not know who else slept with his wife. And the answer, Lewis, is I don't know. Vivian's singular mission is to help James find a nanny, then leave."

"So." Samuels turned to me. "James tells me you and his wife were good friends."

The question surprised me. "Jenny was my *best* friend."

"I'm sorry for your loss. I know how upset James and William are about it."

I looked at him like he had three heads.

"Sometimes," William said, "we don't appreciate the special people in our lives until they're gone. I think my son is beginning to realize just how much he needed her."

Your son has a brain and a mouth, I thought. Why can't he say it? "How touching. I wasn't aware Jenny had met you, Lewis. She didn't tell me."

Samuels sputtered mid-sip in his beer, then seemed non-plussed for a second. He grabbed the drink napkin and wiped his mouth. "We never did meet. Emily and I always meant to invite you and Jenny to dinner, James, but one thing or another kept it from happening. I'm sorry now we missed the opportunity." He turned his gaze back to me. "Would you say Jenny and you were so close that you shared everything?"

"Jenny wouldn't sneeze without checking with Bess first." James laughed.

"She and I told each other just about everything," I said. "But I didn't keep a sneeze count." I semi-glared at James. "It's that Mars versus Venus thing. Women's friendships are deeper. There's such a tight bond."

"Hypothetically," Samuels said, "if a woman were to get in trouble of some sort, maybe something embarrassing, she'd tell her best friend?"

"Depends on the woman, I suppose," I said. "I'm not sure what you're getting at."

"What if a woman had, say, legal trouble. Or let's say, for example, Jenny had a serious financial problem. Would she tell you?"

"Jenny *did* have a huge financial problem," I said. "And yes, she told me all about it. That's what friends are for. To be honest, I'm not real comfortable discussing Jenny right now."

"I understand," Samuels said. "I simply meant—"

William let out an awkward laugh. "I know where he's going with this, I think. Could this have to do with your quasi-rebel daughter, Lani?"

Samuels wore a blank expression, then chuckled.

"Yes," he said. "My little Leilani. My youngest. She's twenty-four and drifting. Emily hasn't a clue how to reach her. We're so worried. She was fired from a great job with an accounting firm in San Francisco. She won't tell us why. Emily thought we should contact Lani's friend, Patti."

"Except you're afraid of alienating Lani further by pumping her friend for information." I sucked the rest of my soda up the straw, stood, and threw the cup into a nearby trashcan.

"Exactly. Sorry if I went 'round the bush," Samuels said. "But do you think Patti would know what happened?"

"Maybe. If she's a true friend she wouldn't tell you, though."

"I'd ask her," James said. "Lani might be into drugs. If you don't find out and get her to a clinic, maybe her whole life will go down the tubes."

"That's a bit extreme." William downed the rest of his beer. "James, you're not helping here. There's an explanation for it, Lewis. I'm sure it isn't drugs. Lani's a good kid."

"Well, we'll figure it out, I guess." Samuels stood and stretched. He glanced at his watch. "It's after five. I'd better get back." He stepped toward me to shake my hand. "I'll call you when Emily and I go to the Kauai place. You'll meet us there, check it out. Do you have a card with you?"

I let go of his hand and reached into the side pocket of my golf bag where I'd stashed some business cards. My fingers felt something else at the bottom, and I pulled it out. A white envelope. I put it back and grabbed my cards, offering one to Samuels. "That would be great. I've love to work with you both on it. Thank you again for inviting me today."

He took the card. "My pleasure. William. James." He strode to the clubhouse and vanished inside.

Our waiter, dressed in a red hibiscus aloha shirt laid the bill in front of William.

"He didn't ask a thing the whole day about my work." I checked my bag to be sure I had everything. "That's odd, don't you think?"

"I told him you were great," William said. "That's all he needs to hear. Emily will use whomever he wants. You're in."

"Thank you." I tried to keep the skepticism out of my voice. "Can't imagine why we had to do this whole golf thing, though. Just so he could ask for my card? I've never worked this way before.

Bidding for a normal job entails multiple planning meetings, research, and fancy presentation boards. A ton of work, and then a load of prayer. He will sign a contract with me, won't he?"

"It'll be fine." William signed the bill and handed it to the waiter. "We need to be on our way as well. You're welcome to stay as long as you like, Bess. Order some dinner. It's on me. The food here is terrific." He picked up his bag and walked toward the parking lot.

"I hope you can forget the stupid things I did." James pushed his chair away from the table and stood. "I know I hurt Jenny. I have to live with that. She was a good mom. Something I didn't have."

"Vivian's, um, an interesting person."

"She's cold. She loves me, but she's cold. Her parents were the same way. Come on, I'll walk you to the car." He slung his bag over his shoulder. "I broke up with Tiffanie."

"Since yesterday?"

"I need someone who's more on the ball."

"You mean, now you're in the market for a step-mom." We reached my van, and I unlocked the back.

"No. I'm hiring a nanny for that. Vivian pre-interviewed some today."

"You're not going to let her choose, are you?"

"She's just narrowing the list for me. See ya." He turned and headed to the Navigator.

"Want my advice?" I called after him. "Pick the one you're the least attracted to. The boys don't need to wake one morning and find you in bed with their nanny."

He turned and laughed, walking backward now. "Why not? I slept with mine." He paused. "Kidding." Then he turned back.

Was he kidding about sleeping with the new one, or with the one from his childhood? I placed my bag in the van. Then I remembered the envelope. Fishing it out, I wondered how long it had been there. I closed the back hatch, got in my van, and started the air conditioning.

The white color of the envelope had yellowed, and it felt like photos were inside. I opened the flap and pulled out pictures wrapped in a note on plain, lined paper. Setting the note aside, I looked at the pictures first.

A gorgeous young woman with gleaming auburn hair and a devilish *come get me* look stared at me from the first one. Naked, reclining on pillows with her legs spread wide, with one hand on her breast and the other much lower.

A mirrored wall behind the bed reflected the naked man taking the picture. The camera and its flash obscured his head.

I had trouble catching my breath as a shock of realization hit me. I knew the woman. Taken before four pregnancies, when she possessed the body of a goddess, it was Jenny.

CHAPTER TWELVE

I took a deep breath. Maybe the man in the mirror was James. They'd been horsing around. Married couples and their private play. Except the photographer didn't look like Jenny's husband, not that I'd seen him naked. But this guy had hanging belly fat, and I'd never noticed an extra pound on James.

I put that picture aside and picked up the other. It showed Jenny and, I assumed, the same man naked together on the bed, in the midst of sexual activity. Somebody blacked out his face with a marker.

Was this a former boyfriend? I glanced at the note on the seat beside me. Something told me this was not a love letter. I picked it up and unfolded it.

Printed in block letters with pink ink, the message read, *Sweetie, you know I hate to do this but I need more. My finances are really strained. Double what you usually do. Whatever Rosie wants, remember? You're a love. Rosie.*

Who the heck was Rosie? And why did her note get wrapped around pictures of Jenny? Was Rosie blackmailing Jenny? Rosie couldn't be playing with a full deck if she thought she'd squeeze any cash from Jenny before the divorce became final.

I checked both sides of the paper. No date. It was in my golf bag. My golf bag had been in Debbie's garage for almost three years. Or was the envelope slipped into my bag today? My brain twisted itself into a tangle with the dozens of questions I had.

Taking time to calm down first, I called Cliff Chang.

"I'm about to eat dinner," he said. "You know where the Zippy's is on Beretania, near Nuuanu Avenue? On the Makai side. Meet me there."

***

"Do you recognize the room? It doesn't look like the Dobbins' bedroom." Chang leaned forward and pushed the napkin the photos lay on across the orange laminate table. With quick, deft handling of his chopsticks, he took another large bite of noodles from his saimin bowl.

When we met in the parking lot, he'd put the envelope in a plastic bag and explained he hoped to find fingerprints, other than mine. After we sat with our food, he used tweezers to place them on the opened clean napkin.

Rounding my shoulders and blocking with my arms in case anyone around us could get an eyeful, I examined them again. We'd tried to get a booth for a more private conversation, but Zippy's was a popular place, and the lone table available was three feet from the next one.

In the pictures, the bedspread lay in a heap at the foot of the bed. It appeared to be burgundy velvet, as were the heavy draperies. The tacky deep-red and gold flocked wallpaper of the room made me cringe. "She hated burgundy. It had to be his place."

"You're sure the pictures are old?"

"Believe me. She never got that body back, even after Paul, the first baby. They were taken at least ten years ago."

Chang drained the saimin bowl and dove into his hamburger-steak plate. The meat, in essence a giant hamburger with no roll, sat on top of a bed of rice and noodles, all of it smothered in beef gravy. A small mound of kim chee garnished the dish.

I picked at my salad and sighed. I'd shared most my questions with him. "It sounds like Rosie got money from her for a while doesn't it? But where did Jenny get the money to pay her? And I don't think that's James with her."

"You forgot one. Who took the picture where they're in bed together? There's a third person involved here." Chang swallowed a forkful of the kim-chee. His eyes widened and began to tear. He gulped some soda, then exhaled.

"Too hot for you? Your ears are turning pink. I bet this Rosie character took the photo."

"No." He coughed the words out. "I like it spicy." He helped himself to another bite of the Korean slaw.

"Do you think Bitsy or James know who Rosie is? Maybe I should ask them."

"Uh-uh." He swallowed again. Gasping, he held out a finger as he drank more soda. "Whew. Okay, better now. Don't ask anybody anything. You haven't shown these to anyone, right?"

"What're you, crazy? Of course not. I came straight to you."

"Good. Not a word to anybody. I'll question people. Got it?"

"Sure, Sherlock."

"Jenny ever talk about boyfriends?"

"She said there was one serious relationship before James. The guy tore her heart out. She didn't like to talk about him."

"Did he have a name?"

"She called him Wobby."

"Wobby? Not Robby?"

"Yeah. He was a lot older than her, but that's all I know. She never told me his real name."

"I hate pet names. Wonder if Bitsy knows of a Robert or a Bob she dated," Chang said. "The guy in the photos doesn't seem her age. Maybe it is the boyfriend."

I finished my salad and pushed the plate aside. My phone rang, and I recognized the incoming number. "Speak of a she-devil. It's Bitsy. Should I answer it?"

"I didn't say you couldn't talk to her. Just don't mention these." He gestured to the envelope and note in the bag.

I nodded. "Hello, Bitsy. How are the arrangements coming?"

"I'm going nuts here. People expect me to do everything. You said you'd help."

"Yes. I am helping. I arranged for the organist and soloist yesterday. They're the same ones who did Aden's grandmother's funeral. I faxed them the list of songs you wanted, and forwarded their price to you. Check your email. Manna Chop Sui will deliver the food on Friday at three. They just need an address to take it to. Have you and James figured out where the mourners are going to congregate after the service? Your house or his?"

"Nobody wants to drive out here. It has to be at James'. But his mother doesn't want people tramping through."

"It's not her house, the witch. How about the reception hall at Jenny's church?"

Chang pointed to his watch.

I mouthed an *okay*.

"Closed for renovations," Bitsy said.

"And Fujimura's doesn't have a larger room for that, right? Looks like you have to tell Vivian to suck it up. I have to go. I'll call you later."

"Things not going so smooth?" Chang asked.

"She's whining, is all. She's mad at me for not doing more. For some reason, it doesn't bother her that James hasn't lifted a finger. Which reminds me. I overheard her talking to someone I'm pretty sure was James on the phone at her house on Sunday. Or Monday morning. The days are smushing together. It is Wednesday, isn't it? Anyway, she called him sweet cakes or baby cakes."

"Odd term for her to use toward him. What else did she say?"

"Stuff like, *it was what it was, leave it alone.* I'm wondering if they had a fling. Except the girls I know he's cheated with are chesty bimbos. Say what you please about Bitsy the bitch, but she's a B-cup at best and not stupid."

He sat back and smiled.

"Do I amuse you?"

"I love your frankness. It's fascinating."

"I thought you had to go." I wasn't in the mood to be fascinating. "Oh, and I forgot. Aden thinks somebody searched my apartment. I promised I'd mention it to you."

"What made him think that?"

"Because so many of my things are in the wrong places."

"You made it sound like you'd misplaced items while dazed from stress. What would anyone be searching for?"

I shrugged. "Whatever they think Jenny had and didn't find?" I sipped at the dregs of my lemonade. "This would be so much better with vodka in it. Aden called my neighbor, Tom, and asked him to keep an eye on me. Tom's a big guy."

"I should have one of my team dust for prints."

I blanched. "Doubt they'd turn up anything now. My nephew got peanut butter all over while he stayed with me. When I got home Saturday night, I couldn't sit still so I wiped everything down. Some women are goofy that way, you know. When we're upset, we clean."

"Oh." Chang took the tweezers from his pocket and replaced the photos in the plastic bag. "Go home and make a drink, hit the sack early, and you'll be ready to roar in the morning." He rose and grabbed the bag. "I'm going to find out what these are about. Come on, I'll walk you to your van."

As we exited the restaurant, a piece of my last conversation with Jenny floated into my brain. "There was something besides the divorce bothering Jenny."

His left eyebrow peaked. "Yes?"

"One of the last things she said to me was, 'It's more than the divorce. Maybe worse.' Then the kids interrupted us. We said we'd talk about it later at her house, and I went to spin with the boys. Think it could be this Rosie chick and her blackmail?"

"We'll find out," he said. "Don't worry. It's hard to keep a big secret on a small island."

Parked next to me was a convertible BMW, dark blue. "I love that car."

"Me, too," Chang said. "Someday I'll get a fancy sports car."

"Alimony payments stopping you, huh? You need to get your ex remarried."

"I've tried." He laughed, then took a step closer. "No one's as stupid as I was."

My nerves jumped, and I moved back.

He looked hurt.

"I'm sorry. It's not I'm not interested. I am, but you getting close to me is trouble."

"You're right." He walked a few paces away and back, then his phone rang as he opened his mouth to speak. "Chang here." He listened for a good minute. "I'm there in ten." He slapped the thing shut, slid it back in his pocket, and his serious detective attitude returned.

"What happened?"

"They found your tattoo man floating face down in the Ala Wai Canal." He hurried to his gray Buick Regal. "I'll call you later."

I watched him drive away, then started my van and drove home. The man with the tattoo drowned? Drunk again and an accident, or infighting amongst the two men who'd robbed and killed Jenny?

Arriving home, Tom Hanegawa popped out of his door as I unlocked mine, same as he had the night before, after Aden called him.

"How was golf with the beautiful people?" he asked.

I rolled my eyes. "It's a beautiful club. Maybe the Samuels' will hire me like James said. Anything new around here?"

"Nope. Been home since four. I'm making shoyu chicken. Did you eat?"

I sniffed the air. "I can't smell anything. Did you forget to turn on the oven again? And yes, thank you, I ate."

"Nah, it's still marinating. I figure I'll put it in at eight, it'll be done by nine."

"I hope to be long asleep by then. Thanks for checking on me. Want to come over early for coffee in the morning?"

"Sure."

"Great, see you around seven."

***

I awoke at five. Surprised that visions of bodies bleeding and floating hadn't invaded my dreams, I felt good. I rose, made coffee, and even did push-ups and sit-ups before my shower.

Tom knocked on the door a few minutes after seven.

I filled my largest mug with coffee, handed it to him, and led him to the lanai. I'd weighted the newspaper down on the table with my mug. "Have a seat." I gestured to the other chair.

"Thanks." He settled himself and took the local section of the paper. "Wasn't sure if you'd want to resume our schedule this week."

"Miss our Thursday coffee-morning? This will help me get the rest of my life back in order. Routine can be a good thing."

He nodded, staring past me.

I followed his gaze. "What are you looking at?"

"My lanai. Could use some sprucing, don't you think?"

"Maybe if you swept all the dirt that's settled on it, you could put it in a pot and grow tomatoes." Our lanais weren't connected. Each apartment had its own, cantilevered over the ninety-foot drop. Four feet away, his greenish blackened-with-mold railing contrasted with my shiny white one. The sole item on his street-soot covered tile was a forlorn plastic planter with some brown stems. "You'd have to remember to water, though."

"Eh. Too much trouble." He turned his head toward the Koolaus in the distance and let out a loud breath. "Lucky we live Hawaii."

I nodded my agreement. Our lanais faced the mauka side. I saw a fine misty rain hitting the mountain peaks and watched as a vibrant rainbow formed before our eyes. "I like having this view better than an ocean view."

"Smart girl. Will you be here tonight? What time should I check on you?"

"Five-ish? I'll call when I'm almost home. And thanks, Tom."

***

By nine, I was on Kalanianaole Highway going to see the kids.

Mikey answered the doorbell and gave me a huge hug. "I missed you, Auntie Bess. Come see the fort I built." He led me to the family room.

Paul and Richard peeked from under a bed sheet covering a card table. Sammy shrieked with delight from the playpen.

"Uh, guys? Where are the grown-ups?" I picked up the baby. She smelled of urine. "Oh, sweetie. You need a change. And you're still in your pajamas."

"Grandpa went to the store. Vivian's in the shower," Richard said.

"Vivian?" I said.

"She doesn't want us to call her Grandma," Paul said. "Dad's in bed. He yelled at me for telling him Sammy was crying, so I carried her down here. That way she wouldn't be lonely."

"Have you eaten breakfast?"

"Paul made us Pop-Tarts," Mikey said.

"Good for you, kiddo." I leaned forward and planted a kiss on Paul's forehead. "I'm proud of you. You're taking great care of your brothers and sister." At least the nine-year-old in the house showed some sense. "While I'm changing Sammy, you boys go make your beds and brush your teeth."

They tore up the stairs ahead of me. The smell emanating from the little girl in my arms made my eyes water, so I detoured into the bathroom. I sat her on the mat next to the tub and turned on the tap. The boys were elbowing each other at the sinks, and Richard spritzed his toothbrush in Mikey's face.

Mikey screamed. "That stings. Ow. That stings. You stupid—"

"That's enough." I stood, stepped to Mikey and brought his face toward the sink. "Splash a little water in your eye, and it'll go away." I turned to Richard. "Say you're sorry."

"He hit me," Richard said.

"I know. I saw. You were jabbing each other. Say you're sorry."

"Sorry," Richard said.

"Good." I gave him a hug. "Honey, your shirt's on inside out. There's a stain on it, too. How'd you do that already?"

"It's from last night."

"You're wearing yesterday's dirty clothes?" I sniffed his hair. "When did you last have a bath or shampoo? Paul? Mikey?"

They stared at me with blank expressions.

"I think at Auntie Bitsy's," Mikey said.

"On Monday? Oh, my gosh," I said. "Everybody strip and get in the tub."

Thirty minutes later, the four of them were downstairs, smelling fresh and in clean clothes. Carrying a basket of dirty laundry collected from the floor of their rooms, I bumped into Vivian on my way through the kitchen.

"I'm sorry. I didn't see you," I said.

"Good morning," she said. "I was enjoying the quiet down here."

"Didn't you wonder where the children were?" I set the basket on the floor of the laundry room.

"No. There was a ruckus coming from the bathroom, and I saw your van out there. What was the noise about?"

"Typical stuff." I wanted to yell at her for not keeping the kids clean, but I restrained myself. "James said you interviewed some nannies. Did you find one?" One who knew hygiene, please?

"I gave him three resumés. He needs to meet them and make up his mind."

The sound of the garage door opening made me look to the driveway. William pulled the Navigator into the garage. A minute later, he came in loaded with groceries. "Good morning, Bess," he said, a bright smile on his face. "How're you?"

"Fine, thanks. Are there more?" I set the laundry down, went out the door, and grabbed some of the bags from the backseat.

William joined me, lifted the remainder, and slammed the car door shut with his hip. We set the bags on the counter with the rest, and he emptied them as I put the food away.

Vivian sat at the table sipping tea and turning the pages of a *Town and Country* magazine. "Bitsy said *you said* we had to let people come here after the service tomorrow." She kept her eyes on the magazine.

"What?" She caught me off-guard. "I suggested this would be the best place. Bitsy lives an hour away from Fujimura's."

"I don't know that we'll find a cleaning service who'll be available today," she added. "This house is a mess. And what about food and drinks? Maybe if we'd had some notice—"

"Manna Chop Sui is doing the food. I'm sure the liquor store would deliver in the morning if you call now." I seethed inside.

"It's only for a few hours, Pet," William said. "Think of how it will look if James doesn't have it here."

"I knew we should have stayed at the Hilton," Vivian said. "Just the thought of all *those kind* of people traipsing in here. How can we be sure they'll stay out of the bedrooms? My jewelry's in there."

"That's it." I slammed a jar of peanut butter on the table and glared into her hard eyes. "I'm tired of holding my tongue for the sake of being polite to you. Jenny was your daughter-in-law. The mother of your four grandchildren. We all know you didn't like or approve of her. But why can't you be compassionate enough to understand there are people grieving for her? We miss her. We loved her, even if you never did, and your spoiled son didn't anymore."

My voice got louder, but I couldn't stop. "Those four babies in there need love and attention. They're hurting. Why don't you get that? You don't have to be here tomorrow, if you don't want to. Take your precious jewelry and check into the freaking Hilton. This isn't even *your* house. But it was Jenny's home, and the very least you can do is allow her friends to say goodbye!" Tears spilled down my face, and I sunk to the floor sobbing.

Vivian's mouth hung open, and she looked like I'd smacked her. I glanced at William and thought I caught the faintest trace of a grin.

"You're mistaken, you know." Vivian's tone was icy and flat. "You think Jenny was some kind of saint. She wasn't."

"How would you know? You never bothered with her," I said.

"Vivian." The imperious and stern quality of William's voice threw me.

James entered the room. Hair disheveled, barefoot, and wearing pajama bottoms, he looked bewildered. He held his cell phone in his palm and stared at it. "Detective Chang called me. He wanted to know if Jenny had a friend named Rosie, or another one by the name of Robby or Bobby. He said blackmail might be the reason Jenny was killed. Blackmail?"

He faced us. "Dad? What's wrong?"

I looked at William. His eyes fixed on James and the color had drained from his face.

"Dad?" James rushed to him.

I scrambled to my feet to help.

We reached William just as he passed out.

CHAPTER THIRTEEN

James and I struggled to lower William to the floor. I put my fingers on his wrist and felt a strong pulse.

"See what you've done?" Vivian said, pointing at me.

"Me?" I reached for my purse and found my phone. "What are you talking about?"

"Your yelling at me upset him so much, he collapsed."

"Jesus, Mother," James said. "Shut up. I think Dad's having a heart attack. Bess, call nine-one-one already."

"I'm on it." My hand shook as I dialed. Two emergency calls in six days. I prayed while I waited.

"Don't you *ever* tell me to shut up." Vivian sounded venomous.

James plucked some towels from the laundry basket and placed them under William's head and feet. "Come on, Dad."

Beads of perspiration glimmered on both James' and William's foreheads.

"What's it mean if he's sweating?" James said. "Dammit. I wish I knew something medical."

"He'll be fine," Vivian said, her voice still icy. "It's probably low blood sugar. He didn't eat breakfast."

I plugged my finger into my left ear to block out the ensuing squabbling. The dispatcher came on, and I gave her the facts.

"They'll be here in five minutes." Whether Vivian and James heard me, I don't know. They continued their sniping. I put the phone on the table and knelt on William's other side.

Paul, Richard, and Mikey scampered in on all fours.

"We're hound dogs," Mikey said. "We're chasing rabbits."

"Hey. What's wrong with Grandpa?" Richard stood and came closer.

"Bess gave Grandpa a heart attack." Vivian hadn't moved from her chair.

James looked like he wanted to punch her.

The boys' happy-puppy faces turned to worried expressions.

"What?" Paul said. "You can do that?"

"No. You can't," I said. "I mean, I can't. Nobody can. *Grandma* is upset, so she's not making any sense right now." I glared at Vivian and rose from William's side. "Come with me, boys. An ambulance is on the way, and we can keep watch for it on the front porch."

They followed me through the door.

"Is Grandpa going to die, too?" Mikey paled.

"I don't think so." I sat on the step and patted my thigh. "Let's sit here. Mikey, you need a hug. Sit on my lap."

He did, and I rocked him, humming *Put on a Happy Face,* the tune his Paddington Bear played when you pulled the cord.

Richard rested his head against my side. I stopped rocking and put my arm around him.

"I don't want Grandpa to die," Paul said. "I like him."

"I'm glad. Your dad and I found a pulse. You know what that is? It's when you can feel the heart pumping blood through a person's body. Right here." I held out my wrist. "Put your finger on top, right below my palm, and press a bit. Can you feel it?"

Paul placed a forefinger on the spot and nodded.

"Can I try?" Richard asked.

"I want to feel it," Mikey said. He leaned forward and put his finger next to Richard's.

"You can check your own pulse the same way," I said.

The time dashed by while they felt for their own heartbeats and each other's.

A siren in the distance announced the ambulance's imminent arrival. We stood to flag it down, then I retrieved Sammy from the playpen.

Within minutes, the emergency crew stabilized William, lifted him onto a stretcher, and trundled him into the ambulance. Vivian allowed the hunky driver to help her to a bench beside William.

"You are such a dear," Vivian said, the poison gone from her voice. Her hand fluttered, and the perfect fingernails landed with a feminine flourish on the driver's chest. "Thank goodness you were here to help. I would *never* have managed on my own."

"No problem," the hunky driver muttered. He sent an eye roll toward one of the other techs.

The kids and I watched from the doorway. Sammy sat on my hip and waved bye-bye to Grandpa.

James decided to follow in his own car. "Thanks for staying with the children." He opened his car door. "I'll call when I know something."

"Come back as soon as you can, please. I've got so much to do," I said. "And James? Pick a nanny from Vivian's list while you're waiting. Tell her to come for an interview today."

I led the boys inside. "Time to clean the family room."

My announcement elicited groans in response.

"Tell you what. When we finish tidying, you can help me sort through pictures."

"What for?" Paul asked.

"Auntie Bitsy needs some photos of your mom to display at the service tomorrow."

"Doesn't she have any?" Richard asked.

Out of the mouths of babes. "She can't seem to find anything appropriate." I didn't share the fact Bitsy said she couldn't put her hands on *any*.

"Are we going to show good ones or bad ones?" Paul looked concerned.

"Why, the good, of course. Although, your mom was so pretty, I don't think she ever took a bad picture."

He seemed to study me, a frown growing on his face.

I pulled him aside. "What is it? Will seeing the pictures upset you? I can do it later."

"I saw bad ones. I only want to use the pretty ones. Do you promise?" Paul asked.

"Yes. I promise." An uneasy feeling arose in me. "What kind of bad photos did you see?"

He dropped his gaze to the floor.

I shifted Sammy to my other hip and cupped Paul's chin with my right hand, drawing his face up until he faced me. "Tell me. It's always better to get the truth out."

Tears welled in his eyes. "She didn't have any clothes on," he whispered. "And there was a man, and he didn't have clothes on either."

"Oh." I put Sammy in the playpen and took Paul into my arms, hugging him close. "It's going to be okay." His brothers sat mesmerized by something on Nickolodeon, so I brought Paul to the kitchen.

"I think I saw those same pictures," I said. "Where did you see them?"

"I found them in Mommy's drawer in her room."

"When was this? Did Richard or Mikey see them?"

He shook his head. "It was after Daddy left." He burst into tears. "I didn't mean to find them. Mommy took away my walkie-talkie 'cause I hit Richard with it, and I thought maybe she hid it under her clothes."

"What did you do with the pictures?"

"I threw them in the trash, and then I thought she might see them and I'd get in big trouble. I put them under my bed, and the next time Quinn came over, I gave them to him and told him to hide them."

"Quinn?" Crud. I felt sick. "Did he see the pictures?

103

"No. I told him they were very bad and he couldn't look. Ever. I made him swear. And I said I'd beat him up, too."

I hoped Quinn honored his oath. I had to tell Debbie, just in case. I didn't know what to tell Paul about the photos. That was way out of my league.

"Am I in trouble?" He quivered in my arms. "Are you going to tell Daddy?"

"No. You're not in trouble." I needed to think about whom to tell. "For now, can we keep it a secret, just between us?"

He nodded.

"Good. Do you think you can look through the box of pictures your mom kept in the hall closet? They won't make you cry?"

"I can do it." He broke free from me, wiped his tears with the back of his hand, and headed for the hall. "I know where the box is."

"Bring it into the family room by the sofa. I'll be there in a minute." I dialed Chang on my cell and waited for the end of his voice mail message. "It's Bess. I know how the envelope got into my golf bag. Call me."

We proceeded to straighten the family room— a monumental task. It appeared that, since Monday when the boys came home to stay with their grandparents, none of the adults noticed the room had a bad case of toy creep. The boys had carried toys in and left them, forgotten because the next activity was more exciting and required yet another accoutrement. War games needed helmets, swords, pistols, and rifles. A fort required a card table, bed sheets, and bed pillows for reinforcement. Cowboys and Indians wouldn't be caught dead without arrows, hats, spurs, and holsters sporting six-shooter cap guns.

Three huge plastic tubs of Legos lay overturned. A partial city sat unfinished under the card table fort. Perhaps a delay in the building permits? The sofa became the city zoo, I assumed, for every stuffed animal they owned lay on and around it.

The mess didn't surprise me. After all, when had William, Vivian, or James *ever* cleaned anything themselves? Magic maid service satisfied their needs. Always had. Always would.

I turned off the television for the third time. Whenever I left the room then returned, Spongebob and Patrick were on. I put the remote on a high shelf and gave the boys my best *don't even think about trying it* look.

I spent the next half-hour wishing I could do that Mary Poppins *snap* thing, and I hummed the *Spoonful of Sugar* song. The boys giggled at me, but kept toting the sorted toys to their rooms. I ran the vacuum and dusted the furniture.

After changing Sammy and putting her down for a nap, I gathered the boys and we settled into the soft cushions of the overstuffed sofa. The picture box sat by my feet, crammed with photos in the envelopes from whatever store developed them.

"Mommy put the new ones on the computer," Mikey said.

"Yes, I know."

"But it's gone now," Richard said. "Daddy said the police took our computer away."

"They want to find the bad man who hurt your mom," I said. "They have to check everything. I'm sure you'll get it back soon. Pick one, Paul. Let's see what we can find."

He took an envelope from the top and pulled the pictures out. "It's a Christmas. See? Richard's riding his new bike in the house."

"Yeah, now it's got a dent," Richard said. "Because of you." He made a face at Paul.

"Wasn't my fault," Paul said. "You made me hit the tree."

"Did not."

"Did too."

"Guys," I said. "Enough." What would they be like when they got to driving age? I snatched two envelopes and handed one each to Richard and Mikey. "Look at these and find the best pictures of your mom. Then we'll decide which to use."

I fished around, pulled a few more envelopes, and perused them. There were beach days at Makapuu, picnics in the lush dark-green shade of the enormous banyans at Ala Moana Beach Park, and Paul's fifth birthday. Sammy's baptism, the day Richard lost his first tooth, and Mikey hugging a dolphin at Sea Life Park.

So many memories in the life of a family, even a fractured one. I'd been there for lots of them. I glanced at the kids. Their idea of idling along Nostalgia Lane entailed flipping through the prints at light-speed, dumping anything with Jenny on my lap, then getting another envelope. They'd turned it into a race.

Boys. I found myself smiling and filled with emotion, half-proud and half-irritated. The truth hit me broadside. These wonderful, irascible, annoying, loving little boys and their sister belonged to me. They were as much my family as Debbie, Quinn, and Aden. Yes, I knew deep down they had to stay with their remaining parent, no matter how inept. But they also were part of me, and I was part of them. Tears welled, and I blinked to stop them before the guys saw.

When the pile on my lap grew to where the pictures slid off, I figured we had enough to choose from. "You can stop now. I think we have plenty." I moved the pile to the coffee table and spread them. "I have room for twenty on the foam board in my car. I'll get it, and you three find the twenty you want posted on it."

They went right to it, and I retrieved the navy-blue board and a tripod stand I'd had at home. In the far corner of the van's well I saw the diaper bag, once again part-buried with decorating samples. "Stupid bag. I'm returning you once and for all." Back in the house, I set the board against the sofa arm and placed the diaper bag by the stairs.

"Your cell phone rang," Paul said.

"That's a cool color." Mikey pointed at the board.

"Thanks. This color will make the pictures show up better than plain white does. Do you have your final picks ready?" I walked to the kitchen and checked my phone. James had called. I punched in his number and rummaged through the junk drawer for a glue stick while I waited.

"This is James."

"It's Bess. How's William?"

"Turns out it was an anxiety attack. He's had one before, but it was a long time ago. He's resting now. They want to keep him overnight."

A memory flooded back. "It was two days before your wedding."

"What was?"

"His anxiety attack. They'd come from the airport, hadn't been here an hour, and he collapsed, remember?"

"Yeah. Huh. Maybe it's got something to do with long flights."

"The funeral's tomorrow."

"I know. We told the doctor. Dad said he'll sneak out if he has to, but he'll be there."

"Can the kids see him? They need some reassurance. I think you should take them to visit. When are visitor's hours?"

"No point. He'll be home tomorrow. I called one of the nannies. She's going to meet me at the house in an hour. First, I'm dropping Vivian at the Kahala Hilton. She doesn't want to stay at the house without Dad."

Because she might have to do something with the kids, I thought. I found a glue stick, its cap missing, the glue dried harder than cow chips. "I see. What's the nanny's name?"

"Toby something. Hang on. Toby S. Munchman."

"Munch man?" I said. "Never heard that one before. You got her name from Vivian's list?"

"Yup. Would you stay and help me check her out? I haven't the slightest idea what to ask her."

"Fine. But then I've got to go."

We ended the call, and I returned to the family room.

"We're done. Can we watch TV now?" Richard asked.

"First find me a glue stick that works, then I'll put on a movie."

He ran upstairs and back in sixty seconds. "Here." He handed me the glue. "I want to watch Nemo."

"That okay with you two?" I asked the others.

"Yeah."

The lower shelf of the bookcase held all their movies and games. I did a quick scan, but didn't see our favorite clown fish.

"Where's Nemo?" I called.

They did a group blank stare.

"When was the last time you watched it?" I checked the DVD player to see if the movie was inside. No luck.

"I know," Richard said. "We were going to watch it in the car." His face took on a strange cast. "On the way home, if we were good. That day at the park."

"What day at the . . . Oh. Right." I knew where Nemo might be. I went to the front hall and looked in the diaper bag. Sure enough, in a zippered side pocket, I found the fish movie. And a video tape in its cardboard slide-on cover. I pulled the tape from the cover. In neat, black, hand-printed letters, the label said, *Rosalie.*

CHAPTER FOURTEEN

Rosalie. I assumed Rosalie and Rosie on the note were one and the same. Did she have more dirt on Jenny? I wondered if the thousands I'd given Jenny had gone to this blackmailing witch.

Hiding the tape under my arm while carrying the DVD in my hand, I did a casual stroll to the kitchen and tucked the tape into my purse, then zipped it shut.

"I found Nemo." I waved the DVD as I entered the family room and crossed to the television.

"Yea," Paul said. "But look, Mikey fell asleep."

I popped the movie in and sat beside the sleeping boy on the sofa. "Mikey. Mikey, honey, wake up. We're going to watch Nemo now." I rubbed his arms, and he stirred, then placed his thumb in his mouth. The doorbell rang.

Richard and Paul were in their customary positions lying on their stomachs three feet from the screen. They seemed content. I left Mikey and answered the door.

Before me stood a young hapa-haole woman with purple and yellow streaked hair, about ten earrings in each ear, and one attached to each eyebrow. She wore no bra to support her generous endowment, and her shorty T-shirt left her faux-diamond belly button ring glittering in the light of the afternoon sun.

"Yes?" I asked. "May I help you?"

"I'm Toby."

"Toby?"

"The nanny. Mr. Dobbins said to come here."

"Right." Behind me, I heard Sammy begin her *come get me, I'm awake* wail. I glanced backward and couldn't decide whether to close and lock the door in Toby's face or invite her in.

"I'm back." James' voice rang out from the kitchen. He approached us and stopped. "What's going on?"

"This is Toby. The nanny you're supposed to meet today. Toby, this is Mr. Dobbins."

Her eyes widened, and she blushed. "Wow. My sister didn't tell me you were hot."

"Your sister?" James stepped forward. "I'm confused. Who is your sister?"

He was probably quick-scanning the names of the women he'd slept with in the last few months.

"I'm getting' kinda sweaty out here," Toby said. "Can I come in?"

Sammy's plaintive wail escalated into a scream. "I'll get her," I said. "Why don't you take Toby to the kitchen? I'll be there in a few minutes." Disbelief flooded me as I ran up the stairs. Vivian met the girls and narrowed the choices down? Jeez, what did the ones who didn't make the cut look like?

When Sammy and I entered the kitchen, James and Toby sat next to each other, drinking iced tea. James seemed to have a hard time keeping his eyes off Toby's nipples, which had announced themselves in a prominent way since I'd seen her minutes before.

"You know, I'll just go make it a little warmer in here. Turn up the AC." I plopped Sammy into James' lap. "You must be freezing, Toby, with that thin T-shirt on."

"So. Where is your resumé?" I sat across from Toby when I returned.

She gave me a look that could have scared the blue off my jeans.

"Who are you?" she asked.

"This is Bess," James said. "She was my deceased wife's best friend. She knows the kids better than anyone, and I asked her to be here."

Toby said nothing, but the set of her eyes told me all I needed to know. This chick would be the kids' nanny over my dead body. I smiled at her. "I believe I asked to see your resumé?"

She dug in her purse and produced a dog-eared, folded piece of paper. She handed it to James. "I didn't think I needed another copy. You're lucky this was in my purse."

"It's fine. Long as I can read it." I held out my palm to James, and he placed the paper in it.

"Vivian gave me copies. They're in my briefcase." He lifted his daughter onto his hip, walked to the counter, and opened his case. "Got it." He sat with a clean copy in his hands.

"Vivian interviewed you?" I said.

"Well," Toby said.

"She never met you, did she?" I asked.

"I couldn't make it yesterday. So I sent my sister, April. She pretended she was me. We look exactly alike." She grinned at James. "But I thought it was you she met, Mr. Dobbins. Not this Vivian person, whoever she is."

"Vivian is James' mother," I said. "Tell me. Does April have as many piercings as you?"

"You can't discriminate based on looks." She glared at me.

"I wouldn't dare. Was just curious," I said. "It says here your name is Toby S. Munchman. Is Toby a nickname?"

"For October."

"Your name is October?" James asked. "That's unusual. What's the S for?"

"Serenity." She sighed. "My parent were hippies out on the North Shore in the late sixties, okay?"

"But you were born in eighty-five," I said.

Sammy wiped a drool-covered hand on James' shirt. He scowled. "Damn. I wanted to wear this shirt tonight."

"Gross," Toby said.

"Where are you going tonight?" I asked.

"I've got plans." His eyes darted at me, then Toby.

"And the children?" I asked.

"I thought I'd have a nanny," he said.

"You thought you could hire a nanny in the afternoon and leave the kids with her the same night?"

"Excuse me," Toby said. "Can we get back to me? I really *do* have plans tonight."

"Sure. Tell me about the last job you have listed here," I said. "For the McKinney's? Why did that end?"

"They sent their youngest, Brad, to a boarding high school in New Hampshire. They didn't need me anymore."

"And that was this past August?"

"Yeah." Toby glanced at her blue polished nails. They had tiny silver stars at the tips.

Sammy shrieked and lurched for me.

"Here. Hand her over," I said.

James seemed happy to do so. "Ever take care of a baby?"

"Coupla times. Just babysitting. Not as a nanny, you know, full-time. But I know I'd be good with her. This is a live-in job, right?" She scanned the room and her head stopped when her eyes lined up with the pool.

"Would it be alright with you if I called Mrs. McKinney?" I noted the reaction she couldn't hide. I rose with the baby, ripped a paper towel from the roll, wetted it, and wiped the drool off her face and hands. "She's teething."

"I'm great with boys. I took care of my little brother, Deecy, the whole time he was in grade school. Plus, the stuff on there." Her forefinger tapped the paper in James' hand.

"Deecy?" I asked. "Let me guess, his name is December."

"We were named for the month we were born in," Toby said. "Like I said, my parents never got over the hippy thing."

I finished reading the resumé. "You've never taken care of more than one child at a time. What makes you think you can handle four?"

"The boys are a challenge," James said. "I mean, they're good kids, and they mostly listen, but even I can't deal with them sometimes."

Sometimes? I took the high road and refrained from comment on James' parenting skills.

"I babysat lots of kids all at once," Toby said. "Just not as a nanny." She smiled at James. "Would my room be upstairs or down?"

"I'm done." Leaving her resumé on the table, I hoisted Sammy and headed for the family room. "I need to make sure Mikey's not napping. He'll never go to sleep tonight otherwise."

"Bess, wait." James followed me. "I don't know what else to ask her."

I pulled him into the dining room. "You're kidding, right?" I whispered. "Is there any way you'd let that girl provide for your children? Think about it. The nanny does homework with them, drives them to lessons, and has a huge impact on how they develop as human beings. She's going to spend as much time with them as Jenny did. They'll emulate her style, her manners, everything. Do you want your daughter dressing like her?"

He cast a glance toward the kitchen. "I hadn't thought about it that way."

"Even Vivian wouldn't hire her. Call the next one on the list and set up a meeting for Saturday. Look at the bright side. Now you can date her."

A look of astonishment came over him. "I would never be interested in her."

"You seemed quite enthralled with her chest."

"Hey. They were at first alert. It's like a car wreck. I'm a guy. I had to look."

I continued to the family room, leaving him to break the news to Toby.

Mikey had joined his brothers on the floor. I put Sammy in the playpen, and we played her favorite game. She threw her toys out with a mischievous squeal, and I tossed them back in.

James sat on the sofa after escorting Toby to the door. He let out a huge sigh.

"You did the right thing," I said. "It might take awhile, but you'll find someone good enough." I rose from my knees and rubbed noses with Sammy, Eskimo-style.

She giggled.

"I need to go," I said. "Everything here is under control."

"Can I talk to you?" James asked. "Out there?" He nodded toward the pool terrace.

"Guys?" I said. "We'll be outside for a moment, okay?"

Paul formed a thumbs-up without taking his eyes from the movie.

I followed James to the pool deck. "What's up?"

"I want to thank you for everything you're doing."

"You're welcome. You know I love these kids." A cloud finished passing. The pool water reflected a blinding glare into my eyes, and I walked to the shady side. "It was necessary to come outside to tell me this?"

"No." James joined me. "Just before Dad collapsed, Detective Chang called and asked if I knew a friend of Jenny's named Rosie."

"I remember."

"Well, who is she?"

"I have no clue."

"Bullshit. Jenny told you everything." He pulled a chair from the table and sat.

"Apparently not. You never heard of this person either?" I mulled it over. "What about Bitsy? Maybe we should ask her."

"She won't tell me. Now you won't."

"Not I *won't*. I *can't*. I don't know who she is. Does Bitsy know and won't tell you, or does she not know Rosie? When did you ask her?"

"I called her from the hospital. She said she didn't know anything." He leaned forward. "What is it with you women? You got a secret code or something?"

"You're confusing me. What exactly did Bitsy say?"

"She said, 'I'm not going there. I don't have any idea.'"

"Sounds like she knows something to me." I sat across from him. "Did you call Chang and tell him?"

"I figured if he was asking me, then he'd be asking her. And you, too. What did Chang tell you?"

"Nothing." It wasn't a lie. I'd told Chang the information we had so far regarding Rosie. I hoped James didn't know about the pictures.

"That's the limit of what I got from him. And I think you *do* know."

I stood and pushed the chair back. "We're going in circles here. Good luck with the kids tonight. Is your mom coming to help?"

He shot me a look. "I'm better off by myself. There's another thing." He stopped and scratched his chin, then took a deep breath. "Vivian said if she were me, she'd be wondering if the children were mine at all. Maybe I should get DNA tests to prove it."

"What?"

"Did Jenny have an affair?"

A sputter of laughter escaped before I could stop it.

"Come on. She told you everything. Did she cheat on me?"

"I'm offended on so many levels. First, it's become obvious that she sure as heck didn't tell me anywhere near *everything*. Second, even if she wanted to have an affair, who would blame her? You hypocrite. You've slept with anything in a skirt since Paul was born. Third, she didn't want to because she *loved* you, you meathead. But if she did want to, when would there have been time? Those children are *two* full-time jobs. Your mother is delusional."

I walked back to the French doors. "On that note, I'm leaving. I'll be here to help Bitsy set up before the service. The kids' good clothes are hanging in the laundry room. Do not let them change tomorrow until after they've had breakfast."

When I pulled out of James' neighborhood, I noticed a rust-bucket special parked in front of one of the mansions and snickered. On the North Shore, authentic-rust was an accepted finish option for cars. In Kahala, a vehicle like that made you wonder if some rich dude was suicidal because his daughter hooked up with a surfer.

The video tape in my purse worried me. I planned to pour a stiff drink, gulp it down, and watch the darned thing. Why would Jenny pay Rosie? Chang and I assumed for keeping her mouth shut about the pictures. But if the naked guy was in fact her boyfriend at the time, before she married James, then who cared? Yes, the photos would be embarrassing, but unmarried people have consensual sex all the time. And many take pictures of it. James would've gotten over it.

Unmarried or married? That had to be it. The guy cheated with Jenny? I wondered if he told her the truth or lied to her. Maybe that was why she took the break-up so hard. So the guy had a wife. Why didn't Rosie blackmail him instead? Was it possible he had no money? Maybe he died. But then why would anyone care if the pictures came out?

Thinking so hard gave me a headache. I turned on the radio and tried to zone out as I turned up the entrance ramp to the H-1. A rusty sedan drove to the top of the ramp four cars behind me. Seemed to be the same one I saw in Kahala. Perhaps James' neighbor's maid was in the car, going home to Aiea or Kaimuki. She probably lived with three other women in a tiny two-bedroom single-wall shack, scraping by, trying to afford living in paradise.

Grateful for my fortunate circumstances, I said a prayer. I couldn't afford to buy a home, but at least my income assured me a comfortable apartment to myself.

Five minutes later, I exited the freeway and made my way to Piikoi Street in Makiki. My twelve-story building dwarfed the surrounding houses. They were single-wall construction, louvered-windowed, teeny houses set on postage-stamp lots. Shimamura Brothers, the developers, named my building the Piikoi Palms. Like it was a resort. It was a box. A big box with no architectural embellishments. They painted it salmon pink. With its nondescript rectangular shape, it stood like a huge block of Spam, sitting on end. The leafy mango and avocado trees wedged into the tiny yards around it formed the green garnish. I'd seen it from the air. It reminded me of a pathetic Easter dinner Mom put together one year when the family finances went through the floor. She'd even scored the Spam and inserted cloves at the intersections.

I parked in my spot in the garage, then walked to the elevator lobby. The two nosiest women in the building, Mrs. Duncan and Mrs. Rodriguez, waved hello and said something to me from their perch on Mrs. Duncan's second floor lanai. A man with a weed whacker buzzed nearby, so I couldn't hear the women. I waved back, shrugged toward the yard guy, then stepped into the building.

CHAPTER FIFTEEN

Tom's door opened as I unlocked mine.

"Hey." He was bare-chested, barefoot, and wore faded, flower-print board shorts.

"Hi, Tom." I turned the handle and removed my key. "How's the surveillance going?"

He laughed. "I think Aden's got a busy imagination. Nothing happening around here."

"Good."

"I'm reheating last night's chicken. Want some?"

"Kinda got myself into a grilled cheese and Spam mood. But, you know what? Not having to cook *anything* is way better. Bring it over, and I'll throw some salad in a bowl." I eyed his wolf-man chest. "Put on a shirt first, please."

He grinned. "Yes, ma'am. Be over in a few."

I set my purse on my bed, mindful of what was in it. Wondering what was on the tape. I thought about calling Chang, but decided to wait until I'd seen it. Maybe it was nothing. Or maybe we'd find out about Rosie.

I cut the top off a bag of pre-washed greens and emptied them into a colander.

A knock at the door sounded, and I opened it.

"You didn't ask who it was," Tom said. "Don't fling the door wide like that."

"I have a peep-hole." I hadn't bothered to check it, but he didn't need to know that.

"Oh. Right."

I held the door as he entered holding an aluminum foil-covered casserole dish. He headed for my little galley kitchen. Old Spice wafted after him.

I placed the casserole in the oven, then handed Tom a knife and a cucumber. "Slice thin."

"How're things at Jenny's house?" Tom took the cutting board from behind the sink.

"Confusing." I told him about William's anxiety attack. I'd been back and forth in my mind deciding whether to confide in Tom. I made my decision. I needed somebody to bounce this stuff off of. "James and his mom now think Jenny had an affair." I rinsed the lettuce.

"Yeah, sure."

"That was my reaction. And even if she had, which she didn't, why does James get to pass judgment? Mr. Screw-anything-but-my-own-wife? He's thinking of getting DNA tests to see if the kids are his."

"What's he going to do? Drop them at an orphanage if they're not?"

"Oh, God. Don't say that."

"Or what if two are his, and two aren't? Then what? Split them up?"

"Stop it. You're not helping. It's silly. Of course they're his kids. Paul's the spitting image of William, and Richard is all James. "I don't know how James and Vivian can't see it."

"You said she never liked Jenny."

"I think she hated her. But I don't know why."

"Some mothers hate any woman who takes their son away."

We watched the news while the dinner warmed. It was a clear evening with a light breeze, so we ate on my lanai.

119

I waited until we finished. "Ono-licious shoyu chicken, Tom. I wonder if you would do something for me."

"Depends."

"I found a video tape at Jenny's today. I'm not sure what's on it, but I am sure I don't want to see it alone."

"A home movie?" Tom's face showed disappointment. "I suppose seeing Jenny again, especially if it's recent, would upset you. Why watch it at all?"

"I want to know what's on it."

"Okay, but if I fall asleep from boredom, don't get mad."

"There's a chance it might have something to do with Jenny's murder. If it does, you have to promise not to tell Detective Chang I even mentioned it, much less let you see it. In case he ever has a need to talk to you. Deal?"

"Deal."

I stacked our plates, put the silverware on top, pushed back my chair, and took a step backward. But I miscalculated, and my foot hit the chair, knocking me off-balance. I lurched sideways, managed to hold onto the plates, but the silverware flew off and sailed over the railing. The forks and knives descended end over end in a nine-story freefall. They made ripples in the dense crown of a huge mango tree next door and disappeared. A dog barked in the yard below.

"Darn," I said. "Don't think I'll find those."

"You could knock and ask to search for them."

I shook my head. "Sounded like a big dog. I need new silverware anyway."

We did the dishes, then I opened the booze cabinet.

"I'm making a vodka tonic," I said. "A double. Like the Irish say, for the courage that's in it. Want one?"

"You seem a bit on edge. Maybe it'll calm you down. Make me one, but I don't want a double."

I served the drinks on the coffee table and spent a few minutes fluffing the sofa pillows.

"You're stalling." Tom took a sip. "It's a vacation video you never saw. Guarantee it."

"I know. You're right." I inhaled my drink and walked to the bedroom. I removed the tape from its cover, then forced myself back to the living room. I took a deep breath, fed the tape to the VCR, found the remote, and sat staring at the blank screen.

After a while, Tom turned to me. "You gonna turn it on?"

I nodded and pressed *play* as my intestines became a Gordian knot.

The screen showed fuzz for a bit. When the picture came on, I recognized the setting as the burgundy bedroom from the photos. I groaned. Music from an opera I sort of recalled played in the background. It seemed the camera was in the wall. The door and the bed were in full view.

The younger Jenny, wearing a pink silk robe, sat on the bed, looking down toward her lap.

"It's not a vacation. Crud," I said.

He nodded.

A light tapping sounded and Jenny jumped to the door.

"Wait," Tom said. "Pause it."

I did.

He looked at me. "What is this?"

"Honest? My gut tells me it's something not so good. But I have to find out, and I don't want to be alone."

"Fine." He squared his jaw and turned his attention back to the video.

I released the pause button.

Jenny opened the door and threw herself into the arms of the man who stood there. I couldn't see his face because her head blocked his. They moved into the room, kissing with great urgency. Moments later, he released her, spun around, closed and locked the door. When he turned to her again, I screamed.

It was William.

Tom grabbed the remote from my hand, hit the pause, and made a quizzical face.

My heart raced, and I couldn't help but stare at the frozen image of William Dobbins, looking as young as when I'd met him at the wedding. "That's James' father," I croaked.

"Holy shit."

Tears leaked from the corners of my eyes. I pulled a pillow to my stomach, wrapped my arms around it, and squeezed. "Play it."

He shook his head, but pressed the button.

William walked to Jenny. He traced her face with a finger and ran his hand over her long auburn hair. "Rosalie," he said, "you are exquisite."

Tom stopped the tape. "This happened a while back, didn't it? Why's he calling her Rosalie?"

"Don't know," I whispered. "Put it on."

The rest I watched under a haze of shock.

William removed and hung his jacket in the closet, then pulled his wallet from his back pants pocket. He removed several bills and placed them on the dresser, weighting them with a perfume bottle.

"I brought you a present." William pulled a small velvet bag from the other pocket and held it in front of her. "For my favorite girl."

Jenny looked excited and opened the sack. She squealed with pleasure. "I can't believe you bought me this. Oh, thank you. I love you." She lifted a sparkling bracelet from the bag. It appeared to be diamonds.

He took it from her, placed it on her left wrist, and did the catch. Then the kissing frenzy began again. They got busy undressing each other. It was obvious what would happen next.

"Turn it off," I yelled. "Now. Off."

Tom, flustered by my shrieks, dropped the remote, scrambled to find it, then hit the right command.

The television clicked off.

Feeling shaky, I pulled my knees up to my chin, and sobbed.

"Are you sure it's him?" Tom said in a gentle voice. "Maybe it's just a guy who looked a lot like him."

"No. It's him." I wiped my tears with my sleeve. "This tape has to be the *it* those men wanted when they killed her. I can't believe she tried to blackmail William. The son-of-a-bitch killed her."

"Jenny slept with her father-in-law? Then blackmailed him?" Tom looked bewildered.

"He wasn't her father-in-law then," I said. "At least I hope he wasn't. I recognize that bracelet, too. She wore it often. Until she sold it."

My mind raced back to that morning. No wonder William had an anxiety attack when James mentioned Rosie. William was afraid of being caught. Now I wished he'd had a fatal heart attack, the bastard. Dozens of questions stabbed at my brain and tortured me.

Tom broke the silence, his voice calm and low. "Did you know Jenny was a prostitute?"

It felt like he'd slapped me. "Jenny wasn't a prostitute."

"Um. He put money on the dresser. Hundreds. He called her Rosalie, so she had a working name."

"He could have been paying her some money he owed her. For something. And I think they were singles, not hundreds. How much does that kind of thing cost, anyway?"

"Don't ask me. I've never been with a whore."

"Uh-huh. And Jenny *wasn't* a whore."

His deadpan expression also showed pity. He pointed to the blank TV screen. "I'm sorry, sweetie, but, yes, she was."

CHAPTER SIXTEEN

"I need another drink." I buried my head under my arms.

"No. You don't." Tom moved closer to me on the sofa and rubbed my back. "Why don't you tell me all that's going on?"

It took some time, and I cried off and on, but I filled him in on everything I could think of. I'd had no outlet for any of it. Jenny was always my first sounding board, followed by Debbie. And telling anything more to my sister would make her worries worse. About Quinn, and me. It felt good to share my concerns.

Tom seemed lost in thought, and I let him absorb the information.

"This is really twisted," he said. "No surprise you've been such a mess."

"Thanks."

"Hey, that's what friends do. You need to call Detective Chang and tell him about this tape. Then don't tell anyone else. Not Bitsy, James, or Debbie."

"I won't."

He walked to the kitchen, picked up my home phone handset, came back, and placed it in my hand. "Make the call."

I dialed, and Chang picked up on the first ring. Leaving Tom out of the equation, I told him what I'd watched.

"Are you alright?" His voice revealed true compassion. "I'll be right there. Don't move. Don't talk to anyone. And Bess? I'm sorry about Jenny. But try to remember we all have things in our past we're not so proud of. Don't let this taint your memory of your friend."

"I know. Thanks."

I clicked off, sighed, and set the handset on the cushion beside me. "He said he'd come right over. I don't want him to know I told you."

Tom nodded. "That's best. I agree." He gave me a light punch in the arm. "You need *anything*, you come over or call, okay?"

"Yeah."

He kissed me on the forehead and headed for the door. "Come lock this after me."

I dragged my body off the sofa, turned the deadlock, and did the security chain, too. I had the kind of nervous energy that makes a person useless. No concentration. I tried answering email. Couldn't do it. Walked outside on the lanai and stared at the moon over the Koolaus. A picture-perfect night. Wasted.

I didn't know what time I'd called Chang. But it seemed like more than twenty minutes. I called him again. It rang and rang, then his voice mail picked up. "Where are you?" I said. "I thought you said you were on your way. Call me."

Now I paid attention to the time. Another twenty minutes went by. Where the heck was he coming from? I had no idea where he lived. Maybe he needed to drive from the other side of the island. I took the tape from the VCR and put in back in its cover. Then I turned my sheets down and wished I could crawl into bed. Fatigue hit me hard.

A full hour after I thought I made the first call to Chang, I called again. On his voice mail, I let him know I was upset. I paced from room to room, until around eleven. I heard a noise outside in the hall, ran to it, and remembering Tom's admonition, checked the peephole first.

Thank heaven I did. Two men, one a haole, stood huddled outside the door, whispering. I couldn't make out what they said. The other man looked Samoan-Filipino to me. The haole had dark-red hair, blotchy skin, and needed to put on weight. Then I noticed the thick reddish hair on his arms, and my heart jumped into my throat. The man who shot Jenny had arm hair like that.

I backed away and tried not to panic. What to do? Think, think, think, I commanded myself. The handle jiggled. They were testing the lock. I ran to my bedroom, retrieved my purse, dug out the phone, then stopped. If I called Tom, they might hear me and know I was home for sure. Plus, I didn't want to waste the time it would take. I wanted to get out of there fast, not get caught huddled in a corner of my closet, helpless.

Chang was on his way. He would arrive any moment. I had to survive until then. An idea came to me. I tiptoed to the door and without a sound, undid the security chain, thinking if they got in, they'd assume I'd left earlier. I tiptoed away, and grabbed Jenny's tape.

The handle jiggled harder. I heard a kind of scraping sound. Picking the lock? I pulled the draperies across the glass slider to the lanai, turned off the lights, and went out, closing the slider behind me.

I found my cell and called Tom.

"How'd it go?" he asked. "What did the detective say?"

"He's not here yet. Listen, there's two guys trying to break into my apartment."

"What? Now?"

"Right now. I think one of them is the man who killed Jenny."

"I'll go knock him flat." He sounded pissed.

"No. Don't make a sound. Don't let them know you're home. Odds are they have guns. I don't want you to get shot."

"Where are you?"

"On my lanai. I need you to help me over to yours. I can wait for Chang there. They're breaking my lock as we speak. Meet me outside. Hurry."

I eased the lanai door open a crack and heard sounds of metal scraping and clicking. I closed the slider again.

Tom came from his lanai door to his railing. "You okay?" he whispered.

"So far, but I think they've almost got it. It sounded loose." I leaned over my railing as far as I dared but couldn't reach his. "It's too far."

"Give me your hands," he said, reaching for me.

I could foresee one of us slipping in our grip and me plummeting into the mango tree below. "No way. I'll land on one of my forks. Here, catch." I put the tape in my purse, then threw the purse to him.

He caught it and set it down. "Now you."

"Hell no. I can't jump that far." I glanced behind me. "We need something I can crawl across. Maybe the table."

"No. I have a better idea." He hurried into his apartment and emerged a half-minute later with a rickety metal ironing board missing a cover. He lifted it over the gap between the railings and placed it. "I'll hold it steady. Hurry."

Swallowing bile, I moved a chair to the railing, stepped on it, then got on all fours on the metal bridge. It made an ominous groaning sound. I ignored my rising panic and scrambled across.

Tom grabbed my hand as soon as I came within reach. He helped me down, lifted the ironing board, and hustled me, my purse, and the board into his apartment. He closed and locked the slider, then drew his vertical blinds shut.

"Is your front door locked?" I asked.

"I'll do the deadbolt."

I breathed a huge sigh of relief, and with it, came shaking and tears.

He approached and pulled me to him, hugging me close. "Shush, shush. It'll be okay now." He stroked my hair, and began to hum, rocking me with a gentle motion.

A crash-like noise reverberated through the wall.

"I think that was my door banging open."

He let me go, and we went to the wall. I put my ear on it, and he followed suit.

I could hear male voices talking in my apartment, but couldn't make out any words.

"They're in there, all right," Tom said. "Call the police."

"I've already called Chang three times. He's on the way."

"Well call him again and update him about this. He'll need some back up if these two have guns, right?"

I dialed. It rang and rang, and his voice mail clicked on. Again. "He's not picking up." I left a message with a brief description of what happened.

What sounded like cursing came from my apartment followed by crashing and smashing noises.

"They're trashing my home."

"Maybe you should stop waiting for Chang and just call nine-one-one," Tom said.

I opened my phone, then slammed it shut. "Wait a minute. Let's think this through. You and I watched that tape. I called Chang, and those men showed up within the hour. Don't you think that's a little more than coincidence?"

"You think Chang tipped them off?"

"No. What if he told someone where he was headed and why, and they reported back to William? He's rich. He could have paid off somebody in the police department."

"Seems unlikely."

"You didn't hear them, that day we played golf. They know Chief Ortiz really well. James said they throw money at the Policemans' Benefit cause. God knows what William could be paying anyone there to keep the truth about him and Jenny out of the public eye."

"If that's true, then you have a problem."

The noise from my apartment died down. "Maybe they're leaving."

"You can't go back there. They'll be watching your place big time, now they know you really have what they want. One light goes on, and they know where you are."

"What do I do then? Stay here?"

"No. They'll watch the building, too." Tom sat on his kitchen counter. "We need to get you somewhere safe until we can figure this out."

"Chang will know where I should go and what to do."

He looked skeptical. "Do you know for sure he's not the one who told those thugs? After all, he hasn't shown up. Maybe he delayed his arrival so they'd be able to get the tape from you first."

Was Chang's interest in me only a ruse so I'd trust him more? The possibility added another layer of hurt.

Tom sighed, jumped off the counter, and disappeared into his bedroom. A minute later, he came back with a set of keys. He opened a kitchen drawer and pulled out a pen and a piece of paper, then scrawled an address and phone number on the paper.

"Can you read my writing?" he asked.

"Yeah. What's this for?"

"Hector will kill me, but I think this is necessary. He's out of the country. In Australia, surfing for three weeks. He left me his car and the keys to his house while he's gone. I'm supposed to check on the house a couple times a week, make sure everything's alright."

"Who's Hector?"

"My first cousin."

"Where's he live?"

"North Shore. Past Waimea, before Pipeline. He's fixed the house up. Total pain in the ass about it, too. You'll have to be extra tidy."

I nodded. Another trip to the North Shore. At night, the dim lighting on the two-laned Kam Highway past Wahiawa made it a journey I didn't care for. "Thanks, Tom."

"You're welcome. Now, what's our plan? How do you get through this without local police help?"

"FBI? There's an office here, isn't there?"

"I don't know. Let's find out."

I followed him into his bedroom where he cranked up his computer.

CHAPTER SEVENTEEN

"There's a field office at the Kuhio Federal Building," Tom said. He clicked on the link to that site.

"Great. But I had another thought." I backed up and sat on his unmade bed. "What if it wasn't Chang or anyone in HPD, but William had someone bug my phone or the whole apartment when they stealthed around my place the first time? Then his guys heard my call to Chang and zeroed in."

"It's possible. Says here the FBI office hours are eight-fifteen to five. Should we call tonight anyway?"

"Worth a try."

He dialed the number and handed me his phone.

"FBI," a female voice said.

I gave her a two-sentence synopsis of my situation.

"I'll connect you to the person on duty," she said.

A moment later, a man answered, "FBI."

I didn't use names, but told him what I suspected. My brief explanation of the men breaking into my apartment and why didn't impress him.

"Breaking and entering is a matter for the police. Period," he said. "Many people don't trust the police department. We get calls like this all the time. But we do not interfere in these cases. It's a

131

very rare occurrence that a citizen has actual evidence in a murder case. Even if it were legitimate, we can't accept that from you. The only thing I can tell you is to make an appointment with the Chief of Police. See if he'll listen to you. I've met him. He's a responsible man, well thought of around here."

Sure. The stalwart Ed Ortiz who cheated on his wife, lied about it, and turned out to be great buddies with William and Samuels. "But what if it's real? The evidence, I mean."

"We'd hand it to the police. That's policy."

We went back and forth for awhile—me trying to convince him that something awful was afoot, and him responding like a robotic brick wall.

I gave up and thanked him for his time.

Tom raised his eyebrows.

"You want me to relay what he said?" I asked.

"Nah. I heard enough from your end. It's after midnight. You need to go. It'll be easier to get you away from the building in the dark."

"Right." I returned to the kitchen.

Tom followed me.

I pulled the tape from my purse. "Here. You keep it. I don't think we should give it to anyone until we know what's what. Do you know somebody you trust to make copies? I'd like to have some insurance."

He looked pensive. "Good idea. I have a friend. He's cool."

"Great. As soon as he makes the copies, send one to each of the local news networks. Do you have a safe deposit box?"

"Yes. Bank of Hawaii. Main branch."

"Put the original in there."

"Do you really want that video of Jenny all over the news? What'll that do to her kids?"

"You're right. I can't do that. Let's both think overnight who to send it to so William can't get away with murder, no matter who he pays. And make sure your friend doesn't put any of the tape on the Internet, either."

"Not a chance." He gave me a black T-shirt to wear over my white one. My jeans were dark blue.

"Take off your shoes and socks." He pulled a black garbage bag from a box under his sink. "Put them in here. There are reflective patches on your sneakers."

He lent me a pair of his flip-flops, which were huge on me, but better than going barefoot in the dark.

"Hector's car is two blocks away on Kihei Street," he said. "Ready?"

"As much as I'll ever be. Oh." I dug into my purse. "Here are my keys. For when Chang . . . or whoever, shows up. Crud. My locks are probably un-lockable now, huh?"

"I'll look at it later." Tom opened his door and stuck his head out. He stepped into the hall, then waved me forward.

I glanced at the closed door of my apartment. It looked as though nothing had happened. I headed right, toward the elevators.

"No, no," he whispered. "Other way. The stairs."

I reversed direction and hurried to the exit door at the end of our hallway.

We eased the fire door closed behind us and started down nine flights. My flip-flops made loud slapping noises on the concrete stairs, so I removed them and threw them into the plastic bag.

At the bottom, he went out first.

"Wait here," he said.

After a minute or so, he came back. "There's a rusty old Monte Carlo with two guys in it parked across the street from our front entrance. I think we'll be okay. The hedges here are a pretty good screen. Keep your head down and follow me."

We threaded our way across the property, dashed to the other side of Kihei Street, and ran for two blocks. We halted at a new red Acura RSX.

I dug the keys from my purse, put the sandals back on, and gave him a hug. "I owe you forever, you know."

"Drive safe and call me as soon as you get to Hector's."

"Oh, my God." I stopped midway into the driver's seat.

"What?"

"I can't go to the funeral tomorrow. He'll have creeps watching there, too. I have to call Bitsy and James and tell them. And what about the kids? Who'll be there for them?"

"You can't call. What if James knows about this? You also said you don't trust Bitsy."

"I don't think you should go tomorrow either, Tom. You don't want them knowing you ever heard of Jenny. Watch yourself, too."

I started the car and pulled away. All the way to the freeway entrance, I checked for any cars that did what I did. It was almost one o'clock.

Traffic on the H-1 didn't exist in the early morning hours, I found out. Anytime I saw headlights behind me, I slowed and moved to the right lane. Each one zoomed by me, so by the time I exited for the H-2 to Wahiawa, I felt sure I wasn't followed.

What was I supposed to do to stop William? Could I trust Chang? Since he hadn't shown up, it made Tom's theory seem right.

Chang turned out to be a rat? He and Smalley were probably dating. Was she in on this? Was she laughing at me as I got moony-eyed when I was with Chang? More humiliation was the least of my problems now.

I tried my best to block further thought. I got off the freeway. The dusty village of Wahiawa looked deserted. At the edge of Kam Highway, leaving the town, I saw two soldiers buying something under the greenish fluorescents at a Seven-Eleven, reminding me of the lonesome, empty feeling of an Edward Hopper painting. Then it was just me and miles of pineapple fields.

No matter the mind games I attempted, the video of Jenny wouldn't leave me alone. Keeping that secret all those years had to take a toll. A prostitute. With William as a client. She'd said on the tape she loved him. Was that for real? Was William the *boyfriend* who broke her heart? She'd called the guy Wobby. I slapped my forehead. How obvious now. William Dobbins. Wobby, for short.

But why blackmail? If she'd known William that well, why didn't she call him and tell him his son was a stingy jerk? William would have sent her money. Wouldn't he? And, what about the coincidence that when she moved to Hawaii, she met James? How strange was that? Jeez, no wonder William and Vivian never visited. Talk about awkward.

Something Vivian said popped into my reverie. That Jenny wasn't a saint. Bitsy said Jenny wasn't like me. Did they both know about Jenny's past? Did Vivian know William was her client? If Vivian knew that, could she be responsible for Jenny's death?

The road headed downhill the rest of the way, and fifteen minutes later I could see the lights of Haleiwa in the distance. I took the by-pass toward Waimea Bay.

By two-thirty AM, I found 1212 Kukunui Road. Cousin Hector's house. It was a pristine white cottage at the end of a short dead-end lane off Kam Highway. The beach was its backyard. I parked in the carport.

I pulled my garbage bag and purse from the RSX, found the right key, and let myself in. I found a light switch to the right of the doorway. The kitchen was new and white, with stainless appliances and speckled brown granite counters.

Setting my bag and purse on the counter, I went into the combined living-dining room. A small hall opened from the living room and led to a bathroom and two bedrooms. The floors were Mexican tile.

The place was a designer's dream. Dual overstuffed loveseats, plush area rugs, well-done Hawaiian art on the walls, every light on a dimmer, and the sound of the surf pounding just beyond the French doors.

I ventured into the hall, walked into what appeared to be the guest room, sat on the bed, and noticed a handset on the nightstand. After dialing Tom's number, I kicked off the flip-flops and put my feet on the bed.

"Good. You made it," Tom said.

"Yes. I'm sure I wasn't tailed, too. Has anyone else shown up at my apartment?"

"You mean Chang?"

"Yes. Did he?"

"Not that I saw or heard. I've been listening for it."

"Well, go to bed. I'll call you in the morning." I glanced at my watch. "Or in about four hours." I disconnected and replaced the handset. There was an alarm clock beside it. I set it for seven, lay back, and closed my eyes.

CHAPTER EIGHTEEN

I woke before the alarm, startled by a dream. In it, Jenny and I had an argument. One that made her cry. But as my night-fuzziness disappeared, so did the elusive gist of the dream.

Staggering into the kitchen, I hoped to find the makings for a pot of coffee. Hector didn't disappoint. There were five varieties of beans in the freezer, including Kona and Jamaican Blue Mountain. The coffee maker and grinder were on a roll-out tray in a lower cabinet.

I drummed my fingers on the granite while I waited. The immaculate counters were devoid of any display except for one flowering plant in a green foil-wrapped pot with a large yellow ribbon. The soil felt dry, so I held it under the tap and added a little water.

I filled a blue mug with coffee, then walked to the French doors and opened them. There was the aquamarine Pacific, lapping the shore, gentle as the breeze ruffling the tree leaves. The surfers were bummed, I guessed, since the roaring waves I heard when I arrived in the wee hours weren't there anymore.

A step down led to a covered lanai that ran across the back of the house. Another set of French doors belonged to the master bedroom. The floorboards were gray-blue, the vertical posts that held the roof crisp white, and the beadboard ceiling pale blue. White wicker furniture with blue-flowered cushions beckoned me.

I sat in a rocker and glanced up. Bright-green leafy plants hung around the eaves. The lanai overlooked thirty feet of lawn with edgings of pink bougainvillea, yellow hibiscus, and blue agapanthus, then the wide, sandy beach.

"Thank you, Hector. And Tom." I couldn't imagine a more nourishing place to escape. If I pretended my life was normal again, and this was a vacation cottage, maybe the dull buzzing of unanswered questions swirling in my head would go away. For ten minutes. For one minute. Turned out I wasn't that good at pretending.

I carried my coffee to the bathroom, then took a shower. Wrapped in an ultra-soft Egyptian cotton towel, I searched the guest room dresser and found a drawer with a few pairs of women's cotton underwear, some socks and T-shirts. Maybe Hector had a sister who visited. The underwear was tight, but serviceable. I washed mine in the bathroom sink, hung them over the shower rod to dry, then slipped on my jeans.

It was seven-thirty. I turned on the television in the living room and sat on one of the loveseats to watch, flipping channels until I found the local news.

"Family and friends will gather today at Fujimura's Funeral Home to say goodbye to Jennifer Cooper Dobbins," Crystal Makena, the On-the-Spot news anchor, said. "Mrs. Dobbins was shot Saturday while on an outing with her children at Kaliki Park." She blabbed a bit more about it, then the station took a commercial break.

I walked out of the room, refilled my coffee, and stared through the kitchen window toward the carport. At least I now knew why she died. William hired men to kill the mother of his grandchildren. That was a hard fact to accept. So he could avoid a scandal among his elite social peers? Why didn't he just give her money? He had plenty. I kept coming back to that question.

"This just in." Crystal came back on. "A rollover crash killed a Honolulu Police Detective last night."

I ran to the TV. They showed a head shot of Chang.

"Detective Clifford Chang was found dead early this morning in his car. The vehicle was discovered upside down in a ditch off Ke Ala Mano Street, near Kapalama Stream. HPD released no further details. It is not known whether another vehicle was involved."

Stunned, I went outside, sat on the lanai steps, and cried. Hector's phone rang. I let it keep ringing until his machine picked up. Then my cell chirped its Lymon tune. I couldn't deal with anything else, so I ignored it.

I cried and cried and cried. Chang hadn't tricked me. I felt overwhelming guilt knowing that I was the reason he died. He was on his way to my apartment when he had his accident.

My cell rang again. I dragged myself to the kitchen and checked the caller ID. Both calls were from Tom. I found some tissues, blew my nose, then called him back.

"Have you seen the news?" he asked.

"Yes."

"What do you make of it?"

"That it's my fault he died."

"No. It's not. I think someone ran him off the road."

"Why?"

He'd watched more of the broadcast than I and paid more attention. HPD updated the info almost right after that first report. A witness said a dark sedan sped away from the site of the crash.

"I still think whoever Chang told about going to your place last night is on the take. We know it wasn't Chang, though."

"Small consolation," I said.

"I called in sick so I could get the video to my friend Fred. Did you have any ideas about where I should send the copies?"

"Haven't thought for a second about that. I feel whammied. I'll try to get my wits together and call you back."

I wrapped some ice cubes in a dishtowel and sat with the cold pack resting on my eyes, which I knew, without looking, had swollen to monster size again. The cold helped with the pressure headache I felt coming on, too.

Who to send the video to? I didn't know anyone at the newspaper. It had to be people who wouldn't benefit from exposing Jenny's secret, so that left out the media. I put the brick wall guy from the FBI on the list. If Tom included a note explaining it, at least it was worth a try. Maybe because a detective had died, the FBI guy might show more interest.

I removed the now soggy towel and searched the kitchen for a phone book. When I found it, I turned to P in the Yellow Pages. For private detective. I picked the two with the largest ads. Tip-Top Detectives, and De Groot Investigations. Both had offices in downtown.

It was nine-forty when my cell rang again. I didn't answer because it was Bitsy. Then James called. Then my sister. Then Steve. I didn't answer any of them. It had to be obvious to them I was missing in action for the funeral service. I didn't want to upset Debbie, but what could I tell her that wouldn't endanger her? She'd badger me for answers.

I thought about the kids and cringed. The boys needed me more than ever this morning, and I couldn't be there for them. My heart broke thinking about it. Would they trust me after this?

My imagination saw William, Vivian, and James escorting the children into the service. The television cameras and reporters vying for photos and quotes. It made me sick.

I called Tom. "I have a list. Ready? But first, I think, if you would, you should write an explanation of what we know and include a copy with each one."

"I can do that."

I read the names and the private investigators' addresses to him. "You'll have to look up the address for the FBI office again." My low battery signal beeped. I looked at the phone and the tiny symbol was yellow. "My battery's going. If we get cut off, call Hector's house phone. Oh, damn. I don't have my charger. It's on my desk."

"Guess you'll have to buy one."

"Out here? Where do they sell phone stuff?"

"I bet there's somewhere in Haleiwa. Maybe even Foodland at Waimea. They have weird things you'd never expect."

"I'll try. I need to get cash and personal items anyway."

"Be extra careful. A red RSX stands out, you know. Try to disguise yourself."

"Okay. Why does Hector have a red car, anyway? Everything in this house is blue or white. He has impeccable taste, too. Does he have a partner?"

"A partner?"

"Significant other. Whatever."

"No, he's single. Why? Are you interested?"

I choked. "In a gay guy? I don't think so. There's a decorator, Joseph, at Mills Wallpaper. Maybe they'd get along."

"Hector's not gay." He sounded insulted.

"If you say so." I let it drop there. Families were often the last to know. But I lived in the design world and had sharp gay-dar.

A disguise. I rummaged through the guest room closet, then Hector's room. He'd have to forgive me the breach of his privacy. There were a number of hats hanging from hooks inside his walk-in closet. I chose a floppy-brimmed fisherman's hat.

I put my hair in a ponytail, then stuffed it into the hat. My borrowed T-shirt said *Surf Naked*. With my sunglasses on, I looked like a tourist.

There were no cars parked along Kukunui Road when I emerged from the cottage. I scanned what I could see of the neighborhood from the kitchen door stoop. A rusty old beater that looked like it started life as a blue car sat two driveways over. The one I spotted following me was maroon. I didn't notice any workmen, repair trucks, or service vehicles that could be faking and in reality, watching me. I'd watched too many movies.

I pulled into the Foodland lot and lucked into a space in the shade, away from the bustle of the entry doors. Glancing at my watch, I realized Jenny's service was in progress. Debbie was there, no doubt in a total panic about me. If I called her cell, she'd pick up and run out of the service, hoping it was me. And I didn't want to talk to her for fear I'd tell her too much.

There was a pay phone outside the store. I dug in my purse for quarters, found them, and dialed Debbie's home phone. This way, she'd know when she returned home I was alright, and she couldn't place the number from caller ID. And she wouldn't call our mother and worry her to death.

Her machine kicked on.

"Deb, it's Bess. I'm fine. Yes, really. I can't explain why I'm not at the funeral, but it's for good reasons, believe me. Don't worry. I've gone away for a few days. Give the kids a hug for me. I'll call you soon."

Guilt got hold of me again, and behind my sunglasses, my eyes filled with tears. I thought of Chang's ardent brown eyes staring at me, missing what we might have found in each other. Lifting the glasses, I wiped at my eyes.

I slogged into Foodland and picked up a hand basket. I needed personal products, make-up, and basic food items. Then I got in the deli line for a sandwich. There was another line twenty feet away for the Starbucks Coffee counter. The baristas worked faster than the deli people. The Starbucks line moved along at a good pace.

I counted fifteen people helped in their line versus only five in mine in the same time. It was prime tourist season, and I had to be patient. My stomach rumbled. When my turn came, I ordered an Italian sub and large Diet Pepsi.

At the checkout, I asked about phone chargers. I hadn't seen any in the store.

The girl shrugged. "Maybe in Haleiwa town."

Figuring it was safer to let my fingers do the walking, I took my purchases to Hector's. I ate outside on the lanai, then searched the phone book again, this time for anywhere on the North Shore that might sell a charger.

There was a Radio Shack in Haleiwa. Glory be. I brushed my teeth, which felt amazing, put my hat on, then got into the RSX. The

Friday afternoon traffic on Kam highway was awful. There was only this one road around the North Shore, and it was jammed.

I turned the radio on, and the jocks discussed the Eddie Aikau Big Wave Invitational surf contest. The ninety-day watch period ended soon, one man said. Rumors of a big swell prediction for the weekend, big enough to hold the contest, explained the massive amounts of tourists and traffic. The best surfers in the world were here, waiting for the big waves to crash into Waimea Bay.

The traffic got worse beyond the bypass. Those of us who wanted to enter Haleiwa crawled to the tiny town where Kam Highway shrunk to one lane in each direction. The road curved inland from the beach park and a long row of one-story wood buildings lined both sides. Crowds of people waited outside the restaurants, and a long line extended from Matsumoto's Shave Ice.

I found the Radio Shack between Pizza Bob's and Bank of Hawaii. How convenient. I needed cash. Finding a place to park was something else. The shopping plaza's lot had cars parked in illegal spots and I saw several circling the lot hoping for a break. I decided to try a side street.

There was a line of four cars ahead of me to exit back onto the road. A sudden slap on the hood of the car startled me.

A dark-haired man in a green shirt stood beside my window and smiled.

I rolled down the tinted window a few inches.

"Hector, dude, when'd you—" He stopped in mid-sentence. "Who are you?"

"Hi. I'm a friend of Hector's."

"He's in Australia. Didn't say nothing to me about somebody driving his car."

"Yes, I know." I gave him my most charming smile. "It's okay. I'm more a friend of his cousin, Tom."

"Hanegawa let you drive Hector's car? Damn."

"What's your name?"

"Mike."

"Well, Mike, it's nice to meet you." I lowered the window more, held my hand out, then noticed there was only one car left in the line in front of me, and a big gap between me and it. "I don't want to hold up traffic here." I pointed to the gap. "Catch you later."

He looked puzzled when I drove forward, but headed toward the IGA Supermarket.

At least he knew Tom's last name. That meant he really was one of Hector's friends. I breathed a sigh of relief. I took a right out of the lot and found a side street. It was a dirt lane, but there were other cars along the side of it, so I eased my way past them and made a space.

Swirls of dust kicked up by my tires hung in the air as I locked up. The lane went west toward Mt. Kaala, and it looked like there were a dozen small homes clustered further down. Two Chinese women using parasols for shade walked down the middle of it toward me. I nodded as a greeting, and they waved. Walking back to Radio Shack, I noticed how many new shops there were. I hadn't been in the town for a while. When going to Bitsy's, I always took the bypass.

T-shirt stores and surf shops seemed to be doing the biggest business, other than the restaurants. I passed tourists speaking German, then dodged around a group of Brazilian men outside a surf shop trying to bargain with the owner. A gaggle of teenage girls stopped short in front of me when one spotted what she *could swear* was Ashton Kucher on the other side of Kam Highway. They ran across the street in hot pursuit.

I went inside the bank to make my withdrawal, not feeling comfortable about taking cash from an ATM with so many people milling around. Not knowing how long I'd be marooned on the North Shore, I took out four-hundred dollars.

I headed next door. I'd never seen such a crowd in a Radio Shack before. After checking every aisle, I didn't see the kind of charger I needed for my phone. No sales-floor people were in sight, so I got into the customer service line.

When it was my turn, I asked about the charger.

The man frowned. "Tell me the model again?"

I did, and he frowned deeper.

"I'll check in back, but I think we're out."

Crud. I cooled my heels for a few minutes and watched the customers. They all seemed to be tourists having a marvelous time. There was lots of excited talk about the surf contest. I guessed they needed to be sure their cameras were ready.

The man came back. "Nope. The manager says we sold the last one this morning. It's the number one thing people forget when they pack for a vacation."

"Darn. When does he expect more? Oh. What about a car charger?"

"Checked. Gone, too. Our shipments usually come in on Tuesdays. But it might be here by Monday. That happens sometimes."

I thanked him and left. A dead cell phone was a pain in the shorts. I made my way back to Hector's car, joined the slow snaking line in the other direction, and turned on the radio just in time for the surf report.

The official word was the swells were indeed coming in. By Saturday morning, Waimea would be breaking.

CHAPTER NINETEEN

I took the liberty of checking Hector's message machine when I returned to the cottage. There was one for me from Tom.

"Where were you?" Tom sounded worried when I reached him.

"Went to Haleiwa looking for a charger. They were out. I ran into a friend of Hector's there. He recognized the car. A scruffy, skinny guy with dark hair, maybe part Filipino. His name was Mike."

"Mike." There was a pause. "Probably Mike Garcia. Stay away from him."

"What's wrong with him? You don't think he has anything to do with the mess I'm in, do you? Am I in trouble? He knew who you were."

"Yeah, I know him. No, I don't think he'd be mixed up with the jerks who are after you, but he's been in some bad situations. Just stay away from him. And maybe you should drive that car as little as possible."

I checked the time. Three o'clock. "Okay. Have you watched the news? Any coverage of the funeral?"

"I did, and there was." His words became hesitant. "The governor was there. Lots of media coverage because of that."

"I'll look for it on the news. I suppose it was a nice gesture. He never met Jenny, though. I guess he went out of respect for William.

I told you they went to college together, right? I wonder what he'd do if he knew William hired people to kill Jenny. Maybe we should send a copy of the tape to Governor Samuels too."

"About that . . ."

I heard a deep breath on his end and sensed something wrong. "What?"

"I watched the rest of the tape."

"Why? Was it titillating?" I felt anger rising.

"Stop. We didn't know what, if anything, was on the rest of it. I didn't want to ask my friend to copy it without seeing it first."

"Fine. You have a point. So?"

"The, um, *encounter* with William wasn't the only thing on the video. A second one happened in the same bedroom with a different man. Lewis Samuels."

Stunned, I couldn't speak.

"Bess? You there?"

"Yeah."

"It looked like the same time frame. There wasn't any background music or any other sounds but what they were doing and saying. What I mean is, I could hear them really well."

"That's great. Spare me the details. I can't believe he was her client, too. The son-of-a-bitch played golf with me and pretended he didn't know her." Then it hit me. "Oh, my God, what if she tried to get money from him, too? He could have hired those thugs."

"I think you may be right. It gets worse." He paused again. "Looks like Samuels liked to play rough in the bedroom. At the height of things, he had his hands around her neck. Jenny's arms were flailing, and she tried to scratch him. I got creeped out. But when he was done, they relaxed and acted like it was normal for them. Then Jenny said, 'You'd never really do it, you know. You don't have it in you.' I should tell you that there was an open bottle of vodka on the night table, and they drank a lot of shots before getting to the sex."

"Go on."

"Samuels answered—but he called her Rosie—by telling her he did kill a girl by accident during sex once. Like it would prove his toughness to Jenny. And she egged him on, saying he was full of it. He told her it happened during his first year of college, when he was home on a break. 'Bullshit,' Jenny says.

"Samuels tells her the girl was local, and her name was Malia. He must have been really drunk at that point, because when he left, they were all smiles and hugs and see you next time. Like he didn't even remember telling her."

"Holy Mother. Think it's true?" I said.

"If it is, and she tried to use it, well . . ."

"His political career and his marriage would be over."

"Not to mention the prison time. If he's the one who hired the goons, then you are in some deep shit."

"He could have full-access to the police department, too." A spike of fear pierced through me. "I need to find out if it's true." I'd seen Hector's computer on the desk in his room. "Do you know Hector's computer password?"

"Good idea. I already brought up the newspaper's website. The archives. But our building's cable went out before I got anywhere."

"The whole building? That's weird."

"Nah. I can see cable company trucks parked on Piikoi from here. I'm going to go down and ask them how long 'til we get it back."

"So, the password?" I asked.

"I don't know. He told me he changes it a lot. But Hector's an organized guy. I'll bet he's got a list of passwords somewhere."

"I'll snoop around."

"Good luck. And please, keep a low profile. I'm dropping the tape at Fred's soon, so if you need me, call the cell."

I rang off, then wandered to the back lanai. I sat in the rocker and shuddered, thinking about what Tom told me.

Did Samuels know this tape existed? Could Jenny have been so desperate as to blackmail the governor? Did Samuels and William each know that the other was a client of hers also? Those two were old friends. Maybe she tried to extort money from both of them, and they teamed up to get rid of her. One thing was for certain—I was in serious trouble.

The sound of waves crashing brought me back from my thoughts, and I directed my attention to the ocean. There was a large set rolling in. It looked like the high-surf predictions were right. If this kept up, by morning every surf spot except Waimea would be closed out and un-rideable.

I went inside and turned on the television, checking the local stations to see if there was any news on. No luck. I'd have to wait until five o'clock.

Hector had a nineteen inch flat-screen monitor mounted on the wall in front of his desk. I turned it on, then started the CPU. It whirred to life, and thirty seconds later, a blue page came up asking for the password.

I riffled through the desk drawers, searching for anything that might contain a list. Hector kept files for everything. I'd never seen anyone so organized. Not even my mother. Besides the normal bills, car, and house information, he had a file for discount movie ticket coupons. There were lists of books he wanted to read, movies he wanted to rent, and hobbies he wanted to try, one of which was needlepoint.

His paperclips were in separate containers by colors, and he had seven different colors of Post-it's. Pens lived in segregated communities of blue, black, and red. Pencils, sharp and ready, resided elsewhere in their own area.

I examined everything and found nothing resembling a password. I took the center drawer out, emptied it, and turned it upside down, hoping to see a taped paper on the bottom.

Disheartened, I walked to the kitchen and seeing Hector's sizeable wine rack, decided to open a modest bottle of Cabernet. My nerves were frayed. I needed it, and I sure wasn't driving anywhere.

The cabinet that held the wine glasses had a shelf filled with cookbooks. I took one that I hadn't heard of and after pouring the wine, perused the recipes in it, trying to push back the fear and pretend things were normal. Hector cooked a lot, I concluded, because there were comments and adjustments written in the edge space of many pages.

The Cabernet was wonderful. I began to think that, if by some miracle Hector wasn't gay, he might be the perfect man for me. My mother would love somebody with organizational skills to enter my life. My mother. Anything she wanted to protect from intruders, she kept in her cookbooks if possible. She'd stashed random addresses and phone numbers, copies of insurance policies, plus tens and twenties into the books on her shelf for years.

I took every cookbook off the shelf, and one by one, went through the pages. Sure enough, in an old *Joy of Cooking*, I found a crisp, folded piece of paper tucked into the back cover.

It was a list of words and numbers. I carried my wine into Hector's room and, starting with the first, tried every entry on the list. The sixth one worked. While the computer did the rest of its warm-up routine, I put the list back and replaced the cookbooks.

When would Lewis Samuels have been a college freshman? He had to be close to the same age as William. They were both in their mid-sixties. I doodled some quick math on a piece of scrap paper. Their college years were the sixties also.

I went to the *Advertiser*'s website, scavenging for articles about murders in the nineteen-sixties. I wasn't the best at online research and ran into a quick dead end. It looked like the newspaper's website had articles going back to ninety-nine but no further.

I tried Google-ing a number of options that might lead me to information, but couldn't find anything about a girl named Malia who'd gone missing or was found murdered.

After an hour, I gave it up, called Tom on his cell, and filled him in on what I didn't find.

"I wanted you to know I'm going to the Waialua library," I said.

"You shouldn't."

"It'll be fine. I'll wear my hat and sunglasses. I look like any of the eight gabillion tourists out here. Did you hear they're running the Eddie Aikau tomorrow?"

"Sure. I'm driving there in the morning. Don't you dare go watch unless I'm with you. From the way you described these guys, chances seem good they'll be at Waimea. No surf troll could resist. Disguised and with me, you'll look like part of a couple. Not what they'll be searching for."

"Maybe we shouldn't risk it."

"Are you joking? There hasn't been one since oh-four. It's history."

"Okay. But keep me safe, dude. Did your friend make the copies?"

"Not yet. I dropped it off an hour ago. I'm working on that fact sheet you wanted me to write to send with them."

I promised to call when I got home again and hung up. The traffic on Kam Highway slowed me down again, but the rest of the trip, once past Haleiwa and into Waialua, was easy. I drove into the library lot at five. There were two other cars parked in front of the building. It seemed the library wasn't the happening place to be, which suited me fine.

It was a small, but cozy-feeling library. One big central room with a few movable wall dividers around the periphery. I wondered if they'd have archives of newspaper back issues. I approached the fifty-something man at the desk and asked about closing time.

"Eight o'clock on Fridays," he said.

"Great," I said. "Do you have microfilm?"

"Depends on what," he said.

"How about old newspapers from the nineteen-sixties?"

"Most of them."

"Can you show me the where's and how's of doing the microfilm? I haven't done this in years."

"Certainly." He escorted me to the section. "Do you have a subject matter and date? It'll make it easier."

"I'm doing a paper on that era," I said. "And young women of the times. Especially those who might have gotten into trouble. You know, I'm impressed that such a small branch would have it."

"When they make the films of newspapers, all the branches get them." He seemed a bit insulted. "Now, women in trouble? You mean, got pregnant?" He looked puzzled. "I don't know if you'll find statistics about that in a newspaper. Maybe a small article. You'd be better off looking up studies."

I smiled and did a fake chuckle. "Oh, no. Not pregnancies, sorry. I meant like women who had bad things happen to them, you know, like as a consequence of bad choices? Maybe runaways, abductions, murders?"

He gave me a disapproving scowl, showed me how to search a subject on the computer, and left.

I keyed in *murder, Malia,* and *unsolved.* Quite a few articles came up from the mid-sixties. I got the correct microfilms for them and sat at a viewer carousel. I searched through a bunch before finding an article about a Punahou high-school senior named Malia London who'd been missing for three days. The date was December 18, 1964.

She'd met a group of friends at the movies and never returned home. There was a photo of her, probably her senior portrait, wearing a black drape and pearls. She was a pretty girl with short dark curly hair. She seemed to be a little cross-eyed, like she normally wore glasses but didn't want to for her picture.

I printed that article, then searched for more. In January sixty-five, there was another. They'd found Malia's remains in dense forest near the base of Mt. Kaala, the tallest peak on Oahu, in the Waianae Mountains. Foraging creatures left little of her, besides bones, to find. Wild boars were the probable culprits. They'd identified her by dental records.

A local-looking guy plopped into the carrel connected to mine, shaking the whole cheap, fake-wood grain assembly. I nodded as a greeting and went back to my search, attempting to ignore him.

He wasn't doing anything. He'd brought no books or material to his desk area.

I glanced his way, and he stared at me. He fit the description of a *moke*. A huge, well-connected-to-the-local-scene kind of dude who no one in their right mind would ever mess with. He wore a muscle shirt and a gold chain around his neck. My guess was he was Hawaiian-Samoan. I moved the microfilm to the next headline I saw, turned my copies over, and pretended to be riveted by an article on stowaway brown snakes from Guam.

Then he smiled. "Howzit?" He spoke with a thick local-pidgin accent.

"I'm good." I flashed a weak smile back. "You?" I'd taken off my sunglasses but left the hat on. My internal panic alarm rang, and I prayed he wasn't somebody sent to look for me.

"Life's a beach." He chuckled.

"Yes." I went back to pretend reading.

"Big weekend coming up, eh?"

I looked up. "The Aikau? Yeah. Pretty exciting, all right." I felt my hands shaking, so I squeezed them between my thighs.

"You know about Eddie?" His question felt like a challenge, as though I was a tourist.

"Of course. The Hokule'a. I don't like to think about his death. The story makes me cry."

He made a slight nodding movement with his head. An approval.

A movement from a partition near the desk area caught our attention, then he tapped me on the shoulder as he got out of his chair, giving me a pseudo-heart attack.

"Rodney," a demanding female voice called. "Get your ass over here."

"I'm coming, Cheryl." He winked at me. "My sister. Bossy as hell. She doesn't like haoles. Maybe I see you at Waimea."

"Maybe." I watched him lumber to where his sister waited. The floorboards trembled as he walked. Cheryl looked very put-out.

She spoke to the man at the desk, picked up a briefcase, and led Rodney outside.

It took a few minutes to slow my heart rate. I found three more articles that had some information about Malia and printed them, too.

I brought the microfilms back to the guy at the desk. "Thanks for your help."

"Sure. Find anything to work with?" He stared at me over his glasses.

"Yes. A few things. Does that woman, Cheryl, work here?"

"Part-time." He eyed me with suspicion. "Why?"

I shrugged. "Her brother seemed nice."

"Rodney's okay. Long as nobody plays in his sandbox, if you know what I mean." He turned and went back to some paperwork.

The sun had set. I scanned the parking lot and now there was only my car and one other. I assumed that was the librarian's. I drove through the twilight, changing directions and turning around a few times, to see if I was followed. Feeling awful, I returned to Hector's preoccupied with unlucky Malia. I'd hoped that Samuels' boast to Jenny was drunken baloney.

My half-full glass of wine was on the granite counter where I'd left it. I downed the rest, poured another, and sat at the table to read the articles.

Near as I could ascertain, Malia's murder went unsolved. Forty-five years later and they never had one viable suspect. Her parents divorced. Her father returned to the mainland, and her mother moved in with her own mother in Makaha so Tutu could help with Malia's younger brothers.

I checked the phone book for anyone named London and found several, including an Apona London in Makaha. I wondered if he was one of Malia's brothers.

Part of me was tempted to call, determine if Malia was his sister, and tell him what I knew. Then sanity came back. I finished the articles.

The police found Malia's parents' car right where she'd parked it in the theater lot. Her friends said she flirted with a guy in the row behind them, and for a few minutes sat with him, giggling, but returned to her seat before the movie ended. One friend said she tried to get a better look at him because Malia gushed about how cute he was. But it was too dark, and when the house lights came on, he was gone.

The girls walked to the ice-cream store afterward. Malia didn't order anything, soon said she didn't feel well, and left before the others. That was the last they saw of her.

CHAPTER TWENTY

"Looks like it's true." I sat on Hector's loveseat with the handset to my ear, flipping channels, looking for local news. I relayed the gist of the articles.

"That's unfortunate," Tom said. "Now what do we do?"

"Right. How do we get this information to people who can prevent William or Samuels from killing me too? I keep coming back to the FBI guy. The trick is how to get him to watch the tape before he does an automatic turn-around with it to HPD."

"I wrote a good letter to go with it. Want me to read it to you?"

"Sure." I listened to the whole thing. "I think on the outside of the manila envelope of the FBI copy you should write in marker, big—*Governor Samuels confesses to murder in 1964 on this tape. Please watch.*"

"If that doesn't do it, I guess nothing will. I'm supposed to call Fred in the morning about picking up the tapes." Tom yawned. "I'm sorry. It's been a long day after the scare last night. Almost forgot. Your ex came by about an hour ago."

"What did Steve want?"

"He said he was worried about you since you didn't show at the funeral, and you're not answering your phones. I heard him knocking and calling at your door, so I went into the hall to talk to him."

"Crud. You didn't tell him about any of this, did you? He's such a do-gooder, he'd go straight to the police and put you and himself in possible danger."

"I promised I wouldn't, remember? Had to think fast, though. I said you'd mentioned going away for a couple of days to get away from the strain of your misery, but you never told me where. 'On the day of Jenny's burial?' he asked. I told him maybe it *was* her funeral you couldn't face."

"Steve's reaction?"

"He looked skeptical. I shrugged and said that was all I knew."

"Thanks."

"Stay in now, would you? Check with me in the morning. And lock the doors."

"Yessir."

I put the handset on the cushion and watched some inanity on the local station, waiting for the news at ten, fifteen minutes away. I closed my eyes and wondered if I should have told Tom about meeting Rodney-the-moke at the library.

The distinctive bell tones of KMBB news startled me. I woke up and turned the volume higher. Tornadoes in the mid-west headlined the news, then a wrong-way crash in Honolulu. They interviewed people facing eviction and highlighted a renaissance festival in Kailua going on through the weekend.

Then I saw the front façade of Fujimura's Funeral Home with lots of people entering. Their camera captured a limo arriving under the portico, then Governor Samuels and his wife, Emily, exiting the vehicle. The reporter asked the governor why he was there.

"The Dobbins are old dear friends of my family," Samuels said. "We came out of respect for them. It was such a tragic death. Especially leaving those four little children without a mother." He looked teary-eyed.

"And how is the investigation of Jenny Dobbins' murder progressing? Any suspects?" the reporter asked.

"That is a question for the Honolulu Police Department. I've been assured they have their best detectives on it, but I haven't been advised of any new information."

In the background, I saw my client, Jocelyn Plimpton, looking like she wanted her turn to talk to Samuels. I didn't see William, Vivian, James, or the kids. They were inside already, I guessed.

The news did catch them on the way out. James and William rushed the kids into a waiting limo, avoiding contact with reporters. Vivian followed, dressed in black. She wore a black hat with a veil and kept her head down.

The children, for the flash of an instant I saw them, looked bewildered. My heart broke all over again. Then the picture changed to something about golf.

I turned the television off and got ready for bed. One day since I ran from my apartment, and I already missed my home. Would the copies of the tape work?

***

I woke at five in the morning with a nagging thought. I didn't know for sure if Jenny tried to blackmail the governor. I didn't know if he knew the tape existed. If she hadn't, and he didn't, then what would exposing him accomplish?

Answers and justice for Malia's family. But at what cost to the state? Samuels' popularity among the many races was unprecedented. By all accounts he was a great guy. He'd made inroads where islanders never believed it could happen. He was the first governor to push hard for the Hawaiian Sovereignty Movement, and had done it in a way that united the disparate groups wanting very different results. That took some serious political talent.

Maybe it was just a very tragic accident forty-five years earlier. Unintentional. Maybe he lived haunted by the knowledge every day of his life and swore to be an outstanding public servant because of it. Malia was still dead, one way or the other. Samuels was around nineteen then. A kid who got scared. Terrified. Nineteen-year-olds make bad decisions most of the time.

Yes, he lied to me about knowing Jenny. But James was there at the table after golf. What was Samuels supposed to do? Say, *why sure, James, I meant to have you two over, but considering the fact that I slept with your wife when she was a prostitute, Emily's not so jazzed with the idea.*

I wondered if Samuels ever told his wife about his past. She did have that world-weary expression so many political wives wore.

Then I remembered my last conversation with James. It sounded like Bitsy knew who Rosie was. I needed to find out how much she knew about it.

I made coffee, took a shower, and borrowed another T-shirt from the guest room dresser. This one was blue with white letters that said, *Get off of my cloud.* It was only six. I'd have to wait until at least eight to drop in on Bitsy.

The constant background noise of the surf grew louder, and I walked outside to look. I strolled barefoot across the lawn, coffee in hand, and used the wooden steps to get down a four-foot drop to the sand. I knew, from other places I'd visited on the North Shore, by the middle of summer, the sand would return and cover the stairs.

I could see the sun starting its ascent to the east. The clouds closest to the horizon glowed pink. There was almost no wind. I looked due north, and it was just light enough to see a faraway set of waves coming in. The tide had the ocean lapping near my feet, almost to the steps.

I moved backward and sat on the bottom step, waiting for the set to arrive. The first wave rose about 50 yards from the shore and formed a consistent ten-to-twelve foot azure glassine face before it curled down on itself.

Shouts came from my right, and I turned to see a group of local guys dropping their gear on the beach. One pointed at the next wave. It was bigger than the last, maybe a fourteen-foot face. They hurried to wax their boards. The next two waves were even bigger. The surfers waited in the churning shore break. Electricity and excitement was in the air. I could feel the anticipation from where I sat.

They were crazy to go out there. The high-surf warnings meant that before long, the huge sets of waves would become un-rideable at this beach or any other except Waimea Bay. If they got caught in the ocean when that happened, well, I wouldn't want to watch.

They waded in further, then lying on their stomachs, paddled out on their boards. I watched until the next set came in. At a quarter to eight, I headed back to the cottage.

I called Tom.

"Ugh. What?" He sounded groggy.

"Did I wake you?"

"It's Saturday." Then he seemed to snap together. "Something happen? You okay?"

"Yes, I'm fine. But I have some doubts." I told him what I'd been thinking regarding Samuels. "Maybe you should wait to send the tape copies until I get a chance to see what Bitsy knows. I'm going there soon. I'll call you when I get back, then we can decide. Maybe only William's after me, and we should delete Samuels' part of the tape."

"The man killed a girl."

"By accident."

"A kinky sex accident. The guy's scum. And a spineless wimp."

"He was a teenager."

Silence ruled for a minute.

"I'm trying to consider what's best for everyone involved," I said. "The greater good. That includes the population of the state of Hawaii. On top of that, what if I open a huge can of worms with it? If he's not the one after me now, then I'm just creating another problem for myself? Maybe a bigger one."

"I don't think there's any question about what to do. But I'll wait 'til I hear from you. Be careful."

I rang off. The possibility of being spotted by William's or Samuels' thugs made me uneasy, so I rooted in the kitchen drawers for a paring knife and tucked it into a side pocket of my purse. It wasn't great, but I didn't have anything else. I switched to another hat from Hector's closet. A Tommy Bahama wide-brimmed straw hat with a flowered band.

First I watched from the kitchen window facing the street for a good ten minutes. I saw nothing unusual. No different cars. The blue rust-bucket sat in its normal place two doors down. No people lurked behind palm trees. This was one sleepy little street.

Red RSX and I took a right onto Kam highway. The traffic slowed as it approached Waimea Bay. Word of the Aikau contest turned the North Shore into the temporary sports mecca of the world. Parked cars lined both sides of the road. There was a long line coming from the other direction, bottled up by people hoping for a miracle spot in the beach parking lot. One van had the ESPN logo. Television news crews swarmed the area, setting up scaffolds and cameras.

Huge banners bearing the names of surfing magazines hung between poles in back of portable booths. People in matching T-shirts unloaded boxes from trucks. My trip back from Bitsy's would be hell. Or maybe by then, the police would have tamed the traffic problems.

I took a left onto Pupukea Road and marveled at how Little Red took the steep hill with no stress. When my van made that climb, I had to shut off the air conditioning to encourage its cooperation.

I drove past Bitsy's street, peering down it as I did. Not seeing anything strange, I doubled back, made the turn, then went well beyond her house, checking every visible driveway along the way. If these guys were on the ball, they'd be watching Bitsy's, too.

At the end of her street, I parked, watched, and waited. An old Korean man left a house a few doors away, walking a huge black poodle toward Pupukea Road. After another five minutes, I left and locked the car.

Avoiding the road, I crept through tall grass at the edge of the last home's lot. Each yard on this side of the street ended at a rocky ridge line that fell off by about thirty degrees. There was a path along the slope, and I kept my head ducked as I passed each house.

I could see the hoopla down at the bay from the path. Short scrubby trees blocked my way several times, and I tried to ignore my imagination's vision of me slipping and tumbling down the mountainside.

At last, I recognized Bitsy's backyard. Again I waited, watching for activity in or around her house, then sprinted to the back lanai

I climbed the steps, opened the screen door, and knocked on the wood one. There was no answer. I put my ear to the door and listened. Nothing. I bet she was still in bed. I picked up a fallen palm frond and walked to her bedroom window.

"Bitsy?" I kept my voice low and tapped at the window with the frond. "Bitsy." I turned the frond around and used the husk end, which made a much louder rattle against the glass.

Her face appeared at the window and registered annoyance when she saw me.

I pointed to the back door. "Let me in."

She met me there and, with wild hair and a sour expression, let me in.

"I have to pee," she said as she retreated from the kitchen. "I hate you now, you know."

CHAPTER TWENTY-ONE

Bitsy let me wait for forty-five minutes before she returned. Showered, coiffed, and with perfect make-up, she breezed into the room wearing a pink tennis skirt and matching polo.

"I made coffee for you." I pointed to her pot chugging away on the counter by the oven.

She ignored me and took one mug from an upper cabinet.

"I'm sorry I couldn't be there yesterday," I said. "I'm here to explain why. It's a really good reason. And I need your help."

She sighed, then turned to the coffee-maker.

"I saw the funeral on the news," I said. "Looks like you did fine without me."

After pouring her coffee, she faced me. "There is no good reason. Nice T-shirt." Her voice dripped with sarcasm.

"Just sit here with me. You know more about Jenny and her past than you're admitting. I know next to nothing about her past, and now I'm in danger."

"What are you talking about?" She sat opposite me.

"You know Detective Chang was killed, don't you?"

"He had an accident." She shook her head. "They say it's going to set back the investigation. In fact, the girl detective, Kelly Smalley, asked me about you. Said they left a bunch of voice mails. I guess she's taking over the case, because she said she needs to talk to you right away. Wanted to know why you weren't at the funeral, too."

Could I trust Kelly Smalley? "Did she seem upset at the funeral?"

"No. Not really. Not that I'd have noticed anyway. But she didn't know Jenny, why would she be?"

"I meant about Detective Chang's death. They seemed to be kind of close."

"She hung out around the periphery of the place, watching people. Like a detective."

"I think Chang was driven off the road." I left Tom out of it. The fewer people who knew he helped me, the better.

"Why?"

"Let me start another way. Did Chang ask what you thought the *it* might be the gunman wanted?"

"Yes. But I couldn't help him with that."

"I found the *it*."

Her eyes narrowed. She took a sip of coffee. "Oh?"

"Jenny was a prostitute?"

The color drained from her face, and she froze.

"So you did know," I said. "She was a call girl. William Dobbins was a client of hers."

Fear showed in her eyes. She held onto the table and took a deep breath. "Who told you that?" she whispered, her voice tremulous.

"No one. I saw it on a video tape. The tape that got her killed."

"A tape?"

I didn't think she could get any paler, but she did.

With slow, deliberate movements, she rose, went into the den, and lowered herself to the sofa.

I followed and sat beside her.

"She video-taped it?" A tear trickled down Bitsy's cheek. "That stupid, stupid girl."

I'd never seen her show that much emotion.

164

"What was she thinking?" She didn't seem to be talking to me.

I gave her a minute to collect herself.

"I think she blackmailed William," I said. "And I think he had her killed."

"No." She shook her head. "Why?"

"Are you kidding? You think William wanted Vivian or James to find out? Think of the social implications if it became known."

"No. I mean, why would she blackmail him at all? Why bring up the past after all this time?"

"She was desperate for money. The judge didn't award her enough temporary support. Hell, *I* lent her four-thousand."

"My God. I didn't know."

"Of course not. You never returned her calls. When was the last time you spoke to her? Three months ago?"

"James told me she had plenty."

"He lied. And that's another thing. You and James. How long were you two sleeping together?"

"Doesn't matter. It never meant anything. Did Jenny tell you that?"

"I don't think she knew about the two of you. But I've got a real problem now because of Jenny. I had to run out of my apartment Thursday night. The same guys who killed Jenny and Chang are after me. They came to my place and broke in right after I called Chang and told him about the tape. They must know I have it. Don't tell Detective Smalley or anybody else that I was here, and if anyone asks, you haven't seen me."

She looked at me, tears now flowing. "I knew it. I knew someday she'd go too far. I thought it was a random robbery, and Jenny's karma had caught up with her."

"I need answers. I'm scared. And I don't know who I can trust."

"What if they followed you?"

"They would have gotten me already. I'm using someone else's car. I parked way down the street, waited to make sure I wasn't seen, then snuck through the backyards. Okay?"

She nodded.

"Tell me Jenny's story. Start at the beginning."

Sighing, she nodded again. "You know Dad left when Jenny was a baby."

"Right."

"Our mother was an alcoholic who tried. She really did. Went to AA many times. It never worked. As soon as I turned eighteen, I left. Didn't bother to finish high school. Made my way to San Francisco and looked up modeling agencies.

"I was lucky and signed with a premier agency. Within months, I made a great income. I sent home money and magazines with my picture in them. Jenny wasn't an academic either, but at least she finished high school. Then she came to live with me." She sniffled. "I need some tissues." She went to the kitchen and returned with a box.

"I introduced her to Libby Barrett, the head of my agency," Bitsy said. "She loved Jenny. They all did. How could they not? Tall, thin, with that gorgeous face? She got the choice assignments right away.

"Soon, Jenny got cocky. And lazy. She'd show up late for photo shoots, when she showed up at all. She thought they needed her, and she could dictate to them. I tried to talk to her about her work ethic, but she wouldn't listen. The situation kept getting worse, so Barrett fired her."

"She told me she quit modeling because she didn't like it," I said.

"Her next job was with a legitimate escort service. She liked it because most the work was at night, and she could sleep in every day. The pay was good. One night she came home, and she'd made far more than her usual amount. That man offered her five-hundred dollars to go back to his room. She did. And had sex with him." Bitsy shook her head. "She wasn't upset. She was excited. I told her I wouldn't allow her to live with me if she did it again. But she kept soliciting the clients. The service found out and canned her. I kicked her out. Then she found Delsey's."

"Delsey's?"

"Delsey Kim ran an exclusive *gentlemen's* club. Everyone knew it was a brothel. Jenny became Delsey's star. Her premier money-maker. The richest and most powerful men in San Francisco requested her. Delsey raised Jenny's fee through the roof. And Jenny thrived on the attention."

"How could I not know this?" I asked. "Is this where William figures in?" It had to be where she met Lewis Samuels, also. "I believed I knew everything about her."

"I told you." Bitsy sighed. "She wasn't like you thought. Two years into Delsey's, William Dobbins comes in. He became her steady client."

"Wait a minute. She told you this? I thought you two didn't get along."

She nodded. "Back then we did. I hated what she did, but she was my baby sister. The only family I had. Our mother lived in a bottle, and it wasn't possible to have a conversation with her. So, Jenny was it.

"Before long, William gave her gifts, like jewelry and perfume. He told her all the right things. As in, his wife was *cold* to him. He *loved* being with Jenny. They *fit* together so well. It was all bullshit, of course. Or maybe he meant that garbage in the heat of passion, but everybody knows you can't believe a word coming out of a man's mouth while he's having sex."

Even I'd experienced that one.

"Jenny believed him and fell in love. Or thought she did."

I sucked in my breath. "Damn. He was *Wobby.*"

"Stupid nickname, huh? I don't know why, but he kept it going. Told Jenny about his life, including the fact he had an unmarried son living in Hawaii."

I gasped.

"I need my coffee," she said.

"I need a shot." I trailed her to the kitchen, where we again sat at the table.

"Wait," I said. "She knew who James was before she met him? But, if she was in love with William . . ."

"I suppose William got bored with her, because he stopped coming." Bitsy looked up from her mug. "Bad pun, sorry. Jenny came to me and cried and cried. She believed he cared about her and fantasized he'd leave his wife and marry her."

"William could be after you, too. Right? I mean, couldn't you blow his life apart like Jenny tried to?"

"He doesn't know that I know. Jenny swore it was between she and I, and she'd never let William know she'd told me. I have to say, she was pretty good at secrets."

"Then she moved to Hawaii, and it was a coincidence that she met James?" I hoped.

She shook her head. "In your dreams. She went after him on purpose. Revenge was her reason for moving here. Her aim was to meet James, tell him anything he wanted to hear, do anything he wanted. He didn't stand a chance."

"You never told James this?" I felt sick.

"No. No one. Until now. But that *is* when Jenny and I had our falling out. I knew someday this would surface and cause trouble, and I wanted no part of it."

"Why did you and Henry move here?"

"Henry retired. He liked Hawaii, and I wanted to keep an eye on Jenny."

"I know Jenny loved James." Nothing would change my opinion on that.

"I think she grew to love him, yes."

"Holy cannoli."

"She told me, when they married, that she was going to have as many children as she could, as fast as she could—so he wouldn't leave her." Bitsy drained her mug. "That strategy worked real well, huh?"

I sat back in my chair and digested the information. "What do you know about the Dobbins' relationship with Governor Samuels?"

"There was a woman at the service who said they'd been friends at college. Other than that, nothing."

"Jenny never mentioned him?"

"Why would she? James said she never met him."

"You sure she didn't know Samuels?"

"With Jenny, you could never be sure of anything. What are you getting at?"

"Nothing. Speaking of James again, why'd you sleep with him?"

She shrugged. "He'd left Jenny. Henry was dead. We were both lonely, I guess. Like I said, it meant nothing to either of us. Do you really think William's responsible for killing Jenny?"

"It looks like she blackmailed him with the tape, and he sure could afford to hire gunmen and pay off someone in the police department. He's got a ton of connections there."

"And how are you going to approach the police with this information when you don't know who to trust there?"

"That's the sixty-four dollar question. I'm working on it." I stood. "I'd better go."

She rose also. We stared at each other for a moment.

"I'm really sorry, Bitsy. About everything."

"Me, too."

I walked to her and gave her a real, honest hug that she returned. And when I stepped back, tears streamed down her face.

"I loved my sister."

"I believe you."

CHAPTER TWENTY-TWO

I traversed the rocky path back to the end of the street, paused in the tall grass, and waited. After a few minutes, I made a dash for Little Red.

Letting my tears spill, I started the car. How had Jenny lived with all her lies and secrets? What would Bitsy do if she knew about Samuels, too? Her shock at learning Jenny videotaped a session with William seemed genuine. It made her cry. I didn't think Bitsy knew how.

Down the mountain, the chaos at Waimea Bay was at full-tilt. Throngs of people stood on the tall rocks surrounding the beach, the rocks that weren't being showered by spray from the giant waves, that is. Crowds jammed onto the beach itself and lined Kam Highway as far as I could see.

I turned right at the bottom of Pupukea toward Hector's. On the way, the surf spots visible from the road were closed out. The huge, choppy sets looked like they'd engulf the Sunset Beach Fire Station and take it back out to sea with them.

The rusty blue car was absent from the neighbor's drive when I pulled into the carport. A gray minivan with illegal dark-tint stopped in front of that house as I unlocked the kitchen door. My heart-rate shot up. I tugged the brim of my hat farther down and slipped inside as fast as I could. Then, ducking down, I watched the van from the kitchen window.

A big local man exited the driver's seat, walked around to the lawn side, and opened the side door. An instant later, three children ran from the van calling in excited voices, "Tutu. Tutu." An old woman met them with hugs in the middle of the driveway, then ushered them into the house. The man followed, carrying an infant.

I called Tom. "My nerves are whacked." I relayed the scene from Bitsy's.

"So what do we do?" he asked.

"Bitsy didn't know about the tape, or that Samuels knew Jenny, much less was a client. I believe her. There's no proof as to which man Jenny blackmailed. Maybe it was both of them. I'm not going to be able to go home until that's figured out. Guess we go forward with sending the copies as is. I hope we're not making a huge mistake."

"You ask me, there's no downside here. Samuels killed that girl. If Malia was my sister, I'd want justice for her. And Dobbins is just scum who lied and cheated and deserves whatever he gets. Fred says the copies will be done soon. I'll get them and drop them off."

"Thanks." I set the phone down and saw the family from the van strolling past Hector's toward the beach access.

I walked through the living room, opened the French doors, and sat in my now favorite spot. The white wicker rocker. The roar of the surf sounded like a train. The tail-end froth from the wild waves spewed up like the wall of water at the end of a flume ride, then rained on the edge of the lawn. The air smelled salty and fresh at the same time.

There was a lot to think about. My best friend lied to me the entire time I knew her. I was there when Jenny *met* James. We went to the party together at James' condo that night. I drove. But I also remembered she was the one who pushed me into going. She heard about it from a patron at the restaurant where she worked in the bar. James' penthouse looked like a set from a Bond movie. Ultra sleek, modern, and rich.

I'm sure Greg, the guy who told her where the party of the *rich and beautiful* people was, expected to sink his paws into Jenny. She showed a slight, passing interest in him, and once she met James, none at all. I talked to Greg a lot that night as we watched Jenny and James.

She wanted me to leave her there to spend the night, but I insisted on bringing her home. We didn't know James, I told her, and wouldn't it be better to play a little hard to get?

"A man like this can have any woman he wants," I said. "Make him work for it. You're the prettiest girl he's ever seen, I'll bet. Give him your number. He'll call."

Within weeks, they were inseparable. Jenny acted like she was crazy in love with him. I believed it.

Small wonder Bitsy refused to attend the wedding. I'd thought she was heartless, mean, and jealous of her sister. And nothing could have prepared William for the shock of meeting James' fiancée two days before the nuptials. He expected a stranger named Jenny. What he got was his former favorite whore, Rosie. The anxiety attack back then made perfect sense to me now.

I wondered how long it took for Jenny's love toward James to be genuine. Was it before or after Paul was born?

And was Paul James' child? Did Jenny sleep with William again after the marriage? Paul looked just like his grandfather. Vivian had hinted about the kids' parentage. Did she know about William and Jenny? I felt in my gut that she did. That would explain a lot, too. Perhaps the two women burned by this twisted plot weren't such horrors after all. What would I have done if I'd been Vivian?

The image of Jenny, my dearest friend, that still came to mind first was her holding her babies. Her unconditional love for them couldn't be faked. I smiled, thinking of the all-encompassing warmth I'd been privileged enough to share.

I ran inside, picked up the phone, and dialed Bitsy's number.

"Hello?"

"It's Bess."

"Oh. I didn't recognize the number on the Caller ID. Where are you? Who's H. Hanegawa?"

"Shoot. Pretend you didn't see that. Please. No one's supposed to know where I am."

"Fine. Make any decisions?"

"Yes, but I called to say that despite everything, I hope you understand who Jenny was. I mean, who she became. She loved James and cherished those kids. She enveloped them in a loving cocoon and reveled in it. What I'm trying to say is, no matter how she started out, what she became was amazing. You didn't see her much in that role, but motherhood was god sent to save her. I wanted to make sure you knew that."

"You and those rose-colored glasses. Jenny always said that about you. I'll take your word for it."

"Thanks. Well, that's all I needed to say. I'll call you when I get out of this mess I'm in."

"Good luck."

For some strange reason I felt a little better than I had in days, but very tired. I shuffled into the living room, plopped on the loveseat, and closed my eyes for a moment.

I awoke to the sound of glass shattering and bolted from the loveseat. I saw the unmistakable wagging of a dog's tail in the hallway.

A happy-looking golden lab trotted up to me and licked my hand. Behind him, one of Hector's tall clear glass vases filled with sea shells now lay smashed on the rug. It had been on the coffee table. Beyond that, I saw I'd left the French doors open.

The dog looked at me with expectant eyes.

"Scared yourself good, did ya?" I petted the top of his head, then rubbed under his chin. "It's not your fault, boy."

A couple in their thirties rounded the shrubs at the end of Hector's yard and waved.

Mindful of the glass shards, I led the dog to the lanai and waved back.

VICTORIA LANDIS

The woman walked faster. "I'm so sorry. He got away from us."

The dog ran toward her.

"I hope he didn't bother you." The man caught up and attached a leash to the dog's collar. "I took him off the leash so he could chase the coconuts I threw, but . . ." He shrugged.

"No problem," I said. Except the panic attack I had.

"We're the Bradleys," the man said. "I'm Dave and this is my wife Marlee. We live a few doors down, on the other side of the street. Are you renting from Hector while he's gone?"

"Yes." I felt rude not introducing myself, but it didn't seem prudent.

There was an awkward moment while they must have realized I didn't want to talk.

"Well, have a nice day," Marlee said.

They left the way they'd come, and I waved again, then closed the door behind me.

I found rubber gloves, paper towels, and a trash bag in a lower kitchen cabinet and took them to the accident scene. With care, I picked from the mess each shell that was still whole, wiped them with a towel to make sure no glass fragments remained, and placed them on the coffee table. Then I plucked the biggest pieces of glass and shell from the rug tufts and threw them into the bag.

The phone rang. I took the gloves off and answered it.

"Okay," Tom said. "I just came back from Fred's. It took longer than he thought. He said to tell you to nail the bastard. Next, I'm dropping off the copies where you wanted, then I'm coming out there to Hector's. How's the contest going?"

"I don't know. But the ocean's gone nuts. You should see it."

"You don't have ESPN on?"

"Hadn't thought of it."

He sighed. "Haole chicks."

"Hey, I'm tired. All I wanted was a nap, but that didn't work out so well."

"Well, stay put. When I get there, we'll go watch the Aikau."

CHAPTER TWENTY-THREE

Tom arrived around one, with a small cooler of sandwiches, water, and soda. He wore a navy-blue T-shirt with the words *Eddie would go* on the front.

"I want a shirt like that. How was the traffic coming through Waimea?" I waited until he set the cooler down, then hugged him. "I'm so happy you're here. It's been kind of unsettling being alone in this situation. The slightest things have me jumping."

"I came from the Windward side. Through Laie. I've tried the other way on contest days before and know better. Got some good news for you."

"Please, tell me." I peeked inside the cooler and lifted a sandwich. "Is this pastrami? Very cool."

He nodded. "I went to the Brooklyn Deli on Beretania. The guys in the rusty car stopped watching our building early this morning. Guess they've given up on your coming back anytime soon. And, hope this was okay, I went into your apartment and took the liberty of bringing you some clothes. Figured you'd need 'em. They're in the car."

"You are amazing. Thank you. As for the guys in the rust-bomb, maybe they just took some time off to catch the surf contest. They looked like the type who'd do that."

175

"Maybe so. It's stuffy in here. I think you can open up the back at least." He headed for the living room.

"Wait," I yelled. "There's still glass in the rug. I haven't finished cleaning it up."

"*Oh, man.* What broke? Hector's a real jerk about his stuff."

I told him about the dog and his owners. "I only closed my eyes for a minute."

He walked around the rug and opened the French doors. "Damn. Look at that ocean. I'll bet Waimea's got thirty-foot swells. We gotta get over there."

"What about the goons?"

"We'll be careful. You know what the one guy looks like, and we'll seem like tourists to them."

"Hope so. Tell me about dropping off the copies. Who'd you give them to?"

He frowned. "No one was at either of the PI's offices. One had an old-fashioned mail slot in his front door, and the envelope fit through it. The other was one of those everybody-shares-a-receptionist kind of places. The person manning the desk said I was lucky because normally she wasn't there on the weekend, but she'd make sure he got it."

"And the FBI?"

"I parked, walked in the door, handed it to a woman at a desk, and asked her to give it to the Agent in Charge. Whoever that is. I felt very strange in there. Like I should feel guilty. I'm sorry, but I didn't wait around."

We brought in my suitcase that Tom packed for me, and I changed into khaki shorts and flip-flops.

"I think you should stay in the T-shirt you're wearing, though," Tom said. "A shirt with writing on it always looks more touristy."

He took one of Hector's hats. With our hats and sunglasses, we did look like visitors. We locked up and left.

"Let's take my car." He led the way.

We drove about a mile before the traffic stopped.

"It's still another three-quarters of a mile. At this rate, we'll never get there," Tom said.

I noticed empty cars on the side of the road. "Wow, this far away they're parking? Let's pull a U-turn and park on the road here, facing the right direction for when we leave. We can walk the rest of the way."

"Works for me." He swung the car around and found a spot.

We weren't unique in thinking that. I saw more and more cars do what we did, their occupants deciding to hoof it.

"Tell me something." Tom grabbed the cooler and a small backpack, swung a pair of binoculars around his neck, and locked up. "Why didn't Jenny just get a job?"

I gave him a look. "A job? Doing what? The jobs she'd qualify for would be restaurant work. Bartending. Or cleaning houses."

"So?"

I stopped walking and glared at him. "Do you have any idea how much childcare costs? She actually did look into it. Waiting tables, I mean. Between the day care for Sammy and the after-school care for the boys, it would have cost her fifteen-hundred a month. More if she had to work nights or dinners, too. She wouldn't gross that much."

"She used to be a model."

"Yeah, there's a business that'll let you back in after your body's shot from having kids."

"Sorry. Didn't mean to upset you."

"That's okay."

We resumed walking.

"Back when James first left," I said, "Jenny and I tried spitballing a few ideas around. Selling Tupperware or Mary Kay cosmetics? Required the ability to be available for evening home parties, etc. And from the people she talked to in those businesses, they weren't earning much, and it takes years to produce enough income to make it an option. Again, babysitters and day care issues."

"Secretary? Receptionist?"

"She applied for a few positions, but she didn't have adequate keyboard skills and wasn't so hot with the basic computer programs, either. No experience in an office setting. One manager told her there were too many good qualified applicants to choose from."

The road curved and I saw an endless line of cars far into the distance.

"Well then, how do the other single moms make it here?" Tom asked. "They don't all have degrees, either. Lots of 'em are waitresses and cleaning women, I'm sure. How do they do it?"

"You've never thought about this stuff before, have you?"

He shrugged. "Nope. My parents are still married. My sister has her degree and a great job. I've only dated professional women."

"How snobby of you." I poked him in the arm and smiled.

"I'm an electrical engineer. I meet fellow nerdy-people, male and female. Believe me, if I thought I could get a model to date me, I'd try it. But, in case you haven't noticed, I'm not the greatest-looking guy around, and I'm hairy. I hear models don't like hairy guys."

I laughed. "I wouldn't know. I'm not exactly one of the beautiful people myself."

"I'm serious, though. How do single moms manage?"

"From what I've seen, 'cause I do work in a lot of private homes, if they don't already live with their parents, they move back in with them. With the kids. Sometimes, there are four generations of one family living in one house. I can't tell you how many second stories with separate kitchens I've done. Those women have mothers, aunties, sisters, and friends. All of whom pitch in and help with the kids. Some of them have zero childcare expenses. Tight networks. Boy, that makes me miss my sister. I wish I could call her."

"I thought those families were in one house because they liked it that way." He shook his head. "Guess I've had my head under a rock."

"Jenny didn't have anybody." I teared up at the thought.

"She had you."

"Wasn't enough." I took a deep breath. "Tell you what I've learned. People are complicated. That one person can do so much good and so much bad in even a short lifetime baffles me."

"Makes me feel I'm kind of boring. Normal. But boring."

"Me, too."

We walked around cars and trucks left in haphazard patterns blocking each other. Some blocked private driveways. I hoped none of the home owners needed to get out in a hurry.

"Did you find out anything else at Bitsy's today?" Tom asked.

With a silent whoosh in my head, his question brought back what she told me. I didn't want to share the whole story with him. "You know the important parts. Bitsy knew about William as her client, but nothing about Samuels. The rest won't make any difference in the outcome of this. I'd rather let it be." I stepped with care past a young man who'd passed out on the ground next to a pick-up, beer in hand. I did a double-take. "Think he's alright?"

"Probably been drinking for two days." Tom knelt and felt for a pulse. "He'll be fine. Just schnockered."

We moved on.

"The talk with Bitsy did remind me of something else," I said. "Not too long after Jenny and James got married, Jenny decided she wanted to do a girls' weekend on Kauai. She'd never been there. James would've done anything for her then, so we took a four-day trip to Hanalei Bay."

"I love that place. And Princeville."

"Me, too. Our room at the resort had an incredible view. We got massages and facials, played a little tennis, explored the area a bit. She loved it. One night, we ventured into the town and found a tiny wooden house converted to a restaurant. No tourists, except us. It had a wide, maybe eight feet wide, front lanai. Around ten, a group of local musicians gathered on the lanai and started playing Hawaiian music. We'd finished eating and sat out there to listen. Two ladies and three men played, I think. There were two ukuleles, a drum, and one improvised bass. It looked like a homemade one. A flat, skinny board with strings running down into a galvanized tub turned upside-down. I don't know how it worked, but it did. The five of them sang together, then did some solos."

"Sounds like the real thing to me, local music-wise."

"They were so good. Maybe it was the influence of the wine we drank at dinner, but the whole experience was beyond beautiful. Soulful, you know? That haunting melodic sound, I couldn't believe how it touched me."

"Guess they didn't mind a couple of haoles intruding, huh?"

"They looked almost pure Hawaiian. Acted like it, too. Full of that genuine kindness and generosity of spirit."

He turned to me. "You were lucky to stumble into that."

"I know. Anyway, after they'd played for about an hour, they stopped. One of the women, the one who'd sung the most, walked to Jenny and looked at her funny. Jenny smiled, then complimented her on the protea lei she wore."

"Oops."

"Yeah, exactly. The woman took it off and placed it around Jenny's neck. Jenny protested, but the woman told her to always pass on the aloha. Then she told Jenny, 'You need much love to heal your deep wounds. Accept the love, don't be afraid.'"

"Some of those aunties are scary with what they know just by looking at a person."

I nodded. "Jenny had tears streaking down her cheeks. The woman struck a nerve. I haven't thought about that night in years. Now, because I know about her past, it beguiles me more than ever."

A minute later, we passed the last house on the right with its palm trees and dense foliage, and Waimea Bay came into view. Sort of. That's where the three-deep crowd standing on the rocky cliff sides of the bay began.

"Holy smokes." I bent and peeked between some bodies. "We're never going to see a thing. It's like this around the entire bay."

"Keep walking," Tom said. "I'll bet we'll find a place on the beach."

The crowd roared, and I crouched to peek through legs. "One of the surfers caught a monster."

"I see." Tom stopped behind a group of women he towered over. "I think that might be Bruce Irons in there. He won in 2004, you know." He pulled me upright. "Come on."

We fast-walked down the sloping road, over the foot-bridge across Waimea Stream, and into the mass hysteria of the beach parking lot.

As we passed the T-shirt booths, a man yelled, "Hanegawa."

Tom turned his head, and I did, too.

"Mike," Tom said. "Howzit, brah?"

Mike Garcia held a beer in one hand and sent Tom a shaka hand gesture with the other, then looked at me. "So, you do know this haole chick?"

"This is—" Tom started.

"Robin. Robin LaForest," I said. "Sorry I had to run last time I saw you."

"Least I know you didn't shit me."

I must have looked confused.

"About da kine red car." Mike gestured ahead. "We got one great place, next to da judges' stand. Made a platform for to see. You want for go?"

"Thanks, but no." Tom pulled me to him and squeezed. "We want to be alone. You understand."

Mike made a face. "Okay. Laters." He pushed his way forward.

Tom yanked me toward the other side of the beach. "Robin LaForest?"

"It was the name I always wished I had when I was a kid."

"Sounds like a stripper."

"I was ten when I made it up. Where are we going?"

"Away from Mike and his friends."

We removed our flip-flops, and I stowed them in the backpack. Tom held my hand tight, and we threaded our way through a sea of bodies to the front.

The official announcers squawked something over the loudspeaker system. It sounded even fuzzier than a fast-food drive-through.

The crowd seemed to be in constant motion, with people moving in and out. We found two men leaving and claimed their tiny patch of sand. We were near the left side of the bay in back of the first line of police tape keeping the crowd away from the dangerous ten-to-twelve foot high shore break. The second line was another five feet closer to the water.

Tom whistled. "Damn. Look."

Out where the waves broke, a contestant paddled from behind the rising crest, leaving the others who weren't in the right position to get there in time. He made it to the top and scrambled to stand as his surfboard began its race down the almost vertical slope.

The loudspeakers sent a shrill, undecipherable excited voice our way.

I couldn't believe my eyes. The surfer looked miniscule in comparison to the wave. "How big is that?"

"The face? My guess is it's fifty, fifty-five foot. So you'd call it about a twenty-five footer."

"Jumpin' Jehosephat. I mean, I've seen big waves before but this is insane."

The drop was too much for the surfer though. He and the board pitched forward a quarter of the way down the face. He flew off and crashed head first into the gargantuan wall of water, followed by the surfboard. Shouts of concern rose from the crowd.

I screamed.

Tom grabbed my arm and pointed to the lifeguards on jet skis already heading toward him.

"How can they tell where he'll wind up?" I couldn't see him or the board in the mighty soup.

"They've got a good idea," Tom said.

The wave collapsed on itself, sending another huge slop of shore break toward us as another wave in the merciless set rose.

Three guys paddled with furious energy to that crest, and two of them made it onto the next face.

More commotion from the crowd diverted my attention back to the ongoing rescue attempt. The lifeguards lifted the limp body from the water. Blood poured from the surfer's leg. Whistles blew, and three more lifeguards stationed on the beach tore into the water to meet the jet skis.

"Jeez," Tom said, looking through his binoculars. "It looks like the board went clear through his leg."

They got him onto the sand and went to work, one guard doing nothing but holding the surfer's thigh together. Within minutes, they had him bandaged and strapped to a backboard. Four of them ran him to the parking lot where ambulances waited for the inevitable injuries.

"Both of those guys caught the next wave," I said. "Do you know who any of them are? That darn squawking loudspeaker is awful."

A loud *whoop-whoop* sounded from a horn of some kind.

"What's that?" I asked.

"This heat is over," Tom said. "Next group goes out." He pointed to the edge of the beach where seven surfers stood holding huge surfboards that towered over their heads.

"They're going to paddle out? In this? How?"

"They wait for the set to pass, then go for it. You'll see."

I shook my head in wonder when a few minutes later, they did. Tom let me borrow the binoculars. "I'm sorry. To do this requires serious insanity."

Tom laughed. "I agree. But it's awesome to watch, isn't it?"

A sudden bump hit me from the rear, and I turned to see a haole couple establishing themselves in the space behind us.

The man removed his backpack. "I'm sorry. Did I get you?"

"Honey, be more careful." The woman smiled. "We're from Georgia. Where're y'all from?"

Tom turned. "Here."

"Oh." The woman looked puzzled.

I returned to watching the contestants. Under normal circumstances, I talked to everybody, everywhere. Not that day.

A few minutes later the woman asked, "Honey, which one of the men out there is the Eddie Aku guy?"

"I don't know, dear."

I cast a sideways glance at Tom. He grimaced.

"Well," the woman said, "why did they name it for a plain old lifeguard, instead of that Duke man with the statue in Waikiki?"

Tom cleared his throat, then turned to face them. "First of all, it's Aikau. Eddie Aikau. You pronounce it *eye-cow*. Second, the man is dead. This is a memorial contest. Eddie was a hero."

"I'm sorry," the man said.

"How did he die?" the woman asked.

They looked sincere, and I saw the impatience on Tom's face go away.

His voice took on a kindness. "In nineteen-seventy-eight, the Polynesian Voyaging Society sent a Hokule'a to retrace the ancient Hawaiians' journey between Hawaii and Tahiti. The Hokule'a was a replica of the double-hulled canoes the ancients used for the journey. They didn't send any backup boats with it. The canoe developed a leak and eventually capsized. Eddie volunteered to go for help on his surfboard. Had to talk the Captain into letting him. The rest of the crew got rescued. Eddie was never seen again."

"Oh, how terribly sad," the woman said. "Is that what your T-shirt is about?"

Tom glanced at his chest. "Yes, ma'am."

"Thank you for telling us," the man said.

We watched the next two groups of seven compete while eating our lunch. A couple of contestants finished up with a few cuts and bruises, but to my relief, nothing like the earlier accident.

"I think we should go," Tom said. "Sneak out before the mass exodus happens."

"Okay."

We managed to pry ourselves from the intense tangle of humans watching the event and retraced our steps past the vendors' booths in the parking lot.

While putting my flip-flops on, before crossing the footbridge, I saw the maroon rusty car parked on the side of the road. I grabbed Tom's arm and pointed. "Look."

"Put your hand down. You'll draw attention to yourself." Tom stared at the car. "Nobody's inside, I think. They must be in the crowd somewhere."

I scanned the people milling about, then checked the mob scene behind us. Just as I decided the guy would be on the beach in the throng of spectators, I saw the glint of reddish-brown hair in sunlight.

CHAPTER TWENTY-FOUR

The man's physique and thick red arm hair made me rather certain it was the same guy I saw at the park with Jenny's purse and outside my door on Thursday night. "It's him. He's right over there." I stopped myself from pointing and did a slow turn so my back was toward the guy.

"Okay, I'm looking," Tom said. "Describe him."

"Shoulder length reddish-brown hair, skinny, no shirt, and black trunks."

"Got it." Tom turned and put his arm around me. "Think he saw you?"

"No. We didn't lock eyeballs or anything like that."

"Good. Now we walk real close like this. Lean into me. Act romantic."

We were about halfway across the footbridge when a big local man passed us going the other way. I did a double-take and so did he. It was Rodney-the-moke from the library.

"Hey. Haole-girl," Rodney yelled, sounding a little inebriated.

His voice had a booming quality that would have been great if we were in a noisy nightclub. But in the open air, even with the background goings-on, it was the type of voice everyone noticed—and turned to see who it belonged to.

I tried to hide behind Tom's bulk, lest the red-haired goon spot me.

"Who is that?" Tom whispered. "He's talking to you."

"Some guy I met at the Wailua library yesterday. His name's Rodney."

"Jesus. I thought you were trying to keep a low profile."

"I'll tell you about it later. Let's get out of here."

"Hi." Tom waved at Rodney, then pointed at me. "She's not feeling so good." He hustled me forward, keeping his arm tight around me.

"Is our creepy guy following us?"

"I'm not going to turn around and find out. It'll be a dead giveaway. Keep moving."

Not until we walked the uphill road leaving the bay did we dare to stop and sneak a peek.

"Is the rust-bucket parked where it was?" I asked.

"Hasn't moved."

"Thank God." I scanned behind us and didn't spot the red-haired guy. "Maybe we got lucky, and he didn't notice me. I don't see him."

We speed-walked the rest of the hill until we passed a few houses.

Winded, I stopped and sat on a patch of centipede grass under a coconut palm. "Sorry. I have to rest."

Tom sat beside me and leaned on the tree. "That's okay. I'm not in such great shape either, I guess." He lifted the binoculars to his eyes and looked behind us.

"You can't see past the curve in the road, can you?"

"A little." He stopped scanning and held the glasses still. "There's a rusty car coming real slow."

I leaned over, pulled the binoculars from his face, and put them on mine. A stream of vehicles labored up the hill. Between a white Mercedes and a blue truck was maybe our bad guy's car. "Wow. Hard to tell from this angle, isn't it? But it could be him."

"Come on." Tom stood, grabbed the cooler, and fled further into the yard behind us.

I followed. We crouched behind a thick hibiscus hedge.

Near the bottom of the bushes the sparse growth of leaves made it easier to watch the road. A pile of debris on the sandy soil clung to the hedge's roots. I spotted a candy wrapper, scraps of tar paper, and a sun-bleached skeleton from either a cat or a mongoose in the mess.

A couple minutes passed. My legs ached from the stationary low squat, but I wasn't willing to sit in the dirt. "I really need to exercise more. This is pathetic. Think maybe he turned around?"

"There's nowhere to do that." Tom leaned out and stared. "Here it comes." He retreated toward me.

Through the bottom branches, I saw the maroon car cruising by in the slow parade of vehicles leaving the event. A big dark-haired man sat in the passenger seat, his arm out the window resting on the outside door panel. He took a sip from a beer can in his other hand.

"Looks like the same car. Can you see who's driving?" I asked.

"Not yet. That guy's head's in the way. Wait. Yes. He's the red-haired dude."

"Shit."

"But check it out," Tom said. "They don't look like they're searching for anything. They're not even looking around. Maybe he's returning to town by way of the Windward side to avoid traffic. Back to watch our building to see if you show up."

"I hope you're right."

We waited ten minutes before venturing to the road for the walk to Tom's car. Tom checked Kam Highway to the east and west with the binoculars. There was no sign of the goons or their car.

I secured my ponytail inside the hat and wiped the salt off my sunglasses. "I'm ready. Let's get back to the cottage. Hector's got a great wine collection. I think we deserve a fine glass after the scare we've been through."

Tom looked at me sideways. "You've been drinking his wine? This little *vacation* of yours is going to cost me. And I didn't have a *scare*. Maybe you did."

"Vacation?" I laughed and punched him in the arm. "Don't I wish. And you were, too. Scared, I mean."

"I'll deny it to the day I die."

It was almost six when we got to the car.

"By now the proverbial shit should be hitting the shinola, don't you think?" I asked.

"The copies of the tape?"

"Yeah. At least one of them should have been watched already. Maybe William and Samuels both have received phone calls or visits this afternoon. Wouldn't that be amazing?"

"It being Saturday, who knows? I can't predict how the PI's will handle it when they see it, but I imagine the FBI guy wouldn't outright call Samuels. He'd need a plan of action. If he even saw the damn thing yet."

We listened to the news radio station on the way back.

I heard something I hadn't expected.

"In the ongoing investigation into the murder of Jennifer Dobbins last Saturday," the announcer said, "HPD has named the victim's friend, Bess Blinke, as a person of interest. Ms. Blinke disappeared Thursday evening, and an inside source suggested she might have fled to the mainland. If you have any knowledge of Ms. Blinke's whereabouts please contact Crimestoppers."

"Oh my God. Turn it off." I felt sick. "How could they?"

"I don't believe it." Tom grimaced.

"Wow. This morning, Bitsy said Detective Smalley asked where I was yesterday, and they wanted to talk to me again. It never occurred to me they'd try and make me a suspect."

"Person of interest."

"Please. Same difference."

Tom parked behind Little Red, and we trudged into the kitchen.

I headed for the bathroom, but froze mid-way through the living room. Bright-red blood stains on the white area rug led my eye to the French doors. One stood open a few inches, the glass pane closest to the door handle smashed. Fear seized my insides.

"Tom?" I stepped backward and tried to sound calm. "Come here."

"What?" He came alongside me. "What the hell?"

"See the door?"

"Uh-huh." Tom pointed the other way, toward the hall. "Look, there's blood smears on the way to the bathroom." He sidestepped the bloody spots and peeked into the bedrooms. "Whoever did this is gone. What do you think the odds are of this being a burglary?"

"Zero. The TV's here. Look in Hector's room. Is his computer there?"

"Unfortunately."

"We need to get out of here. Fast."

"Right. Grab your suitcase and purse."

"How'd they find me? They sure didn't follow us." Avoiding the blood, I used the bathroom, then went into the guest bedroom, put on my sneakers, threw my dirty laundry into the suitcase, and zipped it.

Through the windows, we checked around the yard and the driveway before venturing to Tom's car. We got in. He started the engine, put it in reverse, eased backward, then slammed on the brakes.

"Shit." He twisted his body to see.

I did, too. The rusting maroon car had pulled in behind us parallel to the road, blocking our escape. I slunk below the seat back. "Oh my God. What do we do?"

"Get out, duck down, and run," Tom said. "Watch for the best moment. Try to get to a neighbor's house."

I peeked between the seats.

Tom opened his door and gestured a *how come* to the men blocking us, like he had no idea why they'd blocked him. "Wassup, brah?"

The dark-haired man in the passenger seat got out of the car. "You want for stay outta dis, brah. We only want da kine wahine." He pointed to me.

The red-haired guy got out from behind the wheel and started along the driveway. On my side.

"Go now, Bess!" Tom turned and started running.

I threw the car door open and burst out, headed toward Kam Highway. Mid-way across the next yard, the redhead caught my leg and pulled me down. I tried to use my hands to break the fall, but slammed hard onto my chin, causing intense pain and little lightning bursts in my head.

He was on top of me in a second, sitting on my back.

I scrambled and bucked, trying to pitch him off me. There were sounds of another struggle going on, and I hoped Tom was doing better than me.

"Hey you," an old woman's voice called. "Whatchu doing? Get offa her."

It was the lady who lived next door, the children's tutu.

I heard a gunshot, then felt a hard whack on the back of my head. Everything went black.

CHAPTER TWENTY-FIVE

I came to in a vibrating, dim, confined space. It smelled like fruity surfboard wax, mildew, and something sour-ish-rotten. The back of my head hurt like hell. My mouth and jaw ached. Every pulse radiated new pain.

The vibrating soon registered as road noise and motion. I was in the car trunk. I recognized the coarse texture of cheap carpet against my right cheek. Pinholes of light shone through the rusted sections of the trunk's lid. At least I'd have air. The light meant it was later the same day or the next morning. I thought it was almost sunset on Saturday, because Oahu wasn't big enough to drive an entire night and not get where you wanted to be. Any destination was within an hour or two.

My knees, bent to my chest, felt stiff. I tried to move, got my legs half extended, then scooted and wrestled around until I lay on my back and could stretch both arms. It hurt my head, but I had pins and needles happening in my extremities—time to get some blood flowing.

The car started uphill, and I slid toward the back edge. The grade didn't feel steep enough to be Pupukea, so I figured they were headed to Wahiawa or beyond.

The last thing I remembered was a gunshot and then a whack on the head. Who'd they shoot? Tom? The old tutu? I prayed they both were alive. Maybe it was a warning shot, nothing more.

If Tom was okay, would he be able to get some help and find me? But what if he wasn't? What if he lay bleeding into Hector's driveway even now? I'd never survive the guilt of knowing Tom got hurt or, God forbid, died. Or that innocent grandma who'd had the decency to yell at them to stop. Odds were good she called the police. Would they help? Or let Samuels thugs have me?

A loud snoring came from the inside of the car.

We hit a bump in the road which made my head ache anew and caused a wave of nausea. I thought about trying to kick the trunk lid open and then jumping out, but too many objections surfaced. One, my head hurt too much. Two, if I jumped out, they'd notice, turn around and just pick me up again. Unless I could run fast as hell through a few pineapple fields to lose them. And I wasn't a great runner under normal circumstances. Three, I remembered a scene in *Good Fellas* where the man they threw in the trunk started kicking and yelling. The gangsters stopped by the side of the road, opened the trunk and shot him again, or clobbered him with a shovel, or stabbed him. I don't recall which. I do recall the guy died.

"Gilbert said no earlier than eight."

The voice came from the same direction as the snoring. I wondered why the sound was so clear.

"Right. We got time. So now we get da kine, then deliver da wahine. Then we done," a second voice said.

He sounded like the same local man who spoke to Tom in the driveway. I explored the wall between the back seat and the trunk with my left hand and found on the driver's side, a piece of thin plywood replaced part of the back. It seemed about a foot square. That explained why I heard them so well. But what was it there for? Who cuts a hole in the back seat?

About ten minutes later, we turned from the highway onto a pot-holed dirt road, judging from the constant jostling and bouncing. I knew there were lots of private drives along the highway, fenced with *Beware of Dog* and *Warning – Private Property* signs. When you're bored driving through a place enough times, you notice things. I heard twigs snapping and grasses brushing against metal.

The car came to a stop amidst barking dogs. They wasted no time trailing my scent to the trunk because within seconds, it seemed like fifty canines had honed in on the space just a few inches from my face. Their combined barking reached a major decibel level.

"Jesus," a man said. "Kenny. Call off your freakin' dogs, dude."

"Whatchu got in dere?" another called from a distance. There was a loud whistle and the barking faded away.

The car doors opened, and the frame rose as they exited.

"My cat had kittens in the trunk last week. That's what they smell."

Oh God. I was lying in dried-up cat placenta?

I heard what sounded like a screen door slam and then quiet. How long would they be inside? Could I squeeze my body through the plywood covered hole? I pushed hard on the plywood with my hand, but it didn't budge. Then examined its size again. Too small for me. What the heck was that hole there for anyway?

If I could kick the lid of the trunk open, what were the chances I'd get away, or at least be able to hide? Better than they were if I just waited like a sitting duck.

Getting my leg bent and into position to kick was not easy. There was almost no space to gain momentum, so my first attempt had the power one of those newborn kittens could have mustered. I tried with both feet at once as hard as I could, but the trunk lid didn't even wobble. That surprised me since the rust had disintegrated a good amount of the metal, hence the multiple pinholes of light coming in.

The effort made the ache and pressure in my head feel ten times worse. I gave it one more shot, then rested. The damn dogs would've found me anyway. Wooziness took over.

I guess I passed out because the next thing I knew, the car doors opened, and the guys sat down. The engine came to life, and we zoomed backward before swinging around and going the other way.

Soon after we returned to paved roadway, it was clear we headed downhill. Toward Honolulu?

"What are you doing?" A voice from the front.

"Rolling one joint, brah. Whassit look like?"

"That shit's for da guy. What if he weighs it?"

"He ain't gonna weigh notheen'. Beside, Slow Kenny always give me extra. Kinda tip, you know? One finda's fee." He laughed.

A minute later, the unmistakable aroma of strong Hawaiian pakalolo smoke filled the car, including the trunk. Ten minutes later, I felt a serious disorientation, but the pain in my head was *oh so much* better.

Once the terrain flattened out again, we took several turns on more unpaved roads. Every bump and hole jolted me. The pings of loose stones hitting the undercarriage sounded like when my little brother shot at Coke cans with his BB gun back when we were kids in Florida.

We screeched to a stop amid the sounds of birds squawking.

"Shit-ass chickens. Get out of the way."

Wherever we were, it was country. The car continued for another half minute, then stopped. One of the doors opened, and I heard footsteps walking away on gravel. A moment later, they came back.

"Yeah, dude, we're here, but there ain't a soul around. Thought you said they'd meet us at eight."

Silence.

"Okay. But get 'em here quick, huh?" The snap of a cell phone shutting. "We gotta bring her inside."

CHAPTER TWENTY-SIX

The other door opened and the body of the car once again bounced up after the big man hauled himself out.

I would pretend I was unconscious. They didn't need to know I heard anything. Not that what I heard seemed to be of any use to me at that moment. But maybe they'd talk more, and I could figure a few things out. Pot often brings out the inner Chatty-Cathy.

The trunk opened, and a pair of hands lifted me out, banging my leg on the side of the trunk. I didn't dare crack my eyes open, but I knew it was the big guy. He positioned me over his shoulder in a fireman's carry like I weighed nothing. Kind of like Bluto carrying Olive Oyl. Except you could make three Olive Oyls out of me.

"Jeez, brah, maybe she like die?" he said.

"Nah."

I could tell the redhead walked ahead of Bluto. Now that they couldn't see my face, I peeked. It was almost dark. We were near a group of outbuildings on what looked like a ranch set at the base of the mountains. Which mountains I did not know, but it felt like we were on the North Shore. The red-haired guy led the way to a small single-walled shack. He felt for a key above the frame, found it, and unlocked the door.

He walked in, hit a light switch, and Bluto plunked me onto a sofa, bumping my head on the arm in the process.

I grimaced, withheld my shriek from pain, then let my head sag to the side.

Someone's pakalolo breath came into my face.

"You should come look at her, Joey. She don't look so hot," Bluto said. "How's anybody gonna talk wit her?"

The hot breath backed away. Now I knew the red-haired guy's name.

"Not my problem," Joey said.

Another piece of furniture in the shack groaned. I assumed Bluto sat down and opened my eyes to the merest slit. Joey leaned against the door, texting on his phone. I memorized everything I could about this miserable excuse for a human. I didn't see him do it, but I was very sure he shot Jenny.

With great effort and, I hoped, no perceptible movement, I tore my attention away from Joey and studied my surroundings. Walls with an ancient cracking coat of ivory paint, grimy with grease, smoke, and soot. Two chairs, the ratty sofa, and bare concrete for a floor. There was another door on the other side of the room, opposite the one we came in.

Bluto sat with a magazine on his lap, rolling another joint. He'd taken off his rubber sandals, and I noticed a bloody bandage on the underside of his left foot. Had he stepped on the glass embedded in the rug at Hector's and left his blood all over the floor? It seemed to me he was new at this sort of thing since he hadn't bothered clean it up. Above him, a grimy window higher up on the wall had thick spider webs across its top.

"What he want wit her anyway?" Bluto said. "What she gonna do to heem?"

"I don't know," Joey said. "And I don't want to know. Don't give a crap either. If she's on his shit list, trust me, you ask nothing. From what I hear, that was Darrel's mistake."

"Da kine with da snake tattoo?"

"Yeah. Asked a few questions. Found him floating in the Ala Wai next day."

"Bummer. You want?" Bluto offered Joey the first toke.

"Sure."

I closed my eyes when Joey crossed the room to light the joint. Then little blips and bleeps filled the silence, so I figured Joey for texting again. Bluto seemed sympathetic, worried about me. Joey seemed as impenetrable as lava rock. If he went outside, would I be safe trying to tell Bluto the truth?

Stairway to Heaven began playing, and Joey answered his phone. "Yeah, where the hell are you? It's quarter after."

There were a few moments of quiet where I could hear Bluto take a deep draw from the joint.

"This was not part of the deal. Hang on," Joey said. "Brian, I gotta take this outside. Watch her."

Wow. Talk about getting a wish. I heard the door bang. The big man's name was Brian. I had to take the chance, so I opened my eyes a little, moaned, and let out a convincing, "Ouch."

Brian looked at me. "You're not dead. Good."

"Who are you?" I glanced around. "Where am I?"

"Neva mind."

"My head is killing me. What happened?" I let the words out slow and deliberate. "Was there an accident? Did you save me?"

He snorted. "Not. Somebody need to talk wit you."

"Who?" I wore my most innocent expression. With exaggerated pain and stiffness, I pushed myself to a sitting position, then faked a dizzy spell. "Whoa. I'm really out of it. I think I'd better lay down." And I did.

"Ooh. What did you do to your foot? Did you hurt it when you saved me?" I put a sweet smile on my face. "You look like a friend of mine. You're better looking, though. What's your name?"

He chuckled. "Brian."

"Brian what?"

"Wilson."

"Seriously? Like the Beach Boy?" I giggled. "Can you sing, too?"

"A little. Now and den. My cousin got one band."

The second joint must have loosened him up. "In town? Maybe I've heard them." I acted like I just registered what he'd said at first. "Who wants to talk to me?"

He shot a look at the door. "You piss off somebody very important. Maybe even in da kine government."

"I did?" All innocence and sweetness. "No way." Now I knew for sure Samuels had Jenny killed. Tom was right. But did William have anything to do with it?

He shrugged.

"I know something about the governor." I used a conspiratorial tone. "Wanna know what it is?"

"No." But he looked curious.

"He killed a local girl, like, forty years ago. They never caught him."

The door swung open, and Joey entered still talking on his cell. When he passed in front of me, I saw a gun shoved into the back of his shorts.

Brian cut his eyes in my direction, appearing uncertain about whether to believe me.

Joey shut the phone and slid it into the back pocket of his trunks. He pointed at me. "She's awake? Why didn't you call me?"

"Easy, brah. She just did. And she went cuckoo in da head. Not makin' no sense. I think she got da kine brain damage."

"Shit." Joey walked to me, squatted, and stared.

I giggled. "Hi." If this was Brian's way of helping me, I'd play along.

"Shit. Shit. Shit." Joey paced the length of the room. "That phone call? Change of plans. The two that were supposed to meet us here to take over aren't coming now." He looked at Brian. "You and I have to wait for, well, you know. I don't want to meet him. We were never supposed to meet him. And she's all loony? Shit. This ain't good."

"You hit her, brah, not me."

I laughed. "Hit me. Hit me. Is it poker time? I'm good at cards."

"Damn it," Joey yelled. "Think of something. The man's on his way."

Brian cleaned the mess off the magazine, resealed the bag of pakalolo, and stashed it in a pocket. He pulled himself from the chair and walked to the front. "Better open da doors for some fresh air." He opened the door, then stepped to the back and unlocked that one, and swung it inward revealing a view of bushes and dark emptiness beyond. He fanned the door back and forth.

Joey glared.

"One cross-currant. No smoke. Good first impression, yeah?"

"Coffee." Joey stormed across to a tiny kitchenette and threw open cabinets until he found a jar of instant coffee. "Maybe this'll help."

Two minutes later, Joey set a mug of coffee on top of a dark stain on the floor in front of me.

I smiled at him. "Hi."

Joey slapped his arm. "Stop waving the damn door. Shut it and the front one, too. Damn mosquitoes got in. Then come over here. Help me get her to sit."

With a dopey grin I watched Brian close the doors. He didn't relock either of them. Then he ambled to the sofa.

"I'll pull her up," Joey said. "You sit next to her on that side, so she can't fall over."

Brian watched as Joey yanked me to a sitting position, then sat to my right. I leaned onto Brian's left upper arm, melting into him with a stupid smile on my face.

Joey retrieved the mug from the floor and brought it to my lips. "Drink this. It'll wake you up."

"Am I dreaming?" I took a sip. "You're a good cook." My eyelids went to half-mast. "When do we play cards?"

"Shut up and keep drinking the coffee." Joey handed the mug to Brian and got up to look out the window. He paced the room, checked his phone, then let out a huge, impatient sigh.

I couldn't swear, but it sounded like he muttered the f-word under his breath. Sweat beads appeared on his forehead.

"You shouldn't say that word." I said it like a five-year-old, trying to annoy him. "It's bad manners."

Joey glared my way. "Shut up."

"That's not very nice, either."

He lunged toward me with his hand outstretched and an angry expression on his face, then stopped.

Brian looked at me, then Joey. "Man, she ain't there. Are we gonna catch hell 'cause she ain't okay? 'Cause, if that be the way, then I say we leave her here, and stay go already."

"You wanna be found face down in the Ala Wai?"

"He won't find me." Brian laughed and brought the mug to my lips again. "I got too many cousins, brah. Lotsa places to lay low."

"Great. You lay low. We don't get paid. I need that money. Plus I might get killed. Good plan," Joey said.

"At least if you dead, you don't need no money."

I really liked Brian.

"An if she's all buss-up like dis, maybe he don't pay you anyway," Brian said.

"Shit." Joey opened the front door, stepped out, and slammed it behind him.

Brian winked at me.

"Aren't you afraid?" I whispered.

"Nah. What you said before about da girl. That true?"

"Yes." I stared into his dark eyes. "Her name was Malia London."

His face froze.

"I found a video tape. He confesses on it. That's why he wants me. To find out where the tape is. Then, he'll kill me."

"Jeez."

"What happened to my friend Tom? You guys didn't kill him, did you? I heard a gunshot."

Joey walked in. "Two cars are coming up the driveway. She making any sense yet?"

"Nah." Brian took the mug and pushed me away so he could get off the sofa.

"Here's what we do," Joey said. "We give her over, I collect, and we get out of here before they figure out she's whacked. You got a cousin who'll hide me, too?"

"Yeah." Brian put his flip-flops back on, then stood near me. Joey moved next to him.

I needed to decide how to play my part. Cognizant or dopey?

Light poured in through the window, then died. Car doors opened and shut. Footsteps crunched on gravel.

The door opened. Two chubby men in aloha shirts and cargo shorts came in, followed by a man with a briefcase. After him, Lewis Samuels entered. Wearing a white polo shirt and crisp khakis, he looked like he'd come from another routine day at the office. I could smell his cologne.

"Ms. Blinke." His skewed smile sent shivers through me. "A pleasure to see you again." He turned to Joey and Brian. "One of you morons want to explain why she's not restrained?"

I had a hard time concealing my revulsion at seeing him. I gave him my lunatic smile.

"My partner here had to knock her out when we found her," Joey said. "She's been out cold 'till just a minute ago." He moved toward the man with the briefcase. "So, if you'll settle up, we'll be outta here."

Could Joey be *that* stupid? He threw Brian under the bus by blaming him for my head injury? I guessed when faced with real pressure, a person's character came out. Joey didn't have any. He might have the gun, but Brian could do some real damage if Joey let down his guard. And I was pretty certain that Joey's safe harbor would have to be safe from Brian and his cousins now, too.

"Has she said anything?" Samuels asked.

"No," Joey said. "She just came to."

Part of me wanted to contradict and get him in as much trouble as I could, but that would jeopardize Brian, and he was my only hope.

Samuels nodded to the man with the briefcase, who walked to the kitchenette counter and placed the case on it. Everyone's eyes were on him, except Brian. He stared at me, flicked his eyes to the back door, and gave a tiny nod.

The briefcase guy handed Joey a white envelope, then shut the case.

"Come on." Joey gestured to Brian, headed for the door, and left.

Brian followed, and one of the aloha shirt men went to close the door after them.

"Wait," Samuels said. "You three go outside. I want to talk to her."

The sound of tires trying for fast traction on gravel came through the thin walls. Joey wanted away from this place—bad.

CHAPTER TWENTY-SEVEN

"Hang on," Samuels called as his men filed out. "I want her restrained." He opened a drawer and removed a roll of duct tape and scissors. "Bind her hands and feet."

One of the aloha shirt guys took the tape, peeled a length and tore it, then came over, holding the piece.

"Put your hands out," he said.

He got a blank stare from me. Kicking him in the groin, then bolting for the door appealed to me, but out of the four men there, odds were one had a gun. Even if I made it through the door, I'd never be able to outrun them.

"Put your hands out. Now."

I left them in my lap.

"Chuck," the man said, "get over here."

The other aloha shirt man grabbed and held my arms up while the first one wrapped the tape around my wrists. Then they did my ankles and retreated outside.

Samuels sat opposite me in the chair Brian vacated. He leaned back and stared at me, rubbing his chin with his forefinger. He seemed tense, spring-loaded, and it scared me. "Your friend wasn't so nice, you know."

Watching him made me cringe. His handsome face didn't match the underlying threat in his eyes. Making him think I wasn't right in the head might set him off.

"Rosie—oops. I mean, Jenny, was stupid, too," he said. "She could have destroyed the video she made. Then she'd be alive, and you wouldn't be here now."

I glared.

"How many people know about that tape?" he asked. "Who did you tell?"

"What tape?"

He chortled. "That guy back at the beach cottage? Did you tell him?"

"What did you do to him?" He knew about Tom. Well, of course. Joey would've reported it all. Or a *screw-Brian-over* version, anyway. "Is he okay?"

Samuels shrugged. "Don't know. You should tell me where you hid that tape. Maybe you'll live through this."

"Don't you understand what you did?" I felt outrage welling up. "There are four little kids with nobody now. Their father doesn't care about them."

"He's rich. They'll be raised by a nanny. Big deal. Better than a whore for a mom."

I went to kick him, but with my ankles bound it knocked me off balance, and I tipped a little to my left. I righted myself. "You are disgusting. To think I voted for you."

He laughed. "Thank you."

"Do you even *have* a daughter named Leilani? That was total bull at the golf club, wasn't it?"

He leaned forward and placed his hands on his knees, a sincere-looking calm replacing the venom I sensed earlier. He was again the charmer I met at the golf course. "You have no options here. But I can be fair. You didn't start this mess. Tell me where it is, and maybe I'll reward you. I can guarantee you more business than you'd ever dream of. Multi-million dollar contracts."

The more time it took for him to get anything out of me, the better. If Brian could help, he'd need time. If Tom did get away and tried to find me, he'd need time. If the FBI guy took the note seriously, he'd need time. My best strategy, my only strategy, was to delay. Not for a second did I believe Samuels would spare me, but clearly he thought I was dimwitted, so I played along.

"Ah." He narrowed his eyes. "You're thinking about it. Good. Imagine your work in *Architectural Digest.*"

"How do you know I won't tell your secret later?"

"Money works wonders on the human mouth. You'll love the lifestyle of mixing with the elite who frequent the islands. Lots of celebrities, too." He stood and walked to me. "And once I have the tape and destroy it, you *could* say whatever you want. No one would believe you. I'd cast you as a home-grown wannabe cold-case detective." His voice was calm and measured. "Then, you'll have a terrible accident. I'm sure all sorts of inappropriate material will be found in your apartment after that. Might be embarrassing for your family."

I nodded. "Got it."

"Thought you would. So where is it?"

How could I tell him I didn't know where Tom put the original after picking up the copies? He said he would put it in a safe deposit box. Samuels didn't know about the duplicates. Or about Tom seeing the tape and making the extras. Or did he? Was Tom stashed somewhere now? In which case, had they already searched Tom's apartment? What about Tom's friend who made the copies? Had I endangered that poor guy? I needed to stall for thinking time.

"You know, I'm having a hard time remembering," I said.

He lurched toward me with his jaw clenched, eyes on fire, and his right hand balled into a fist.

I shrunk back and covered my face with my bound hands. "Stop. I'm not being a smart-ass."

He stepped back.

"That jerk Joey clonked me good on the back of the head." I leaned forward and bent my head down. "Look. Bet I've got a bloodied goose egg back there. I'm dizzy and nauseous, and I'm having a hell of a time trying to recall some things."

"And one just happens to be the location of the tape." The anger in his eyes intensified. He stood and walked to the kitchenette. From the same drawer as before, he removed a folding pocket knife.

"When I ran away from my apartment Thursday night," I said, "I had it with me."

He returned to the chair, sat, opened the knife, and began cleaning under his manicured fingernails with the blade. "Go on."

"It was in my purse." That was the truth. "I made my way to a bus stop on Ala Moana Boulevard, hid behind some bushes, and tried to get some rest. Then I hopped on the first bus to the North Shore."

"Really." He sounded sarcastic. "What about your friend, Tom Hanegawa?"

"What about him?"

"Quite a coincidence you ran away to his cousin's house, don't you think?"

"Of course not. I asked him to help me."

"Didn't he want to know why you needed a place to stay?"

I wished I knew if Tom had said anything. "There was a gunshot back at the cottage when your clunkheads took me. Was it Tom? At least tell me if he's alive."

"Answer my question."

"Will you answer mine, then?"

He nodded, sat back, and appeared to relax. "Sure. I'm a great deal maker. That's how I get things done."

"I told Tom I was afraid the guy who killed Jenny was after me, too. And I had to get away. Right then. So he gave me the key to his cousin's place, and I left. I didn't think about the tape again until today, assuming it was still in my purse. But when I looked this morning, it wasn't there. I don't remember taking it out. Maybe it was stolen?" I hoped my lies were convincing.

"That would mean someone else knew about it. You want to tell me who?"

He had the look my father did when he caught me lying. Very skeptical.

"When I saw Joey at the murder scene, he was talking on his cell. He said he didn't find *it*. Did you know I heard that? I had no idea what he'd been looking for. There's your guy, I think. He broke into my apartment, been stalking me for a week. What makes you think he didn't manage to take it from me? Maybe he has plans to blackmail you also. Did you see how anxious he was to get out of here?"

He seemed to accept that as a plausible possibility.

"Now can you tell me if Tom's okay?"

"You lied, so I lied. I don't care about your friend and what might have happened to him. You don't understand how this works, do you?" He stood in front of me with the extended knife and stared at my neck.

Did he mean he knew about Tom and the copies? That he didn't believe my story?

He sighed and glanced around the room. "I don't like the way things turned out here. It's unfortunate."

At first I supposed he meant my situation. I watched as his eyes misted over and realized he was lost in thought while I connected the dots.

"This is where it happened, isn't it?" I asked. "Malia died right in this room, didn't she?"

He snapped back and glared at me. "Don't you judge me."

"I'm not. I know it was an accident."

"You don't know anything." He leaned in and touched the tip of the blade to my cheek. "Your nephew is a cute little boy."

"My nephew?"

"It would awful if anything happened to him, don't you think?"

Was he threatening to hurt Quinn? "You wouldn't."

"Tell me where the tape is. Now."

I felt a sting as he pressed harder and broke my skin.

The distinct loud crack of a large branch breaking stopped him. Then a heavy-sounding thump hit the roof.

"What the—" he said.

We both looked toward the ceiling.

The window behind Samuels shattered. Glass flew across the room and smashed against the wall. The staccato sounds of gunshots followed. He served as an unwitting shield for me, then fell forward, his head hitting my knees, and landed on the floor. Blood bloomed through his shirt where a shard of glass pierced his back.

CHAPTER TWENTY-EIGHT

The shooting stopped, but my pulse felt ballistic. I twisted and glanced at the wall behind me, then checked out the rest of the room. Not seeing any bullet holes or damage other than the window, my guess was the shots weren't aimed into the building.

Samuels moaned, tried to push up from the floor, then lay his head back on the concrete.

"God damn it," he mumbled.

His knife had landed near my feet, so I scooped it up as best I could and pushed myself to a standing position. His men would burst into the shack to check on him any second. This might be my one chance to escape. I tried to position the knife to cut the tape on my ankles, but with my hands in such a tight bind, I couldn't coordinate them. It would take too long.

I hopped—bent over—below the window, since the shooter could still be there, made it to the back door, and opened it a crack. Peeking out, I saw nothing out of the ordinary. A nearly full moon lit the area. Ten feet away was a sloppy growth of bushes where the mountain's upward slope began. Behind me, jumbled voices came from the other side of the front door.

I hurried outside, closed the back door, and hopped to the shelter of those bushes and scrunched my way about twenty feet further through the undergrowth.

"Hey, wahine." Brian's voice came in a whisper.

"Brian? Where are you?" I whispered back.

"Over here. To your right."

I crawled, shrimp-like, another twenty feet to him. "Here's Samuels' knife. He was about to cut me when something hit the roof." The realization of what a close call it was sent a shiver through me.

"Dat was me." Brian took the knife and cut through the duct tape on my wrists and ankles.

"Wow. That feels better." I pulled the tape off, rubbed my hands together, and put the closed knife in my pocket. "What were you doing on the roof? And how'd you know I'd run this way?"

"Closest place to hide from that door. C'mon, we gotta move dis way." He pointed to his left. "Out of here. Dis the first place they gonna look for you."

He crawled under low-hanging branches, favoring his right leg.

"You got hurt? Are you okay?"

"Shhh. Laters. Follow me. And don't make so much noise like you did before. I thought you was one wild boar, da way you crash through. Think dey heard you in Wahiawa."

Chastised, I followed, being as quiet as I could manage. Brian, despite his heft and an injured leg, moved through the brush like a Native American stalking a deer.

We soon came to place where we could stand. I spotted the shack through the brush. "It's quiet back there. Maybe they're moving Samuels out to the car."

"What happen to heem?"

"Piece of glass hit him in the back. He was talking when I left, so he's alive."

"Too bad."

"Why were you on the roof?"

211

He let out a soft chuckle. "Joey left in da car. Left me, da shit. I was gonna find a way to go for help for you. But den I figga it take too long to walk, so I stick around and think of something. Sometimes, I forget I'm big. So I climb da kine tree." He pointed to a huge mango tree whose branches overhung the shack. "To see who is where. But da branch break, 'an I fall on da roof."

"And his guys shot you? Are you bleeding?"

"No, no. They miss. I got hurt jumping off da roof."

"Thank you for believing me." I gave him a huge hug, knocking him a bit off balance. "Oh. I'm sorry. I forgot about your leg. But thank you also for helping me."

"It's all good, seestah. We got to get going." He turned and nodded toward some houses in the distance. "Out dere. I got cousins in Mokuleiea."

"So we *are* in Waialua. I wasn't sure where you brought me." I looked up the hillside. "And that's Mt. Kaala up there."

"Yup. Shit. Get down. Be quiet." He sunk to the ground.

I did, too, causing the earthy smell and tickle of decomposing leaves to my nose. I stifled a sneeze. Light poured from the now open back door of the shack. I heard low voices and rustling brush.

"See how you can hear dem?" Brian whispered. "Da sound travels."

"How do we get out without them hearing us?"

"Shhh."

We watched. A cloud obscured the moonlight. As the voices came nearer, I could make out the faint outlines of three people stooped over, searching the bushes and stopping to listen every few feet.

"My God." I whispered at a level a dog would have trouble hearing. "They'll hear us if we move even a little."

"Shhh."

Panic invaded my brain. I worried about Brian. If they came any closer, we'd have to make a break and run—take our chances. With his injured leg, he'd never get away. I steeled myself for what I needed to do.

Still whispering, I said, "We need to run that way, right? To get to Mokuleiea?"

"Yeah. But not yet."

One of the men moved within ten feet of us. He could've been the guy who'd taped me, it was hard to tell in the dark. My heart pounded. He was sure to find us any moment.

"Stay here," I said. Before Brian had a chance to rebut my decision, I turned and burst from our hiding spot, making as much noise as I could crashing through the underbrush. They didn't know Brian and I were together. I wanted them to follow me away from Brian.

"There," a man yelled. "She's over there."

As I reached the open field behind the main house, the clouds cleared, and the moonlight lit the scene.

"She's headed for the road," one shouted.

I wouldn't have known where the road was if he hadn't said that.

"I'll go around and cut her off," another yelled.

A car up on blocks sat in the driveway of the main house. I ran to the far side of it, and, chest heaving, scanned the area. My options were—continue running in full view of them toward a road and a man with a gun waiting for me—or find another route.

A ramshackle chicken coop stood in front of a red hibiscus hedge. In the opposite direction, between me and the shack, was a small garden enclosed by a low picket fence and an empty clothesline. A big black sedan sat on the drive in front of the shack.

Running footsteps came closer as clouds covered the moon again. I grabbed a handful of gravel from the driveway, then threw the stones as hard as I could toward the chicken coop. Rewarded by the sound of them hitting the wood roof and riotous angry squawks, I eased my way around the car as the footsteps hammered by toward the coop.

I ran across the open area, past the garden and clothesline, and ducked as I approached the sedan. Was Samuels in it waiting for these guys? Or was it empty? It wasn't running. Maybe the keys were in it, and I could drive it for a few miles, then dump it. I crawled to the driver's side door and reached for the handle.

The window rolled down a bit, and a man's left hand holding a lit cigarette flicked ashes outside.

I ducked back.

"Why the hell did you idiots shoot the window?" The governor's voice sounded weak.

"You awake again? Good. I patched your back. It's not that bad. You'll need some stitches."

"Thanks. About the window? Who aimed at me?"

"Chuck hit it by accident, trying to get the big local guy," the man in the driver's seat said.

"Stupid ass. What local guy?"

"The one with Joey the Weasel. Joey peeled away without him, and the guy walked to the road. Joey probably stiffed him his share. I figured it's their problem. So I went back to watching the door of the shack here. A while later, who falls out of the goddamn tree but the big guy. Chuck tried to shoot while running, but yeah, he's never been a good shot."

"As of now, he doesn't work for me anymore. Understand?"

"Perfectly."

The driver's door opened, hitting me and knocking me back on my bottom. The driver looked as shocked as I felt.

"Hey," he shouted. "She's over here."

I jumped to my feet and fled toward the mountain.

He kept yelling at the other men while chasing me. Shouts from the others became louder.

"Get the flashlights from the trunk," the driver said. "Hurry."

I tore through the brush again and didn't stop until I ran straight into a barbed wire fence. I screamed with surprise at the sharp jab. The impact cut my left arm, but otherwise I was all right. I felt for the metal horizontal strands and, with great care, maneuvered my way through them, snagging my shorts and shirt a few times.

The slope increased, and I climbed as fast as I could—grabbing small trees and bushes as handholds to keep from slipping. Not far below, flashlight beams swept the area. Between their voices and careless crushing of the vegetation, they made so much noise themselves that I didn't think they could hear me. I also hoped with all the commotion, Brian managed to escape.

"She went up there," one shouted. "Any sign of the moke I shot out of the tree?"

"Not yet."

"I think I hit him in the leg, he won't get far."

A light beam came much too close to me. They used a lot of the f-word as they maneuvered their way through the barbed-wire. Sweat dripped from my head and down my neck. I pulled myself over a four-foot-high exposed section of rock. Above it, what seemed to be a path opened up. I ducked and peeked below. They weren't far behind.

"We don't have to climb that shit in the freaking dark," someone said.

"Yes, we do," another voice said.

"Damn it. But there's nowhere for her to go up there. What we gotta do is be here when she comes down. That way's just a cliff, no getting anywhere in that direction."

"What if she climbs all the way up?"

"Then she's more stupid than you. I told you, she's gotta come down, and there's only a few accessible places to do it. I know where they are, so I'll stay down here, call in some more guys, and we'll watch for her. Chuck, you and Henry keep going after her just in case. And Leon, you get back to the car. Take the gov to Doctor Lum. He's expecting him."

The crunching underbrush sounds resumed, and I scrambled higher, checking often for their telltale flashlight beams. I could see them trailing me, but the men's pace slowed and I got further and further ahead of them. No doubt the considerable extra weight around their middles worked in my favor.

An hour later, I stopped to watch behind me. I didn't see any lights, but kept climbing, slower, for another hour.

CHAPTER TWENTY-NINE

I replayed what the one man said about the ways off the mountain. Great. If he was correct, I was stuck. The additional men would camp out at the accessible trail-ends until I got too hungry or tired. There had to be another way.

By not coming down for as long as I could stand it, I increased my chances that any of my would-be rescuers would catch up with my pursuers. As if to emphasize the point, my stomach growled. When did I last eat? I was thirsty, too.

I knew from friends' hiking accounts there were fresh water ponds and streams in these mountains. They'd told of skinny-dipping in the pristine water, then finding passion fruit vines and guava growing wild. There were other stories about narrow paths, losing their footing and almost falling down the steep mountainside, but I didn't want to think about that.

Mosquitoes buzzed near my face, and one bit my arm. I became aware of the itching from many bites already covering my body I'd been too preoccupied to notice before. The itching increased the more I concentrated on them. Arcane facts about mosquitoes, remembered from heaven knows when, came to mind. Like—only females bite, the males are vegetarians. It would take over a million of the bloodsuckers to drain a human. And, they stay at the lower elevations.

I'd been thinking it might be best to climb higher and further away from Samuels' men anyway. I hadn't seen a light or heard a human-like sound in a while, but didn't want to tip them off in case they were closer than I thought. I tried to be like Brian and marshaled my inner Native American, then rose in silence. Enough moonlight showed through the trees that I could manage not to smack into a tree or rock. Taking my first step, I felt with my foot for twigs or leaves, brushed them aside, then placed my foot on the ground. Repeating this process, I inched up the mountainside, thanking God for the little trees I clutched for help along the way, and wondering if I'd stepped over the spot where they found what was left of the unfortunate Malia London.

I knew Mt. Kaala was the highest peak in this range and on the island. Most trails led to it and the restricted access FAA Radar station located at the top. The radar station. Seemed reasonable to assume it would be manned. Or was it? I'd never seen a road to it. What did they do, drop people off by helicopter for occasional inspections? Still, it was better than staying where I was. If someone was there, I could call Tom—I so wanted him to be alive—or Aden and Debbie, tell them what happened and maybe get some help. It was worth a try.

Double checking every step before making it, I climbed for yet another hour. Then heavy clouds covered the moonlight again, turning the skies back into night. I held onto a trunk and sat, waiting for them to pass. There wasn't anywhere I could go or anything I could do until they did. After twenty minutes of waiting, I felt for the flattest space around me and settled in a more comfortable position. The altitude helped the mosquito situation. They'd stopped buzzing in my face and around my neck.

I awoke to a tickling sensation on my calf and the awareness that my face was in the dirt, right cheek down. I snapped to a sitting position almost before my eyes opened. It took a moment for the scene to register. Blessed breaking daylight streaked the sky in the east. Wild and raucous bird calls made it sound like a rain forest, which I guess, in a sense, it was. A movement near my feet caught my attention. A fat, six-inch centipede crawled near my leg.

I jumped up and back, a shriek escaping. I kicked the foul insect into a bush, a shiver radiating through me. First I brushed off my shorts, then my shirt, reaching as far as I could around my back, in case any more of the creepy creatures had found me. I hated centipedes. I'd been bitten once, and it stung like hell. They won't kill you, but it's unpleasant. My legs and arms displayed numerous scratches from my escape. Some had welts and crusted blood over them. More dark, dried blood marked the gash from the barbed-wire. My arm ached. No wonder the mosquitoes went nuts for me. Their swollen bites made me look like I had a giant case of the measles. And I couldn't remember when I'd had my last tetanus shot.

My stomach registered a strong and loud complaint. I surveyed the area, hoping for one of those fruit vines my friends raved about.

The sun rose fast. Through the trees I saw Waialua below, and Mokuleia in the distance to my left. Tiny figures on windsurfing boards sailed near the coastline. I'd gotten further in the dark than I imagined. Several ranches with their clusters of buildings were visible, but I couldn't tell if any were Samuels'. I listened, but didn't hear anything human. Had the men turned back during the night, opting for a bed? I hoped so.

On the ground nearby, mint-green air moss grew in springy formations, competing for space with an unbelievable number of ferns. Ridiculous amounts of emerald-green carpet moss covered everything else, including the bases of the tree trunks.

The air smelled sweet and clean. I picked up the scent of something earthy and—apples? Hawaii didn't have regular apple trees, but rose and mountain apples grew there. I climbed and searched for them. Soon a group of five mountain apple trees were within sight, bursting with massive clusters of the small red fruit. Smashed ones lay on the ground under and surrounding them. I hurried closer, hit something slick, slid downhill, and landed when my back slammed into a tree trunk. The impact made the pain in my head throb all over again.

Gathering myself, I realized something smelled disgusting. As I sat up, I saw there was almost as much manure around the trees as apples. A lot of it was fresh. Now I had dung smeared on me. I examined the trees. The bottommost branches looked stripped of all fruit. Both wild boar and mountain goats lived in the mountains, and I hoped it was the goats that frequented this spot, not the pigs.

The trees were about thirty feet high. The animals must have learned to grab at the branches and yank them down to reach higher fruit. The bark on the trunks showed deep scrapes. I climbed one and shimmied along a main branch until I could grab an apple.

Nothing ever looked so good to me. I ate the little pear-shaped apple in a minute, savored every crunchy, juicy morsel, spitting the brown seeds on the ground. I picked another and wolfed down that one. When I finished six of them, I picked another whole cluster and climbed down.

I didn't have anywhere to put them to keep my hands free for climbing. As I thought about how best to carry them, in spite of the ever-present cacophony of bird noise, I heard a snort from behind me. On alert, I turned to see a large boar with huge tusks about twenty feet away. Its snorting increased. I dropped the apples, raced back to the tree, and climbed as fast as I could.

The boar charged forward and rammed the tree before I reached the branch I'd been on before. The hit shook the tree, almost knocking me out of it. Several clusters of apples fell to the ground. I scrambled higher and held on as he backed up and charged again.

He made an awful groaning sound, and the tree reverberated when he hit. I could smell him now that he wasn't downwind anymore, and the stench overpowered me. I gagged, leaned over the branch, and threw up. He backed up a few steps, and beyond him now were two smaller boars, maybe two feet long, with no tusks. They looked like they each weighed over fifty pounds.

The *he* boar must have been a *she*. A momma boar. No one could blame her for protecting her babies, but I needed her to go away. The smaller pigs edged closer and snorted in a junior-boar way, and the mother sent them a stern snort. They backed up.

They'd come to eat their breakfast and the mother wouldn't let them near the trees until I wasn't a threat. How was I going to escape without getting hurt? The way that made sense was to freeze where I lay on the branch until she determined I wasn't going to move. Then the pigs would eat and leave. I hoped.

Now I knew how the deep scrapes got into the tree bark. The boar rammed the tree twice more, each time more ripe fruit dropped. Pinching my nose against their revolting odor, I breathed through my mouth and stayed still on the branch. She ignored me and ushered her young to feed on the newly fallen fruit.

When they at last wandered down the slope, I picked two clusters of apples and came down from the tree. I didn't waste time eating then, moving far away from the animals' known food source was more important. Boars sometimes traveled in packs. I had no desire to meet momma boar's friends.

I took off my T-shirt, turned it inside-out so the now-dried manure wouldn't contaminate my fruit, wrapped the apples in it, and tied the ends around a belt loop. I felt ridiculous climbing a mountain in my bra, but no one could see me, so it didn't matter. My back and leg muscles were stiff and sore, but after a half an hour, they warmed and no longer bothered me.

Hiking in daylight was a great improvement over climbing in moonlight. If I hadn't been in so much trouble, I could have enjoyed it. The scenic views expanded the higher I went. An hour later, I emerged onto a well-worn trail. I breathed a sigh of relief, sat on the volcanic-red dirt, and opened my T-shirt bundle. I took my time eating the apples. Opposite me was the Koolau mountain range that framed the Windward side of the island. Kam Highway was a ribbon cutting through the pineapple fields below.

Saving half the fruit in case I didn't find more food, I retied the shirt to my pants and resumed the hike. Following the path was a joy after trailblazing through the forest.

Until I came to the narrow—*you could fall off the mountain*—part. Ahead of me, the trail shrunk to a foot wide, curving around and up until, in the distance, I saw it widen again and disappear into the trees. The reason for the narrow trail was a tall rock face on its mountain side, and sheer drops of more rock on the other. The skinny ledge wasn't level, either. It looked to be slanted at steep angles in sections.

Ropes, power cords, and computer cables dangled at intervals along the way. Previous hikers must have tied the strange array of devices to tree trunks. I could see the tops of those trees above the rock face, but there was no way to know if they were secure enough to rely on.

I stopped a few feet away from where the foot-wide trail with the ominous drop-off began. Did I have the courage to try it?

CHAPTER THIRTY

In the midst of the bird and wind noise, another sound wafted my way. Faint, but there. Male voices. I hurried in the direction I'd come from and peered down the slope, trying to see through the trees.

Was it Brian and maybe some friends looking for me? Wait. No. Not with his hurt leg. Could Samuels' chubby henchmen have caught up with me so fast? I'd had such a great lead on them. Waiting for a minute, I did hear it again. The rustling of leaves and the cadence of local inflections, then a glimpse of two men climbing. Thinner than the governor's guys from the previous night, they could have been everyday normal hikers, but I didn't want to take the chance Samuels' men found fitter recruits to chase me.

I had no choice now. It was the scary way or maybe die. Remembering not to look down, I took the first step onto the ledge trail. My stomach sunk. The narrow path was anything but smooth. Jagged ends of rock protruded, making each step a challenge. Facing the rock wall, I moved my left foot to the left, looking for a secure place to land and hold my weight while I placed my right foot where my left used to be.

It was slow going. Loose bits of rock littered the surface making each step an unsteady, slippery guess. The first slanted section corresponded with the first dangling power cord. I grabbed it and gave it a good hard yank. It held. I clung to the cord, thanking God someone had the courage to venture up the rock face to tie this lifeline in place. The path shrunk to a mere six inches for a few feet and without that absurd looking lifeline, I'd be at the bottom of the abyss.

About halfway across the perilous path above the deadly drop, I reached a blue polypropylene rope. The reality of what I was doing hit me hard. I started hyperventilating. I glanced down. A huge mistake, but I couldn't stop myself. Panic seized me. I felt faint, and disoriented, and frozen.

In the midst of taking deep breaths to calm my anxiety, I saw movement from the far right of my periphery. The climbers, two young guys with backpacks, emerged onto the path.

"Hey," one of them said. "There she is."

They ran toward the ledge.

"And we get a show," the other said, laughing and pointing at me.

Adrenaline flooded my body, and I moved faster. I reached the next line—a gray computer cable—grabbed it and slipped. I screamed. For a terrifying second I dangled, hanging onto that cable. I got one foot in place, pulled myself up, then the other foot. My pulse hammered in my head.

The men stopped at the edge of the precarious shelf. Their backpacks seemed very heavy. They took them off and set them on the ground.

I moved another few feet. Glancing left, I had about fifteen feet until I reached the end and wide terra firma. On the right, one man removed a black gun with a long front. I squealed in panic, shuffled faster, and thought my heart would explode from sheer terror.

Seven feet left. I grabbed the last lifeline, a green Christmas extension cord, and checked to the right again.

The man with the gun dropped to one knee, aiming the weapon at me.

I screamed, "Don't shoot me. Please. You don't know what he did."

The muffled shot hit the rock near my right arm with a zing. Little splinters of rock hit my body.

"Fuck," the non-shooter said. "You asshole."

Three feet to go. I hustled, clutching at crevices in the rock to steady myself, and made it to the end. Tears of relief streamed down my face as I ducked behind the first bush I saw.

The men put their backpacks on and eased their way onto the ledge. It seemed they'd done this before, because they moved faster than I had.

There was another path that led upwards. I followed it and found the trees anchoring the safety lines above the sheer rock wall. I ran to the side that I began my crossing on and tried to untie the first power cord I'd used. Then I realized it was slack. No one at the moment using it for support. I moved to the second one. It too, was slack. My pursuers had passed these points already. The guys were making great time.

I went to the blue polypropylene and could see the strain from someone pulling on it. The knot was a hopeless nest of turns. There was no way I'd untie it in time. Then I remembered Samuels' knife. I felt in my pocket. I hadn't lost it. I flipped it open and sawed at the rope, but it went slack before I finished.

Last ones first then, I thought. I ran to the end and cut the green Christmas cord. Then backtracked to the next, and cut through that one, too. The third from the end went taut as I got to it.

I had never hurt anyone on purpose before that moment. But this was me or them. I sawed into that cord with savage intensity. Saw the strain on it help tear it as I cut, and it split apart.

A hideous scream filled the air. I imagined his fall and shuddered.

"Danny," a man yelled. "Danny!"

As I ran into the woods, I hoped that the second guy would move a lot slower with no lifelines.

Further up, the wind increased, and the temperature dropped. Although the day was sunny, I felt chilled. Shivering, I removed the apples from my shirt and turned it right side out again. It was stiff and stinky, but I put it on and carried the fruit. Hiking fast and checking behind me every few minutes, I neared the Radar Station. I could see its fencing in the distance.

Half an hour later, I reached the station. They'd cleared at least five acres for the site. The chain-link perimeter fence had rolls of razor wire attached to the top. A white metal sign said, *FAA Facility. No Trespassing.* Inside the fence was a blacktopped area with a designated helipad circle. Several corrugated metal buildings faced the black top. The place looked deserted.

On the west side, opposite me, a closed gate seemed to be the only access. I hustled around the fence and approached the gate. It was padlocked from the inside. Another padlock, not in use, hung facing the outside. A road led up to the gate. I figured it came up from Makaha, on the west side of the Waianae Mountains.

Many locals lived on the Waianae coast, which included the towns of Makaha, Waianae, and Nanakuli. I'd been there exactly twice, both times for events leading to Debbie and Aden's wedding. The locals welcomed few white people. Tourists were advised to stay away, unless they went to a couple of golf resorts located there. Smart visitors never ventured beyond the resort boundaries.

Hesitant to yell, I waved at the FAA buildings, hoping someone would notice me. The wind was a constant whine in my ears, but I listened for the man who might be tracking me. Finally I hollered as loud as I could. "Hey anybody? Help. Can you help me?"

I kept it up along with the waving for a few minutes. I was so cold at that point, my teeth began chattering. I couldn't control them. If there was a person in one of those buildings, they either couldn't hear me, or were napping, or who knew?

My legs felt like they'd fall off if I walked another step, but staying exposed in the chilling wind wasn't an option. Moss and lichen grew in the few inches of mud that covered the skinny two-lane road in patches. Heavy-duty tires had left deep tread marks in the muck. I headed downhill, often checking behind for unwanted company.

The mud and moss made the going slick and difficult. I skidded and lost my footing, landing with a painful thud on my rear. Shivering, teeth knocking together, and exhausted, I fell apart. My arm now throbbed around the puncture from the barbed wire fence. My throat felt parched. I let the tears loose. I wailed and sobbed, wishing for help, warmth, and water.

Ten minutes later, I was only colder, and no closer to help. I ate my remaining apples, then picked myself off the road, every muscle screaming for relief, and began the journey downhill.

Soon, the wind stopped howling, and the sun felt warm. Almost two hours later, I saw a house not far from the road. The sun had begun to set. The house, a single-wall construction with green peeling paint and jalousie windows, had concrete blocks as steps to the front lanai. Chickens and ducks pecked around the weed-ridden yard, unperturbed by my approach.

The front door was open, and I knocked on the wooden screened door.

"Hello?" I said. "Anybody home?"

I saw movement in the house, and soon an old Hawaiian-Chinese looking woman came to the door. She made a face as she saw me.

"What you want?" Her voice wasn't kind.

I knew that haoles weren't welcome on this side. "I, I'm sorry. I need help."

"Who is it, Emmaline?" a man's voice asked. He came alongside her. "Whoa. What happened to you? You in an accident?"

"Ooh. She stinks," Emmaline said.

"My brother-in-law's mom lives out here. Dorothy Kaikau? His name is Aden Kaikau. Do you know them? I need to find her." At that point dark fuzziness closed in around me. I sunk to my knees and passed out on the lanai.

CHAPTER THIRTY-ONE

I awoke to the uncomfortable sensation of being dragged across rough boards. It was almost full-dark, and a mosquito buzzed near my face. Aden's mother, Dorothy, stood over me, smiling. Thank heaven, I thought. I'm off that damned mountain. A tear ran down my cheek.

"You're okay now," she said.

In the porch light, Dorothy's curly brown hair shone like a halo around her serene cocoa-brown face. She looked like an angel. Next to her was the man who answered the door, and Emmaline, who still wore a disapproving frown.

"I was about to try to lift you into Dorothy's car. Can you sit?" the man said.

"I think so." The effort hurt my head and my back, but I managed. My throat felt cracked-desert dry. "Water?"

The man gestured toward Emmaline, who sighed and went into the house. She returned with a plastic cup and handed it to me.

"Thank you." More tears escaped. I drank the water.

"I'm bringing you to my house," Dorothy said. "Aden's on his way."

"Debbie, too?"

"No. She's staying with Quinn. But Aden said she cried when he told her you were alright." Dorothy crouched and examined my eyes. Then she felt the lymph nodes by my ears, and with gentle fingers, checked the back of my head.

"You got one bad headache?" she asked. "This is a big bump here."

I nodded. "It hurts, yes."

Dorothy and the man helped me to my feet, then supported me as we went down the steps toward her Honda. She opened the front passenger door. There was clear plastic sheeting on the seat and its back.

"Emmaline told me you stunk. She was right." Dorothy laughed. "What did you do? Roll in shit?"

"Kinda, yeah." I grinned. "Thank you for helping me. It was horrible, all of it. First—"

"Wait. I want to hear your story. But wait for Aden. Then you won't have to repeat it."

I thanked the man, who said his name was Vernon, and I waved goodbye to Emmaline. She ignored me and went indoors, slamming the screen door.

"Wow, Emmaline really doesn't like haoles, huh?" I said after Dorothy pulled away.

"No." Dorothy smiled at me. "Don't hold it against her. She hasn't had any good experiences with white folks. Can't stand to drive to Honolulu anymore. Heck, she won't even go with Vernon to Pearl City for a movie. She doesn't approve of their lack of integrity, their greed, lack of manners . . ." She waved a hand in the air. "You know the way it is for some locals. They feel like they got squeezed out and forgotten."

"And they have a point. Some of the rich from the mainland think this is a play land made just for them. I've done design jobs for them. They have no desire to understand Hawaii's people or its history."

"And that, my dear Bess, is why we welcomed you and your sister into our family. You cared enough to learn and to respect us."

228

We drove toward her home in Makaha, a few miles down Farrington Highway from Emmaline's. On the way, I wondered if any of our tape copies were viewed. Did anyone of any consequence know about Samuels' crime yet? I wasn't sure if I was really out of the woods. What if Samuels knew about our efforts, and it had pissed him off worse? He might have more men after me now.

As luck would have it, our destination might have been the safest place on the island. No paid goon, even at the governor's behest, would dare take anyone from the Kaikaus in Makaha. The local community was a tight brotherhood. Every man with so much as an ounce of Hawaiian or Samoan blood would hunt the fools down. It would have nothing to do with me and everything to do with respecting the Kaikaus.

We passed shacks that looked as though they'd cave in any minute beside nicer, sturdier, maintained ones. The yards had rusted cars and VW busses, strange lean-to's built of corrugated plastic and tin, an occasional sofa, and lots of concrete hollow block.

Dorothy's house was a tidy three-bedroom on short stilts with a meticulous, postage stamp-sized front yard. When she swung the car into her driveway, the headlights highlighted three large local men sitting in white resin stack chairs in her carport, drinking beer.

I sucked in a breath, and she gave me a strange look.

Then she seemed to understand. "That's just Aden's cousin Rudy, my son-in-law Morton, and Aden's friend from high school, Fuzzy. You've met them. They won't hurt you."

"Sorry." I felt awful. "I've never been afraid of local guys before, but after the last two days . . ."

"Must be one heck of a story." She parked, walked to my side, and helped me out.

"Boys," she said, "remember Bess? Aden's sister-in-law?"

"Right," one said. "You da one went missing since Friday, yeah?"

"That's me." It was Sunday night, and the past three days felt more like three months.

Dorothy led me by the hand past them to the back door. "First, a shower. By then Aden will be here."

"Hoo. Good idea, Auntie," Rudy said. "She smells like one dump."

She ushered me past the kitchen table where I noticed a half-full plate of food.

"I interrupted your dinner. I'm sorry." It smelled like garlic heaven in her house.

"Oh, please. No problem to heat it up. Come."

I followed her to a pink and white bathroom. She gave me some of her clothes to change into and left a bag for my ruined ones. "You okay to stand in the shower? Need help?"

"No," I said. "I'll be fine. Thanks."

When I emerged from the bathroom, Dorothy's living room was full of big men and two more local, older women. The three men who'd been in the carport had moved inside, and on the brown leather sofa sat Tom Hanegawa and Aden. I screamed with happiness and ran to Aden.

He stood, then hugged me hard. "You had us so worried." When he released me, his eyes were glassy. "Debbie was beside herself. Your mom flew in from Florida today. I made her wait with Deb."

Tom hugged me next. "I've never been happier to see anybody." He had a purplish bruise on his right cheek.

"I didn't know if they killed you or what," I said, beaming. The Old Spice never smelled so good. "Thank God you're okay."

"Killed him?" Dorothy asked. "What's been going on?"

"Just in case," Tom said, "I haven't told anybody anything yet. Except I called Aden and Debbie to tell them you were taken."

"I want to know why Tom said we couldn't call the police," Aden said. "Your mom is driving us crazy wanting to call the authorities."

"We didn't know if they'd help or hurt," I said.

Tom whispered, "Do you think it's safe to tell them all of it?"

"I think these are the only people who actually can end this nightmare," I whispered back.

Dorothy sat me in a recliner and bandaged the gash in my arm from the barbed wire fence. I explained what had transpired starting Thursday night. I told them about the governor's confession on the video tape.

A room full of incredulous faces greeted me. Then a chorus of denials and *no ways* followed.

"I didn't want to believe it, either," Tom said. "But I saw it. Samuels admitted it. And he's been trying to kill Bess ever since."

He didn't say Samuels had Jenny killed. I didn't mention that Jenny was the prostitute who recorded the tape. I had no desire to revisit those facts. With so many details to relay, I hoped no one would ask. Sooner or later though, the truth would come out. When I got to the part where I found out Brian Wilson's name, Rudy stopped me.

"Brian Wilson?" he said. "Hell, I just saw him a couple hours ago. Auntie, call his mom and get his ass over here."

"No, no." I said. "I mean, yes, have him come over, but what I'm getting to is, he listened to me and tried to help. He's the reason I escaped. He hurt his leg doing it."

I finished the telling of it and sat back, exhausted anew.

"Who was the girl Samuels supposedly killed?" Aden asked.

"I looked at the news accounts of the murder at the library," I said. "It was real. Her name was Malia London."

A collective gasp filled the room.

"No," Fuzzy said. "I know her brothers."

"We all know the family." Dorothy had come back in from calling the Wilsons. She rushed across to where the Japanese looking older woman stood against the hall doorframe.

The woman slumped in Dorothy's arms.

CHAPTER THIRTY-TWO

"Wake up now, Kiku." Dorothy patted the older woman's face.

Kiku, the lady who'd fainted, stirred and shook her head. Aden and Rudy had carried her from Dorothy's arms to the sofa.

"Auwe." Kiku sat up. "I cannot believe it. After all these years. I went to the movies with her the night she disappeared."

"I'm sorry," I said.

The screen door in the kitchen slammed, and heavy footsteps advanced toward the living room. Floorboards creaked under the weight. Brian Wilson limped in followed by four huge Samoan men.

Tom glared at Brian. "Hey. Remember me?" He pointed to his bruised cheek.

Instant tension flashed through the crowded room, like an electrical jolt. I thought Tom might leap across the room and punch him if it weren't for the guys with Brian.

Dorothy stepped forward. "Stop. No beef in my house." It was a command, not a request.

Brian's face showed acknowledgement to Dorothy. He shook his head, then looked at Tom. "I didn't know. Joey told me lies about Bess and you to make me help him. I'm sorry, man."

Tom nodded. "All right."

The invisible ruffled feathers calmed.

Then Brian turned to me. His voice softer, he said, "You okay, haole-girl? Auntie said you climb da freaking mountain to get to this side? Damn."

"I'm happy to see you got away from those goons, too," I said. "I was afraid they found you."

Brian let out a loud, hearty laugh. "Haole-girl, you got da fools so mixed up and turned around, they didn't know I was there." He scanned the room. "You had to see it. She went crazy, running like one no-head chicken. To da road, back to da shack. To da car, then to da woods. And these guys are kinda fat, too. No good shape. Clutching their opu." With a broad smile, he imitated the men bent over holding their stomachs and catching their breath. His gaze returned to me. "I had plenty time to get out."

"Great," Aden said. "Now that everybody loves everybody, we have a problem to deal with. What do we do about Lewis Keala Samuels?"

There were over twenty people crammed into the room. Four women, and the rest—big local men. I hoped the old wooden floorboards could take the strain. With all the jalousie windows cranked open, the evening breeze carried mixed scents through the house. Night-blooming jasmine, tantalizing garlic from the kitchen, and the tang of sweat from male bodies.

No one spoke. Dorothy left the room.

"My wife's sister was terrorized and almost killed because of Samuels," Aden said, pointing at me. "He might still be after her. She's my family. That makes her as much a part of this community as any of you."

Dorothy returned with a tray full of food and placed it on my lap. "When's the last time you ate? You must be hungry."

"I found some mountain apples," I said. "But I'm starving. Thank you."

"Dis," Fuzzy said, "is not so easy. We been friends for—*evah*, Aden, but the governor . . . Dude—he's Hawaiian. Like us."

I looked down at my plate. It smelled wonderful. Shoyu chicken, garlic rice, and fresh papaya with a lime wedge. Pretending to be more interested in food, I listened while I ate.

"Yeah, I mean, no offense or nothing," another man said, "but we finally have a governor who wants us to reclaim the sovereignty."

"No, he doesn't," Rudy said. "He's the first one with a good plan. A good compromise."

"What?" Dorothy said to the man. "You want to be the new king?"

"Sure. I'll be da king," the man said. "I'll rule all haoles must leave." He cast a sheepish look at Aden. "I mean, except for da ones we like."

Dorothy laughed. "And that, my friends, is why we make sure only people with an education actually run things." She walked to the man, gave him a playful slap on the head, then kissed his cheek. "Honestly, Leo, you need to think more, talk less."

Kiku cleared her throat. "You know, if you banish the haoles, then you have to kick me out, too. My father was Japanese. Moved here at fifteen. My mother? Filipino. We have no more claim in these islands than the haoles do. In fact, lots of haoles families have been here longer than most so-called locals."

"Malia London was a hapa-haole," Brian said.

"We're getting off subject," Aden said. "What do we do?"

"Aw," Rudy said. "Bess, why did you have to come here and make this *our* problem, anyway?"

I looked up from my plate and saw the whole contingent staring at me. I swallowed and put my fork down.

"That's not fair," Aden said.

"Yes, it is," I said. "I had a lot of time to think when I was alone the last few days. I realized how lucky I am to live here. How much this island, this state, means to me.

"And how lucky it was for my sister, Debbie, to meet and fall in love with Aden Kaikau. Because if she hadn't, I wouldn't know first-hand how beautiful, loving, and fair the Hawaiian people are.

"This island has become my home. The only place I've ever felt *connected* to. And I'm proud to say I'm even a minute part of the Hawaiian culture, because of my brother-in-law. When I moved here sixteen years ago, I knew almost nothing about Hawaiian history, except it fascinated me. I read and learned everything I could because I thought it was important.

"Along the way, I watched and listened. And when things go bad, who are the first ones to help? Who would literally give you their last dollar if you needed it? Who are the people who understand the preciousness of all children? Who are the people who are so tolerant and forgiving that it's taken them two hundred years to get damn good and mad about their land, their power, and their sovereignty being stolen away?"

I looked at Dorothy, then Aden. "I knew if I could survive long enough to get here to you, that you would help me. Even if it means losing the governor who represents the best chance yet of regaining much of what you've lost. I voted for Samuels. I liked him. I thought he was the right one for the right time. But I also know that you as a people won't tolerate gaining your desires through a man who's capable of cold-blooded murder to cling to power."

There were a few moments of quiet.

"But, I thought you said Samuels admitted to killing Malia by accident," Fuzzy said.

"Yes," I said. "But I now know he also hired that Joey creep—to murder my best friend, Jenny Dobbins."

"The rich haole lady from town?" Rudy asked. "The one on the news?"

"Shit." Aden said. "He's the one behind Jenny's death? Why?"

I looked at Tom for help.

"Jenny was the one who, um, found the tape with Samuels' confessing to killing Malia," Tom said. "It's a long story."

"It gets worse," I said. "I think he arranged for Detective Chang's deadly accident on Thursday night. And the guy who was with Joey at the park last Saturday turned up dead in the Ala Wai. I don't think that was an accident either. And Aden? Samuels even threatened to hurt Quinn if I didn't tell him where the tape was."

"Son of a bitch." Aden's face filled with rage, and his hands formed fists.

"He threatened my grandson?" Dorothy sounded incensed.

"I would have told him what I knew at that point," I said. "To save Quinn? The game was over. But that's when the shooting started and the window broke."

"Jesus, you should have told us that first." Aden pulled his cell from his back jeans pocket.

"You're right." I fought back tears. "I'm sorry. Do you think they'd go to your house? It wouldn't do Samuels any good to hold them unless he could let me know—to draw me out of hiding. Would it?"

"I've got to warn Debbie, just in case." Aden walked to the kitchen. "I'll be right back."

The group fell quiet. I listened for Aden's conversation and breathed a sigh of relief when it became evident Debbie answered. I watched the faces around me wondering what they thought, imagining their disappointment. They all wore T-shirts, shorts or surf trunks, and flip-flops—*slipahs*, looking as inconsequential as the budget tourists who stay in the cheapest hotels. The truth belied their appearances. Some, I knew, were from old, established families with money. Some had nothing. But every one of them had great influence with their state legislators, the governor's office, and the Office of Hawaiian Affairs.

Aden came back in. "Bess, your mother called Steve earlier. She wanted to see him. He's at my house. I told him to lock everything and stay until I got there."

I nodded. "Yeah, sounds right." I looked at Dorothy. "Mom loves my ex. She thinks I'd be better off back with him."

"Aden's not so fond of him," she said. "But at least Debbie, Quinn, and your mother aren't alone right now."

"So what are we going to do?" Fuzzy said.

"I know what I'm gonna do," Brian said. "Find one shithead Joey."

"He can wait," Dorothy said. "First we go to the capitol building. Gather everyone. Your mothers, fathers, cousins, everyone. In the morning, we drive to town and confront Samuels. He'll have to face us. Morton, your cousin is still a cop?"

Morton nodded. "Just made detective."

"Perfect. Call him and tell him what's happening."

"Wait," Tom said. "One of the reasons we were afraid to alert the cops in the beginning was because of Samuels' influence with the police. He's close friends with the chief. Then we decided to drop a copy of the tape at HPD, thinking if they saw it, they'd have to do something, right? But remember just yesterday, the detectives went on the news and announced Bess was now wanted as a *person of interest?* Do any of you think the police believe she had anything to do with Jenny's death? Morton, tell your cousin not to say a word at work yet. I don't want him to have a car accident, too."

"I can't believe the police chief would go along with Samuels, but okay, tell him to wait," Dorothy said.

"After everything I've heard, I totally believe it. Don't tell your cousin-cop where Bess is," Aden said.

"Where's the tape?" Dorothy asked.

"I put it in my safe deposit box yesterday morning," Tom said. "After I dropped off the copies."

"In the morning, get it, and bring it with you."

"Um," I said. "I really think it would be best if no one else saw it. I mean, no one here."

Dorothy gave me a strange look.

I put my tray on the floor beside me, walked to her, and whispered in her ear. "There's some explicit sexual activity involving Jenny. I don't want it to become common knowledge if I can stop it. For her children's sake. Can I explain later?"

Dorothy nodded. "I'll hold the tape tomorrow. If we have it with us, Samuels will think we saw him confess. You're staying in my guest room tonight, and Rudy, you and Fuzzy sleep here, too."

"Debbie and her mom wanted me to bring Bess home with me," Aden said. "They'll have to wait until morning. I need to get home and protect my family in case our *esteemed* governor makes a move toward my son. You coming, Tom?"

"Yeah. I'll guard your front door," Tom said.

They each hugged me and headed for the car.

CHAPTER THIRTY-THREE

After the crowd left, I insisted on helping Dorothy with her dinner dishes while Rudy and Fuzzy argued over who'd sleep on the sofa in the living room. Rudy won. Fuzzy unrolled his sleeping bag on the carpet in the hall outside my door.

Tucked into Dorothy's guest bed, I felt protected and loved. Feelings I hadn't had in a long time, even before Jenny's death. Stillness settled over the house, and the sounds of the night became audible through the louvered jalousie windows. Wind rustled the palm fronds. A dog barked in the distance. Cicadas chirped. Fuzzy snored.

The sensation of the cool, crisp sheets against my clean skin made me promise myself I'd never take such simple luxuries for granted again. It took longer than I thought to fall asleep as I couldn't help but worry about my sister and her family, and the next day's events. Would Samuels see the locals and realize his secret reign of terror had backfired on him? Dorothy seemed so sure. I wasn't.

***

A hideous squawking-screeching woke me, and I bolted upright. My heart pounding, I wrapped the sheet around me and opened the bedroom door. Fuzzy slept on his side, undisturbed. The sounds of water running and cups clattering came from the kitchen. I stepped over Fuzzy and glanced out the living room windows where the early dawn sent pale light to crystallize the dew on the grass. Chickens pecked at corn scattered on the bare ground near their coop and made contented clucking noises. Rudy slept face down on the sofa.

Dorothy smiled when she saw me enter the kitchen. "Good morning. Did the donkey wake you?" She filled the coffee pot with water.

"If that's the creature that screamed like a banshee, then yes." I sat at the table and yawned.

"You slept through my rooster then. The donkey is my neighbor's. My rooster wakes his donkey every morning." She laughed and opened the freezer, removing a gallon Zip-Loc bag full of coffee beans. "I assume you want some?" She held the bag up. "From my cousin Sylvia on the Big Island."

"Yes, thank you." I looked over my shoulder toward Rudy and chuckled. "So much for my bodyguards."

She measured out the beans into a grinder. "They're used to animal noises. Watch this." She pressed a button and a loud whirring filled the air.

"Auntie Dorothy, stop." Rudy pulled the pillow over his head.

"See? That, he heard. Rudy, go collect the eggs for me."

The pillow hit the floor, and the big man sat and rubbed his eyes. "Yup. Okay." He yawned, then looked my way. "You all right?"

"Sure," I said.

"Then I did my job." He snickered as he stood and stretched, then headed for the back door.

"You heard me?"

"Of course. I'm one great da kine bodyguard." He winked at me and went outside.

Dorothy cranked the jalousie over the sink so it opened further. "Rudy? Pick a couple more papayas and an avocado, too, if you see a good one."

I walked back to my room and dressed, noting Fuzzy and his sleeping bag no longer lay on the floor. Then Dorothy and I made breakfast.

The three of them chatted during the meal, and I listened some, but thought about the day ahead more. Rudy and Fuzzy excused themselves as soon as they'd finished. They headed home to organize the carpools for their families.

"You're too quiet," Dorothy said. "What's on your mind?"

"Everything," I said. "Jenny. And what'll happen when we go to town."

"Tell me about Jenny. She was your best friend, but you didn't know her like you thought you did. That's it, right?"

I nodded and took a deep breath. "Turns out I knew what she wanted me to know. That's all. I'm guilty of blind loyalty. Because she resented and maligned her sister Bitsy, I did, too. We were so mean to her sometimes. I feel awful about it. Bitsy filled me in on Jenny's past."

Her eyebrows went up.

"You don't want to know, except she lied. About everything. And I'm having a hard time reconciling the Jenny I knew with what Bitsy told me Jenny did. My Jenny was kind, considerate, patient, generous, and such a loving mother. Bitsy's version of Jenny is cunning, conniving, sneaky, revengeful, and downright cruel.

"I can't blame Bitsy for keeping her distance. In fact, I find it amazing she kept the little contact she did. I feel like a fool. Like my judgment is so far off, I can never trust it again."

She patted my hand and stood. "I can see why you'd think that." She retrieved the coffee pot and poured more for both of us.

"Maybe my suspicions about Steve are wrong, too. My gut tells me he's more interested in Debbie, but my mom thinks I'm way off base. Am I paranoid? Do I have unresolved issues making me run from a man who says he wants me? I mean, look at him. He's gorgeous, and I'm . . . well, you know—kind of dumpy. Plain."

Dorothy returned to her seat and sipped from her cup. "Is that how you see yourself? Auwe. No wonder you're all mixed up in the head." She leaned in and kissed me on the cheek. "You're a fine looking woman. Learn to love what you've got, and you'll find someone who thinks you're the most beautiful woman he's ever seen."

She sat back and gestured to her face and body. "Look at me. No great shakes, eh? But my husband, Kanoa . . ." She rolled her eyes. "To him I was Marilyn Monroe." She chuckled. "He was a good man."

"I think you're very beautiful."

"Thank you. Going back to Steve, if you think he's gorgeous . . ." She waved a hand. "I trust your instinct. Aden and Debbie trust your feelings on this. The most important thing is to believe your gut reaction. We tend to ignore it, because we want to believe something else, but that can lead to worse trouble."

"Then how come my gut didn't sense Jenny's deceptions?" I stirred sugar into my cup.

She smiled a Cheshire Cat smile. "Have you considered maybe you were supposed to believe her, because she needed you to teach her?"

"Oh boy, there you go all cosmic and akamai on me."

"People come into our lives for a reason. Your friendship helped change her, shaped her into someone capable of unconditional love for her children."

"I did that?"

"Remember, I did meet her at Aden and Debbie's wedding, then years later at yours. And no one is all bad or all good. The good things you saw in her really were there." She took my hand and squeezed it. "I believe you each brought a lesson for the other to learn."

"Huh." I mulled it over. "What was mine?"

She laughed. "Only you know the answer."

***

An hour later, cars, SUVs, and vans lined Farrington Highway near the Kaikaus. At least sixty people milled about on Dorothy's lawn and driveway. Rudy and Dorothy arranged, then rearranged the seating for maximum capacity.

"Parking stinks near the capitol building," she said. "And the underground garage? Forget about it."

"I think our best bet is the lot near the palace," Rudy said.

Morton and his wife Kanani—Aden's sister—stood beside Rudy drinking from travel mugs. I stayed close to them, feeling maybe some of the group resented me for having made this *their* problem, as Rudy put it the night before. Once he heard the threat to his little cousin Quinn, that changed. I didn't think everyone in the crowd knew all the details, so a few of those stern faces intimidated me.

By nine-thirty, the Makaha contingent snaked its way toward Waianae and Nanakuli. The caravan reorganized itself in both those towns, and soon we headed for downtown Honolulu.

I rode in a green van with Dorothy, Rudy, Fuzzy, Morton and Kanani, and a man named Wylie. I sat by the driver's side window in the third seat with Kanani and Morton. Aden and Tom would meet us on the palace grounds.

"Hey," Fuzzy said. "What if Samuels isn't there this morning?"

"I called his office earlier," Dorothy said. "He's supposed to be in all day on Mondays."

"You didn't tell them we were coming, did you? Like this, and why?" I imagined Samuels might be pretty sore about his glass wound and my escape. He had to know I'd tell his secrets.

She turned from the front passenger seat and gave me a look. "I wasn't born yesterday."

My nerves twisted my stomach around. We passed Pearl Harbor, and it reminded me of when Jenny and I brought the kids to the Arizona Memorial. I wondered who now had charge of Paul,

Richard, Mikey, and Sammy. Did James and Vivian find a suitable nanny? Were the boys back at school this week? I missed them. I missed my friend Jenny more. Dorothy's words earlier helped me understand a lot.

While we sat on the bench at Kaliki Park, two Saturdays before, Jenny said I was her only real friend. I blew it off at the time as a throwaway comment. Now I wished I'd paid attention. From what Bitsy told me, it sounded like Jenny had never had a friend. No best buddy in high school. Nothing. Her older sister moved away, and her mother was a drunk. I couldn't imagine how alone she felt growing up. I'd had five siblings and a slew of good friends.

"Put your headlights on now," Dorothy said.

Rudy, who drove, nodded.

We exited the H-1 at Kinau Street, and turned right onto Ward Avenue. The tourniquet gripping my insides squeezed tighter. I looked out the back window and all our cars, about twenty of them, had their headlights on.

Our van made the turn onto Beretania Street past the capitol building, then a left on Richards Street. The parking lot near Iolani Palace looked half-full. Maybe we'd fit the cars in.

The knots in my intestines hurt as I climbed from the third row seat. I paced on the grass nearby, hoping to relax my nerves. One by one, the others in our caravan filed into the lot. In the mix, I spotted Aden's car. He, Tom, Debbie, and . . . Steve got out. Tom saw my *what's he doing here?* reaction and shrugged.

"Bess." Steve ran ahead and embraced me before I could stop him. "We've been so worried." He scanned me up and down. "You look horrible. Did you walk into a beehive?"

Debbie came behind him. "My turn." Steve backed away, and Debbie's eyes filled with tears. "I thought we'd lost you."

My eyes watered, and we hugged each other. "I'm so happy to see you."

Dorothy, Aden, and Rudy stood at the front of the crowd. The last of the cars parked on the grass and the occupants joined the group.

"Where are the Londons?" Aden called. "Laka, Apona, and Inoa. We want you in the lead."

Malia's brothers, now men in their sixties, walked through the parted crowd to the front. The others nodded their respect to them. Some recited quiet blessings. One man looked angry and murmured something like *go get the bastard.* The Londons' solemn faces seemed stoic, but I watched as they passed, and their brown eyes betrayed them. Emotions long sequestered lurked far too near the surface.

CHAPTER THIRTY-FOUR

I tried counting heads but lost track after one-hundred-twenty-five. The group decided not to approach the capitol building by walking through the adjacent Iolani Palace grounds. Because of several takeover attempts by native Hawaiian groups in the recent past, they knew the guards of the grounds were on hyper-alert. Rudy argued there was no sense in making anyone think we were about to occupy it.

"How's your stomach?" Debbie asked.

I'd told her how awful it felt. "Same. Hurts."

We set out toward the capitol building, three abreast on the sidewalk, walking beside the iron fence surrounding Iolani Palace, its gold-tipped points gleaming where the sunlight dodged the palm fronds to touch them. I took the tour several years earlier and fell in love with the koa wood staircase. Most the windows had their original glass. I tried to remember in which room on the second floor the self-appointed provisional government imprisoned Queen Lili'uokalani in 1895. Then they forced her to sign a document of abdication by threatening to shoot some of her supporters.

The way the United States acquired Hawaii caused most of us transplanted mainlanders to cringe. It was so wrong, and in today's world, so hard to untangle and resolve in a fair way. Governor

Samuels had worked a miracle in getting a compromise. Native Hawaiians voting as a separate body. One of their votes counting as two of everyone else's. An advisory council made from proven Hawaiian Alii descendants. Now would it go through without him?

The few tourists on the palace grounds took notice of us, pointing and taking pictures. I guess to see Hawaiians not in a hula show twirling fire, hosting a pretend luau in Waikiki, or leading a tour to Hilo Hattie's aloha wear factory was a surprise.

We passed the royal barracks building and turned onto the concrete mall separating the capitol building from the palace. The statue of Queen Lili'uokalani stood in the middle of the mall on its raised circular grass dais, facing the capitol. At her feet were bundles of tropical flowers bound with ti leaves, leis, and notes attached to single flowers. A purple crown flower lei hung from her outstretched right hand.

As we approached Lili, four uniformed security guards came down the makai steps of the capitol building. They must have seen us coming. Dorothy, Aden, Rudy, and the London brothers stopped us at the front of Lili's statue. I stood a few feet behind them, to the left of Lili, with Debbie on my left. Tom came to stand between me and the statue. The rest of our group filled in around and behind Lili. Steve, who'd been several layers back from us on the walk, finagled his way to stand beside Debbie. He smiled a giddy smile at both of us, like we were on a middle school field trip. Debbie gave me a look, and I refrained from the eye roll I wanted to send. Tom poked me in the side with his elbow.

"We didn't come to start trouble," Dorothy said to the security men. "We are not armed."

The security guards reached the bottom of the stairs and stood in what I'd call military stances. Arms crossed behind their backs, chests out, feet shoulder width apart. They *were* armed.

Dorothy waved at the Londons to join her. Aden and Rudy stepped forward with them.

"Do you have a parade permit?" one of the security officers asked.

"This is not a parade," Rudy said. "These gentlemen," he gestured to the Londons, "would like a word with the governor, please."

"Tell them to make an appointment, like everybody else," another officer said.

One of the Londons started to step forward.

Dorothy put her arm out. "No. Wait. Samuels can't know that we know until we see him."

The man took a deep breath and nodded. Impatience emanated from the brothers. I felt the tension in the group go up a notch.

"We'd like to see him now, please. Will you allow us to enter the building?" Aden said with respect and calm.

"It's very important. We are Hawaiians. Blood of his blood. If you tell him we are here, I'm sure he'll want to see us," Dorothy said. Her purse dangled from her shoulder. Inside, I knew, was the video tape.

Loud voices came from behind us. I turned. Curious tourists stood by the open palace gate.

The squawkish sound of a mobile device made me face the makai steps again. One of the security guys, who looked a bit Hawaiian himself, spoke into his phone. I couldn't decipher the words. I leaned toward Dorothy. "Do you think he's calling the fifth floor?"

She nodded. "I hope so."

I felt a tap on the shoulder and twisted around. Brian Wilson stood behind me, grinning. "You think it'll work?"

I hugged him, then introduced him to Debbie.

"Oh." She turned and hugged him, too. "You are my new most favorite person. Thank you so much for helping my sister."

Brian blushed. A rosy flush actually bloomed in his brown cheeks. Debbie had that affect on men. This time, it made me laugh, and when I turned to Debbie again, Steve had a strange look on his face, and his fingers fidgeted at the edge of his jeans pocket. He saw that I noticed and let out a nervous laugh.

The realization hit me. He was jealous. He couldn't handle being so close to Debbie and watching yet another man enjoy her company. A final resignation and sadness joined my already full plate of emotions.

"He says he'll come down here," the security officer on the steps called out.

"Thank you," Dorothy said.

"Maybe this will work," I said to Debbie. My nerves settled some.

While we waited, I studied the capitol building. It was meant to be for all the people. The architects went too far with the design of the building, trying to make every aspect of it represent something. It was a metaphorical nightmare.

The eight tall tapered columns represented palm trees and the eight major islands of Hawaii. The conical-shaped congressional chambers represented the volcanoes. The shallow reflecting pond surrounding the building represented the Pacific, nurturing life on the islands. Fed from the brackish water of nearby streams instead of a chlorine-based recycling system like most pools and fountains, they never figured out a good way to keep it clean. They tried adding fish, but they all died. It stank from the proliferation of algaes, brown and green. Pond scum. Some said it was now a perfect representation of the local state of affairs.

More security officers appeared at the top of the capitol stairs. The crowd hushed. Then Chief Ortiz of the Honolulu Police came forward. In the periphery, about a dozen uniformed police officers made their way around the sides of the building and spread out on the lawn facing us.

"I don't think they believed you," I whispered to Dorothy.

She stepped forward. "We'd like to talk to Governor Samuels. The other man said he would. Is he coming?"

"Yes," Chief Ortiz said. "I couldn't talk him out of it. Said you were his people and he must honor your request. So," he gestured to his officers on the lawn, "this is a precaution. My job."

"Freaking unbelievable," Tom said.

"Yeah, like we're da ones who did something wrong," Brian said.

"They're trying to intimidate us," Aden said.

"It's working," I said.

A news van pulled up along Richards Street and parked in the nearest traffic lane. The crew jumped out and began to unload equipment.

"What's going on?" a loud voice demanded from the growing gaggle of tourists.

"This isn't good," I said to Tom. "I've got a bad feeling about this."

The news crew set up its cameras at the edge of the crowd nearest the street.

I wondered if Samuels had his office call them. They would report the magnanimous way our beloved governor behaved toward his fellow Hawaiians who showed up without an appointment. Despite his busy schedule, he'd taken the time to see them at a moment's notice. Samuels was a talented politician.

A few minutes later, Samuels walked from the open-air lobby to the top of the stairs accompanied by four men dressed in aloha shirts.

Cheers went up from the tourists in back of us. Samuels must have thought we all cheered, because he gave a humble nod and gestured with his arms wide to welcome us.

"Brian," I said. "Look. The two guys on the end. They're the same ones from the shack Saturday night, right?"

"It's them."

Dorothy set her purse on the ground between her feet and pulled the tape out of it, keeping it by her side.

"My fellow Hawaiians and esteemed visitors," Samuels began. He walked down a few steps.

The tourists cheered again.

"I understand your concerns and urge patience. It must be an important matter for you to come here, taking time from your work and your lives. I want you to know I'm ever pushing forward with the legislature the peaceful resolution of our sovereignty issue. The revisions to my Restoration Bill have been sent to the state house and we're working as hard as we can to pass a solution that helps everyone."

Samuels paused and scanned the crowd, seeing for the first time, I guessed, the familiar haole face in the second row. Me. His expression froze. He leaned toward one of his men and whispered to him. The man signaled to the other three, and they retreated into the lobby.

"Where are they going?" Tom asked.

Samuels put a broad smile on his face and stared at the news camera. "Unfortunately, I have a very busy schedule today, and I have only a few minutes."

I spotted one of his men working his way along, among the palm trees behind the police officers. "Look guys, there's one of them on the right. Watch for the others."

I studied Chief Ortiz, and it looked like he saw the aloha shirt men, too. His face stayed blank. He knows, I thought.

"These men would like to ask you a question, Governor Samuels," Rudy said, pointing at the Londons.

Samuels looked at him, then back at the TV crew. "Of course. Ask your question." His pasted smile made me want to gag.

The three brothers walked out a few steps. "Governor," Inoa said, "we want to know why you have never done the right thing and come forward to confess to killing our sister."

Loud gasps came from the tourists. A few of the policemen looked confused.

"I'm sorry." Samuels let out a nervous sounding laugh. "You must know something I don't. I'm sorry if someone did kill your sister. Or are you inferring that my policies have affected your sister?" He shrugged toward the camera, then looked at his watch. "I'm due inside. Thank you for coming." He turned toward the building.

"We have the video tape, Governor." Dorothy waved the tape in the air. "We know everything. We are your people. You must confess."

"Come back here and face us," Laka said.

"You son of a bitch." Apona London leapt forward, followed by Laka and Inoa.

"You're not getting away with murder." Inoa waved Laka onward.

Rudy and Aden sprinted to catch them.

"No," Aden shouted.

A loud pop and shots rang out. The tape flew out of Dorothy's raised hand, the plastic casing splintering in mid-air. A metallic zing came from Lili's statue.

Shrieks erupted.

"Everybody get down," Aden shouted.

The Londons dropped to the ground with the rest of us.

Samuels yelled, "They've got guns." He started to run up the steps.

"Don't let him get away," I shouted to the police. None of them paid me any mind. I never took my eyes off Samuels. The policemen had their guns out and pointed at the crowd as they approached us.

The security officers surrounded Samuels and escorted him into the building.

"There are four more copies," Aden yelled. "We can prove he killed Malia London."

Chief Ortiz's head snapped toward Aden, then looked at the news camera. The expression on his face changed. "Okay men," he told his officers. "Let them stand with their hands up until you check them for weapons. Everyone up. Now."

As I rose with the others, Steve screamed, "Debbie."

With my hands up, I turned to see my sister lying on the concrete, blood oozing from her upper right arm. Her eyes closed, she lay still. Steve crouched beside her, and looked at me with tears in his eyes.

I screamed, then started to move toward her.

"Hold it," a policeman said in a commanding voice.

I froze.

"That's my wife." Aden, with his hands in the air, spoke to the officer. "Can I go to her?"

The man nodded. He yelled up to the chief, "Call an ambulance. Gunshot wound." He scanned the crowd. "Is anyone else hurt?"

No one answered.

Aden pushed his way through.

Steve stroked Debbie's face and cried. Through his sobs I heard him say, "Don't leave me. Please. I love you."

"Get the hell away from her." Aden shoved Steve aside.

Steve fell backward and stared wide-eyed at me.

I stared back. For the first time since I'd met him, he didn't seem attractive. In fact, he looked ordinary. Nothing special.

"She's breathing," Aden said a moment later. He took off his T-shirt, wrapped it around Debbie's arm, then cradled her head in his lap.

"Thank you, God." I turned my back to Steve.

As the officers finished patting down each of our group, they instructed them to sit a few yards away. An officer came to check me.

"If you find those four men who came out with Samuels," I said, "you'll find who shot into the crowd. None of us have a weapon. Tell that to your chief."

"Is it true? About the governor?" the officer asked me in a hushed voice.

"Yes. And he's killed three others trying to hide his secret."

He directed me to sit with the others, then went and whispered to the other officers doing the pat-downs.

I sat beside Dorothy facing the capitol and leaned on her shoulder. "I can't believe he's going to get away with it."

"He won't," she said. "How's Debbie?"

"She's alive. I think maybe she hit her head when she fell, because she's unconscious. I'm worried."

"Me, too. But her arm? It looks good, bad, what?"

I shrugged. "I'm no expert, but the blood wasn't spurting out. More of a trickle."

She sighed.

"By the way, I was *so* right about Steve."

"I saw him crying on her." She rubbed my back. "You'll find someone who deserves you."

"Just now, I realized how crooked his nose is. And he's got huge pores. Why did I think he was so gorgeous?"

She smiled. "I don't know."

Three cars pulled in behind the news van, parked in the shoulder lane, and four men and two women jumped out of the cars. There were in casual dress, but the way they moved was all business. Five split off, bounded up the steps, and showed ID to Chief Ortiz.

"Who do you suppose they are?" Dorothy asked.

"It's the cavalry," I said. "At last."

She looked puzzled.

"I think it's the FBI. They finally listened. Or watched. Whatever."

The sixth one, a tall man with dark hair, dark eyes, and medium-brown skin, headed our way. He spoke to the officer guarding us, gestured to his companions talking to the chief, and showed his ID to this policeman.

Another car pulled ahead of the news van. The driver got out and opened the back driver's side door, craning his neck to see— something. Maybe into the capitol building? Then he sat sideways in the driver's seat, tapping his foot on the curb.

"You know," Tom joining us after his pat-down, "if we'd parked in an active lane on that street, our cars would have been towed in a minute flat."

An ambulance, siren wailing, came down Richards Street and pulled into the growing queue of cars. EMTs hustled out.

I raised my hand to the officer in charge of us.

He and the tall dark-haired man stopped talking and stared at me.

"That's my sister who's hurt. Can I go over there, please?"

The officer glanced behind him where only a few of our group waited to be searched, nowhere near where Debbie lay, and nodded. "Sure."

I got there as the EMTs did. Aden placed her head gently on the ground and stepped back next to me to let them do their thing. I put my arm around his waist and hugged him.

"It was those guys in the aloha shirts. The ones with Samuels, right?" Aden asked.

"Yeah. I'd bet on it. Two of them Brian and I know from the other night. Did you see them sneaking behind the police? I think I was the target. A shot hit Queen Lili. I heard it ricochet off her. My guess is that bullet hit Debbie's arm."

They placed Debbie into a neck brace and bundled her onto a stretcher.

"You with her?" one of the medics said to Aden.

"My wife," Aden said.

"Come on then," the medic said. "You join me in the back."

I watched them wheel Debbie to the ambulance with Aden walking alongside and holding her hand. I followed at a distance, wishing I could be in it, too.

"Haole-girl."

I turned to see Brian and Tom catching up with me. "We're allowed to move around now?"

"All of a sudden, they're being real nice," Tom said. "We have to stay until they get a statement from every one of us, though."

The ambulance pulled away from the curb.

"I think the people in those cars behind where the ambulance was, are the FBI. Did you see them?"

"Yes. Suppose they went to the fifth floor to find Samuels?" Tom said.

"Maybe. They won't find him," Brian said. "Look." He pointed down the street side of the capitol.

Hustling across the lawn between the street and the reflecting pool, Samuels and his henchmen headed our way. The building blocked the line of sight for the police, who had gathered near Lili to take statements. Brian, Tom, and I were the only ones close enough to Richards Street to see Samuels coming.

"Shit," Brian said. "What we do now?"

"Don't let them know we saw them."

"I'll go tell the police," Tom said.

"Hurry," I said. "I bet they're going to that car with the back door open."

Tom walked until he was past the building, then ran to the police officers.

"What do we do?" I asked. Samuels and his men increased their pace. "They're almost to the mall."

"We go stay over there." Brian nodded toward Lili. "Come on."

He limped toward the statue. The police ran our way just as Samuels' crew cleared the building. Samuels shouted something, and the one thin man with him sprinted ahead with his gun drawn.

Samuels and the others raced for the open car door. The police shouted at them to halt, and I spun in time to see the thinner man within a few feet of me.

With a harsh and painful grip, he grabbed my left arm on top of the bandaged gash and rammed his gun against my head. "Don't say nothing. Walk backward with me."

I nodded, wanting to scream from the pain in my arm. My breakfast rose into my throat.

"Put your guns down," he yelled at the police. "She dies if you don't."

The officers looked angry, but laid their weapons on the concrete. Tom, Brian, and Dorothy stood together with shocked expressions.

I took small steps backward with the man, so petrified I couldn't hear anymore. I felt light-headed. I saw lips moving, mouths wide, people gesturing and waving. My heartbeat pounded in my ears. The palms swayed in the breeze behind the crowd, but they seemed so distant. Everything so distant.

In the seconds before I passed out, I registered a dark blur coming from the left. A hell of a shove knocked us to the ground.

CHAPTER THIRTY-FIVE

My head ached. My arm stung. I opened my eyes. Dorothy, Tom, and Brian kneeled over me. A gorgeous dark-haired man in a black shirt stood a couple of feet behind Tom.

"This is getting old," I said. "Let them kill me already." I wiped sandy dirt from my mouth.

"You stay funny," Brian said.

Tom held out his hand. "Come on. Can you sit?"

I took a deep breath, grabbed his hand to pull myself up, and surveyed my surroundings. The crowd looked prepared to leave. On the mall, a single cop lingered. "How long was I out? Where'd all the policemen go?"

"Two minutes, maybe. A lot happened real fast. The police and the FBI chased after Samuels' car," Dorothy said.

"He got away?"

"Not for long," the dark-haired man said.

I realized he was the guy who showed up with the FBI. "Who are you?"

"This," Tom said, "is the man of the hour. He's the one who knocked the gunman over."

The black blur I'd seen.

"Zeeman DeGroot." He stepped forward, leaned, and put out his hand. "Nice to meet you finally."

He had a deep, sexy voice. I shook his hand. "Finally?"

"DeGroot Investigations." Tom helped me stand. "You picked him out of the phone book, remember?"

I studied his smooth coffee-colored skin, his almost black eyes, lashes, brows, and shiny, thick black hair. "Wow. I'm good."

He smiled and crinkles formed at the corners of his eyes. He had high cheekbones, an angular chin, and wore black jeans with sneakers. He stood taller than Tom, whom I knew was six-three. Zeeman seemed to be in his forties. He wore no rings.

I saw Dorothy's eyebrows raise and smiled at her.

"Does she need an ambulance?" The officer approached us.

"No," I said.

"You need your head examined." Dorothy laughed. "I always wanted to say that." She turned to the cop. "One of us will take her. Thank you."

I peeked under the bandage on my arm. "Along with inspecting my now rather lumpy head, I think this needs stitches, and it might be infected, too. Boy, it hurts. That stupid man tore it open more." A quick scan around the mall told me the guy was gone. "Speaking of the jerk who put yet another gun to my head, where is he?"

"Handcuffed and escorted into a police vehicle, ma'am." The officer grinned. It was the same one who'd asked me if the allegations against Samuels were true.

"So this nightmare is over? I can go home?"

"After the hospital," Tom said. "They took Debbie to Queen's Memorial. If we go there, maybe we could check on her."

"I'd love that." Out of habit, I felt for my purse. It wasn't there, of course. I'd lost it on Saturday when Joey and Brian ambushed Tom and me. And it hit me that my ex wasn't there. "Where's Steve? Did he follow Debbie's ambulance or what?"

"I told him he should go home," Dorothy said. "He looked upset, but he went."

"Thank you. Tom, would you have any idea where my purse is? My wallet has my Island Care insurance card inside. I'm pretty certain I'll need it."

"I took it home with me after I woke up from the knock on *my* head." He gave Brian a look.

"Brah. Dude." Brian backed up a step. "A thousand sorries, man. I told you I owe you one plenty."

"Yeah. We're cool." Tom looked at me. "I can go home and get your purse."

"Jeez," I said. "My mom's at Debbie's with Quinn. I wonder if Aden called her yet. If he did, she's going crazy. If he hasn't, somebody should be there with her when she finds out Debbie's been shot."

Dorothy moved in front of me. "Calm down. Here's what we'll do. Brian, you can go home in the van with Fuzzy, Morton, and Kalani. I'll take Aden's car, give Tom a ride to his apartment, then go stay with Bess' mom until Aden, Debbie, and Bess return from the hospital. Tom, you fetch the pocketbook and bring it to Bess at Queen's in your own car. And Zeeman?" She winked at me. "You get Bess to the hospital in a cab. Tom will meet you there. Everybody clear?"

CHAPTER THIRTY-SIX

The cab pulled up to the curb, and Zeeman opened the door for me.

"You don't need to come," I said. "I'll be fine."

"What if you pass out on the way?" He pointed to the back seat. "Get in and move over."

Shrugging, I did as he said. Part of me loved the idea of sharing a back seat with him. The other part told me to get real.

He sat beside me. "Queen's Medical Center," he told the driver. He turned to me. "Now. Tell me about Bess Blinke. Your name is Dutch, like mine?"

"Yes." Blood rushed to my face when I caught him giving me a once-over. I felt so embarrassed. What an awful time to meet this man. I wouldn't, under normal circumstances, dream he'd be interested. The way I looked that day—impossible.

I gestured to my un-made up face, Dorothy's old-lady flowered blouse and jeans, and let out an awkward laugh. "I don't always appear this glamorous, you know. The swollen bug bites and scratches really add to the effect." I wanted to disappear into the seat.

He smiled. "They'll go away. How did you know to send me the tape?"

"I'm not sure what you mean. I just picked two PI's from the Yellow Pages. You and . . .Tip-Top? You had the biggest ads."

"Oh. Huh. Dumb luck, then." He folded his hands in his lap.

"I guess. Why?"

"Because I might be the sole PI in town that the FBI listens to."

"Yeah, they don't listen to anybody. Believe me, Tom and I tried. The agent in charge kept repeating, 'Take it to the police. Show it to the police.' The guy was a robot. And I told him it was about the governor and was afraid maybe Chief Ortiz would bury it."

He laughed. "That sounds right."

"Why do they listen to you?"

"I'm ex-FBI. Worked out of the Honolulu office for ten years before I started my business."

"You're the reason they took this seriously? Thank you."

"I'm sorry I didn't get to it sooner." He cleared his throat. "I, uh, had plans all day Saturday, but watched the tape yesterday afternoon, and ran it to them. I didn't know whose jurisdiction it was. There's been some back and forth on that one between HPD and the FBI."

He'd had plans Saturday. His way of telling me he had a girlfriend, no doubt. I turned redder. "We sent one to HPD, to Chief Ortiz. I'm willing to bet he knew all about Samuels being after me. I watched Ortiz at the capitol. He knew."

"To save face, he'll claim they never received it."

The cab drove into Queen's Medical. I opened the door as soon as the vehicle stopped. I realized I had no money.

"I've got it." Zeeman walked to the driver's window, fished out his wallet, and paid the cabbie.

"I'm sorry. I forgot I didn't have anything with me." I headed for the Emergency Room entrance. "Well, thanks again, Zeeman. I'll send you a check for the cab fare."

He caught up with me. "My friends call me Zee." The automatic doors opened.

"Okay. Zee." I stepped into the building.

He followed.

I turned and gave him a questioning look.

"If you don't mind," he said. "I'd love to hear the whole story from the beginning."

"Sure." I registered at the desk, then asked about Debbie. The woman wouldn't tell me much except Aden would be upstairs in the surgical waiting room. I deduced that meant Debbie went to surgery. I sat beside Zee on a polyester imitation-tapestry seat in the E.R. waiting area. For forty minutes, I told him everything that happened starting with the afternoon at the park.

"You might be the bravest person I know," he said.

"Oh, please. I'm a chicken from day one."

"You sell yourself short."

Tom came into the waiting area, walking with an affected gait and swinging my purse from his hand.

"Boy, it's a good thing you're not gay." I laughed. "You'd be scary."

"He'd need a lot of waxing, that's for sure," Zee said.

Tom tossed the purse onto my lap and sat on the other side of me. "Did they look at you yet?"

I shook my head, found my wallet, and went to the desk with my insurance card.

When I returned, Zee stood.

"Think I will move on now that Tom's here," he said. "A pleasure to meet you both."

I liked Zee a lot. He had smarts and looks. And he believed me. Too bad he had a girlfriend.

***

The nurses had fun poking at my head lumps. A technician ran me through a scanner. A doctor put five stitches in my arm and prescribed an antibiotic for the infection.

When they finished with me, Tom and I found Aden. He looked exhausted.

I hugged him. "How's Debbie?"

"They had to operate to remove the bullet. It lodged in there. Someone came out a minute ago and said she's fine. In recovery. I can take her home in a couple hours."

"We are so lucky. Have you called my mom?"

He rolled his eyes. "Oh, yeah. My mom's at the house with her now."

Tom and I sat on either side of him.

"These last four days, I've seen more excitement than ever in my life," Tom said. "And that includes the time we tried to surf naked in the moonlight at Pipeline."

Aden and I stared at him.

"We, who?" I asked.

"Doesn't matter," Tom said. "But wait till the guys at work hear this story."

I leaned back on the uncomfortable chair and stretched. "I can't wait to sleep in my own bed."

"Oh. About that," Tom said. "When I went home, the police were in your apartment. Now that they know what's been going on, they're searching and fingerprinting. You might not be able to stay there tonight."

I wanted to cry. "That stinks."

"You can stay at our place," Aden said. "It's going to be a hell of a gathering anyway. Both our moms there? Hey, Tom—maybe I could bunk in with you. I'm being overrun by women."

"Nice try. If I have to be there, you have to be there," I said. "Think the police would let me in my place to get some clothes?"

"Worth a shot," Tom said. "I'll take you home. At least you can drive your van to Aden's house."

***

Aden's Element was in its place in the driveway next to Debbie's Highlander. I parked behind Debbie, figuring if anyone had to run out for anything, it wouldn't be her.

I knocked, then opened the screen door. Dinner making noises and loud voices came from the kitchen. The smell of onions and garlic sautéing in butter made me realize I hadn't eaten since breakfast. If that kept up, I might become as thin as Debbie.

I stood outside the kitchen for a moment, taking in the scene. Mom and Dorothy, their backs to me, hands moving as fast as their mouths, chopped and stirred whatever was in the pans. Chicken, beef, eggplant, I didn't care.

Debbie, seated at the table, her right arm in a sling, saw me and shrieked. "Bess, it's about time."

My mother whipped around and screamed. "Honey." She set her knife on the chopping board and ran to hug me.

"Hi, Mom." I held her tight. "I'm sorry you had to travel so far and leave Dad."

A tear escaped from Mom. "From the time Debbie called, all I saw in my head were those headlines when young women disappear. I promised myself I wouldn't cry." She wiped it away with her sleeve. "There aren't words for how worried I've been."

"I'm thirty-eight. No self-respecting molester wants me."

"You're hilarious," Debbie said in a flat tone. "No, a regular criminal wasn't good enough for you. You had to be terrorized by a serial-killing governor. Yeesch."

"Auntie Bess!"

Aden and Quinn entered the room. I stooped to pick Quinn up using my right arm and squeezed a bit. "You're a sight for sore eyes, kiddo."

"Your eyes hurt, too?"

I laughed, pecked him on the cheek, and set him down. "No. They might be the only things on my body that don't hurt."

Mom hustled back to her cooking. "Come here and talk to me while we finish this."

"Show her the lump on your head," Dorothy said. "It's first rate."

I bent and, with care, moved my hair aside. The shaved area around the lump had a dressing over it. "Here." I grabbed her hand. "Feel it. Gently."

Mom gasped. "How did you get this?"

"On Saturday, Samuels' goons . . ." I hesitated, remembering Brian's part. "A man named Joey hit me with his gun when I tried to get away."

Mom's face showed bewilderment.

"We haven't told Mom many of the details," Aden said. "And maybe," he nodded at Quinn standing in the doorway, "you should wait until later."

I'd thought the little guy went back to his video game as usual and kicked myself.

"Was it a real gun?" Quinn asked.

I walked to him and knelt. "You know what? Now that I think about it, maybe it wasn't."

"Did they catch the man?" Quinn said.

"Yes," I said, hoping it would be true soon. "He won't hurt anybody else."

***

After we finished the dinner clean-up, and his parents tucked Quinn into bed, we sat on the back lanai enjoying the peace and quiet. Mom sat beside me and patted my leg and my good arm at regular intervals. She'd never been very demonstrative, so this constituted an emotional milestone. It felt great to know she loved me, despite her frustration with me regarding the Steve situation. She hadn't mentioned my ex all night. I wondered why, but I sure as heck didn't want to bring it up.

The house phone rang. Aden ran in to answer it.

"It's for you, Bess," he said, stepping outside with the handset. "It's James."

CHAPTER THIRTY-SEVEN

The next morning, the television news showed continuous repeats of Samuels' Monday afternoon apprehension at the Water Taxi dock. He'd been trying to get to his place on Kauai, where he kept his yacht. His lawyer gave a statement—it was all a huge misunderstanding. Joey's wanted picture popped up every ten minutes on the local channels.

HPD allowed me into my apartment at nine. Detective Smalley, now in charge of the Dobbins murder investigation, met me there at ten.

"They really trashed it, didn't they?" I wandered around the living room, wondering where to start the clean up.

"Not my people," Smalley said.

"No, I meant Joey the Weasel. Would you like coffee? I'm in need of some caffeine."

"Yes. Thanks." She sat at my kitchen table.

"Thanks for announcing I'm no longer a *person of interest* on the news. When I checked my answering machine and charged my cell, I had some rather discouraging messages from clients wanting to cancel their contracts. I hope now that I'm exonerated I can talk them into coming back. Otherwise, I'm in big financial trouble."

"For what it's worth, I never thought you did it," she said. "The order to name you came from way above my head."

I sat across from her and waited for the coffee pot to do its thing. There was an awkwardness between us I wanted to dispel. "I can't tell you how sorry I am about Detective Chang. I know you really liked him."

She sighed and looked at the table. "Yes. He was special. One of a kind."

"If I could go back and not make that phone call, I would. I should have waited and brought in the video the next day."

"You couldn't know Samuels had your apartment bugged. It's not your fault." She brought her head up and gazed at me. "Chang wanted to ask you out after it was done. He told me."

"Fool," I said. "He couldn't see how you felt about him?" I smiled. "He must have been out of his mind. You're so pretty. Men mystify me sometimes."

"Me, too."

I poured coffee. She assumed her official persona, and I told her about the whole ordeal, leaving out one detail.

"Think they'll ever catch Joey?" I asked.

She chuckled. "Maybe not. You've been here long enough to know about *local justice* haven't you? We'll keep searching, but my guess is he's already dead, and we'll never find him."

I hadn't said a word about Brian. I knew Tom and the others wouldn't either. I doubted the governor and his men knew his name. As far as the police knew, Joey's helper was a nameless, faceless moke. No chance they'd ever arrest him.

When Smalley left, I picked up the cell, called Aden, and asked for Brian's number. The least Brian could do was get his bottom into Honolulu and help me clean up the mess in my apartment. Maybe I'd get him to sing something for me.

***

I met James for lunch at the Outrigger Canoe Club in Waikiki. The Dobbins family had been members of the old-guard exclusive enclave forever. The Maitre D' escorted me to the table. Bitsy sat with James, both of them smiling at me.

They stood and greeted me with hugs and kisses on the cheek.

"I didn't know you'd be here," I said to Bitsy.

She patted the chair next to her. "Sit."

Our view, through a huge window with no screen or glass, looked onto forty feet of sand populated with tall palms leading to the peaceful, lapping Pacific. The sounds of children squealing in the waves and birds squalling and diving in the water for fish faded away as a Hawaiian trio began to strum and sing in the corner of the room. The singer, her haku lei made of tiny white pikake blossoms and maile leaves, swayed as she picked the notes on her ukulele. I recognized the song, *Ku'u Home O Kahalu'u*..

"This is lovely," I said. "I was here once, but it was years ago. With Jenny."

We made small talk and ordered lunch.

"I want us, the three of us, to mend fences," James said.

"I thought Bitsy and I already had," I said.

She smiled. "Yes. Then, on Sunday, I told James everything I told you."

My eyebrows went to my hairline. "Everything?"

"He deserved to know."

James' face clouded. "A bizarre set of events."

"That's an understatement," I said.

"It explains one hell of a lot, though," he said. "Looking back, I can make sense of so many things I couldn't before."

"Are your parents still here?" I asked.

He shook his head. "No. I told them to leave. I needed time to assimilate the truth. Too hard to look my dad in the eye. Jenny had been pushing him for more money. He finally broke down and told Vivian about it, removing the threat. He knew Jenny wouldn't go public with it because she'd be dragged into the dirt in the process."

"Explains why Vivian was so cruel to him and the way she spoke about Jenny, doesn't it?" I said.

"Jenny was crazy-foolish to try and blackmail Samuels after that," Bitsy said.

"I don't want to upset our new-found camaraderie, James," I said, "but have you taken any of the blame in this? If you'd simply been fair with the support payments, none of this would have happened."

His eyes watered. "Yes. You're right. I listened to a team of vicious lawyers, and I behaved like a total asshole. I got caught up in the nastiness. The rest of my life I'll regret it. Is that what you want to hear?"

"That'll do." I exchanged glances with Bitsy. "Thank you." I took a sip of water. There wasn't anything to gain in belaboring the point. The tragic truth was the tragic truth, and wallowing in *you coulda shoulda* wouldn't bring back Jenny. "So, who's watching the children?"

"An older woman, Tutu Kim, for now. The boys don't like her, but she at least knows how to care for them."

The waiter arrived with our food, fussed over us, and left.

"The kids are the other reason I wanted to see you today." James tapped his fork on the table. He glanced at Bitsy.

She nodded. "Go on."

"We've been going 'round and 'round on this. And the best solution we've come up with is—*you* need to be the kids' nanny."

I stared at the two of them. Thought for a moment. "What?"

"They love you," Bitsy said. "You love them. You're a whiz at childcare."

"I have a business. And honestly, I couldn't afford to live on what nannies get paid."

"Lucky for us their father is rich," James said. "I'll pay you whatever you need. You can live in the master suite if you want."

"Wrap up whatever jobs you've got going, or hand them to someone else to finish," Bitsy said. "It's not that hard."

"You *will* live there, James, right?" The client cancellations and complaints I'd listened to in my voice mail echoed in my head. The faces of Paul, Richard, Mikey, and Sammy popped in.

"Yes," James said. "I know they need me."

"Then—maybe." I picked up my fork. "Let me think about it."

We finished lunch and took a walk down Kalakaua Avenue toward the crumbling Natatorium. Bitsy found a bench in the shade and sat. "You two go on. I'll wait here. These shoes are not meant for this."

I glanced at my low sandals, then at her four-inch stilettos, and laughed. "Ever the fashion plate. You think you're in New York?" I sat on the other end. "You know what? I like your quirks."

She stuck her tongue out at me.

The bench wobbled when James plopped between us.

"There will be conditions," I said.

"You mean you'll do it?" James said.

"If you agree to my terms. You and Bitsy have to take a stronger role in the kids' lives. No more of the hands-off stuff. You need to know when their birthdays are and be responsible for choosing their presents from you. No delegating. You have to show up for the birthdays, Thanksgiving, and Christmas. No more ski trips with the new girlfriend during the holidays. You'll be at every school play, open house, and soccer or baseball game, or whatever sport they're in. And James? Do not introduce any woman to them unless you think she's going to be a major part of your life for a very long time. Paul and Richard are truly scarred from the last few years."

"Is that all?" Bitsy said. "Piece of cake."

"Anything else?" James asked.

"Yes. You and I have to be on the same parenting page. What I say goes, but if it's a problem, we discuss it privately first. And when Sammy goes to kindergarten, I can go back to work part-time. Oh—none of them gets a new car when they turn sixteen."

"I got a car at sixteen," James said with a crooked smile. "Had some good times in it, too."

"Didn't you wreck three of them by the time you were twenty?"

He shrugged. "You made your point. Deal." He stretched and put one arm over Bitsy's shoulder, then one over mine. "Man, it's a beautiful day."

We sat in the shade watching the tourists wander by, checking maps and pointing at everything, leaving the smell of tropical fruit-scented sunscreen in their wake. Cars and busses blew past. Ocean waves crashed in the distance. Local men approached oiled white people on the sand with trays of drinks in coconut shells adorned with bright-colored paper umbrellas.

I closed my eyes and saw Jenny's face. She approved.

CHAPTER THIRTY-EIGHT

Two days later, while I organized my files, my cell rang. The ID feature said *private number*. An awful lot of my clients did that.

"Bess Blinke."

"How are your bug bites? Almost gone?" The deep voice sent warm tremors through me.

"Zeeman?"

"'Cause if they are, maybe you'd consider going out in public with me."

"Um." No more words would come out.

"I thought Saturday night, if you don't already have plans. Do you like jazz? There's a new supper club open on Monsarrat. Food's supposed to be ono-to-da-max and the music great."

Say *something*, I nagged myself. "Um. Yes. Jazz is nice." I sounded like an idiot. I felt like a fifteen-year-old.

"Did I catch you at a bad time?"

"No. Not at all. Saturday is great. Thanks."

"Wonderful. I'll pick you up at seven."

After I picked my shocked ego off the floor, I dialed Bitsy.

"Hi, Bess," she said.

"You have two days to make me gorgeous."

By the time I stepped toward Zee's black convertible Porsche at seven on Saturday night, I felt stunning. Bitsy had me waxed, plucked, polished, and made up to look like I had never looked. I wore a tight skirt with a silk tank she made me buy.

Zee's eyebrows rose when he saw me, and a devious smile crept onto his face. "This is going to be fun," he said.

THE END

ABOUT THE AUTHOR

Victoria Landis writes both fiction and non-fiction in multiple genres, including a monthly humor column for *The Parklander* magazine. Credits include Chapter Nineteen of *Naked Came the Flamingo,* co-edited by the late, great Barbara Parker, and *The Easy Little Diet Book - A Prep Course for Easy Weight Loss Success.* She has been a member of Mystery Writers of America since 2003.

Victoria lives in South Florida. She is also an artist.

www.VictoriaLandis.com

CPSIA information can be obtained
at www.ICGtesting.com
Printed in the USA
LVHW110931230619
622070LV00001B/107/P